SKYWORLD SAGA
FOUNDATION

SKYWORLD SAGA
FOUNDATION

ALAN PRIEST

Library of Congress Control Number: 2022906731

ISBN: 979-8-9857113-0-1

Published by ACP Strategy Group.

Cover design: Daniel Schmelling / reedsy.com/daniel-schmelling

Interior formatting: Mark Thomas / Coverness.com

DEDICATED TO JULES VERNE, H. RIDER HAGGARD,
AND ISAAC ASIMOV, WHOSE STORIES ARE
THE FOUNDATION OF THIS ONE

"So I learned then, once for all, that gold in its native state is but dull, unornamental stuff, and that only low-born metals excite the admiration of the ignorant with an ostentatious glitter. However, like the rest of the world, I still go on underrating men of gold and glorifying men of mica. Common place human nature cannot rise above that."

Mark Twain – *Roughing It*

PROLOGUE

The 7A return capsule plunged toward Earth's outer atmosphere. The heat shield covering the lower half of the tube-shaped module turned a bright yellow. As it continued to race toward the Tucson International Airport, the compression and friction of the air around the heat shield increased its temperature to five thousand degrees Fahrenheit, turning it orange, then red.

As the heat on the capsule subsided, the grid fins extended and maneuvered it above the launch pad. Seventeen hours prior, the robotic arm of the 7A probe had extended its rotary percussive drill with hollow coring bit to extract a pencil thin core sample and place it into the capsule within a capsule, then ejecting both toward Earth. Now, as the return capsule approached the ground, thrusters fired to slow its approach, and the landing fins folded down. One of the three landing fins stuck halfway out and, as the capsule touched down, it toppled over onto its side, hard.

"Oh, no."

Robert Stewart dropped his binoculars and ran over to the capsule. He saw fluids leaking out onto the platform, and even though the thrusters had shut down, everything was hot. He opened the panel to the control touchscreen. It showed internal damage and temperatures increasing. Switching to the asteroid sample container menu, he entered the sequence to open the panel. It faced toward the ground and opened halfway.

Robert kicked over the capsule onto its other side. The panel jammed and stopped moving. Robert pulled out his multipurpose tool and unscrewed the cover around the jammed panel. He had half of the eight screws out when he saw the smoke. The multi-purpose tool slipped out of his sweaty hands.

"Too many screws!"

Four, five, six screws fell to the ground and then the fire started at the rear of capsule. He looked at the asteroid sample container stuck inside a half-open panel door. The capsule just completed a five hundred-thousand-mile round trip journey, the asteroid core was now a less than a foot away, but it might as well still be in space if he could not get the panel door open.

"Come on!"

Robert stripped the seventh screw, and it stuck in place.

"No, no, no, no!"

He took off his wind breaker, wrapped it around his hands, and pulled on the panel, yanking against the last two screws holding it in place. The panel bent, but the screws would not budge; it was built for space travel. He bent the panel as far back as he could and kicked it. The half-open panel door moved a quarter inch and no more. He stared at the container right in front of him, lodged behind two inches of a faulty stainless-steel panel door.

The orange and yellow of a fire flickered over the back of the capsule. It was a matter of seconds before everything went up in flames, or worse, exploded. Robert stabbed the container with the pliers in his multi-purpose tool, shredding the perforated metal wall. He could see the core sample suspended by a rubber clamp.

There was a *pop*, and then flames moved up from the rear toward him. He wrapped his windbreaker around his left hand and shoved it into the container, pushing the shredded metal inward. He released the windbreaker, feeling for the core sample. His index finger touched it, he tuned his hand up, shoved his arm in as far as it could go, and wrapped his fingers around the metal bar.

"Got it!"

He tried to remove his hand slowly, but it got caught on the torn metal, sharp edges pushing into his forearm. He turned his arm, feeling for a clear path to remove his arm. Then his peripheral vision saw the flames coming up the sides. He turned his arm more, and the flames were in front of his face. He yanked his hand out, shredding his wrist, palm, and knuckles.

He stumbled back as the flames shot across the capsule. Robert stood, held his wounded hand against his chest, and ran. He made it halfway back to the hanger door when the capsule exploded and the thrust of the ignited fuel threw him against the door, shattering the upper glass panel and creating a two-inch dent in the lower steel panel. After the glass stopped falling on his head, he found his glasses next to him, put them on, and pushed himself up to sit with his back against the door, watching the flames. Looking down at his bleeding hand, he opened it to stare at the small metal rod.

To anyone else, it would be nothing more than an interesting trinket, maybe even junk. When he heard sirens approaching, he slipped it into his pocket. The capsule fire was dying down, but the heat picked up as the metal hit twenty-five hundred degrees Fahrenheit and melted. Nothing but a puddle of molten metal would be left once the fire burned itself out. A series of fire trucks and cars pulled up. Milton Tripp, chief executive officer of Outside Earth Exploration, Inc., jumped out of one and ran over to his chief scientist.

"Robert, you okay?"

"I'm fine.

Robert stared at the remains of his space probe's final return capsule.

"So, it was a total loss?"

"Unfortunately."

PART I

How did Earth become covered with floating countries as large as the continents? It began with a small asteroid and a very large earthquake.

SkyWorld, Jubilee Celebration (2150)

CHAPTER ONE

SEPTEMBER 9, 2070

The detent escapement's locking ruby moved 1/96th of an inch, which released the escape wheel. It rotated, forwarding the wheels of the movement, which shifted the hands on the silvered brass dial by one second. The sub-dial second hand moved to point at sixty, the minute hand at twelve, the hour hand at eight. Eight p.m. Coordinated Universal Time, or UTC, which was also high noon at the watch's current location in the middle of the North Nevada desert. Routine and unspectacular.

What *was* spectacular was that the Hamilton model 21 marine chronometer's mechanisms operated in the same manner for every second of every day, losing virtually no time, just like when aboard U.S. Navy ships crossing the Atlantic and Pacific in World War II. The owner of this precise instrument, Benjamin "Ben" Dawson, wound the chronometer each day at the same time with the same number of turns to keep the main spring and fusee chain powered and the time precise.

"That's it," said Ben as he screwed the glass cover back onto the watch face, placed the watch back into its brass cover, and secured the cover to the gimbals in its polished mahogany box. Ben had stared at the inner workings of the chronometer for the past ten minutes with a focus that was either genius or imbecilic, depending on who was asked.

Ben owned and maintained, among other things, the Hamilton model 21, which he had secured onto the desk in his ship's cabin. There was no practical reason to have a mechanical working chronometer on board. He could more easily identify his longitude with three onboard computerized mapping devices, one of which was on his wrist.

These devices gave longitude and latitude locations down to five decimals of precision, or inside of four feet. But staring at the antique device that kept UTC, which succeeded Greenwich Mean Time, or GMT, was staring into history. This small device, the result of hundreds of thousands of hours of innovation and labor across an army of craftsman, scientists, and engineers, was the solution to a problem that stalled world exploration.

Longitude, scourge of the seventeenth century. Once sailing ships were truly seaworthy in the sixteenth century, trade and discovery became national priorities. The location of these massive ships on the ocean was critical. While latitude was accurately measured for hundreds of years observing astronomical movements with cross staffs, back staffs and, eventually, sextants, a ship's longitudinal location became a mystery once out of sight of land. A mystery costing thousands of sailors their lives. Accurately measuring longitude became a worldwide obsession and early in the eighteenth century, fortunes were offered by European governments to whomever could solve the problem.

Ben loved that an uneducated, small-town carpenter turned watch maker solved the longitude problem. Although now recognized as a mechanical genius, John Harrison was considered one of the least likely of individuals to prove Sir Isaac Newton and other astronomers wrong by providing precise longitudinal measurement with a timepiece. John Harrison's various talents in carpentry, mathematics, and mechanics all came together to create the marine chronometer.

A random talent stack provided John Harrison the necessary background to create a clock keeping precise time regardless of temperature, humidity, or the position of the rolling ship it sat on. And like so many obstacles in human history, which drove countless men to madness, once longitudinal measurement was solved, it became commonplace and a forgotten historical footnote.

Ben shut the lid on the chronometer as he looked at the elegant ship's controls at his desk and the vintage nautical items on his cabin's walls, not even a measurable fraction of man's accomplishments, but each with their own fascinating history. It was these inventions and many others that were the foundation of his technological miracle, the Skyboat®.

Like many inventors before him, Ben was unremarkable in appearance, walking down the street unnoticed until his Skyboats became famous, and him along with it. Looks and charm matter only to inventors when fundraising, even if they must paint it onto themselves, which is frequently the case. Not that Ben was void of those qualities, they just showed up at the edges of his personality, like his autism, while his relentless drive sat front and center.

A natural problem solver, nothing excited Ben more than a mystery, especially if it involved technology. Early in his career, he made technical discoveries with incredible potential. Growing up in a small city, he believed in supportive and collaborative relationships, but after being cheated out of his first inventions, always the case when fortunes are involved, it hardened him. Over time, Ben pursued dreams only if he was in control. Complete control. Then, did it matter if he wasted hundreds of millions of dollars and years of his life pursuing fantasies like flying a sailboat in the sky? No, because it was his time and his money. So what if it all burned to ash? It was his ash. And that sort of conviction resulted in the generational breakthrough happening today.

Ben turned around, walked up the stairs leading out of the small cabin to the front of the open cockpit. He looked at the other Level Five Skyboats behind him. The highest and smallest level of Sky City began with Ben's *Blue Darter*, a forty-foot cruiser-racer and the first working Skyboat. Except for *Firefly*, center of Level Five and a seventy-eight-foot cruiser flown by his wife Paige, the other Skyboats were the same size as *Blue Darter*. His son, Jason, was to the right of Paige in *Sky Dancer*, his daughter Angie, left of Paige in *Freedom*. Ben's mentor, Daniel Nguyen, sat behind Paige in *Serenity*. They all looked for Ben to signal the launch.

Instead, Ben turned and walked out to the front deck, putting his hands on the railings, admiring the view. A perfect late summer day in the desert with crystal clear blue skies and a warm breeze. Ben looked at the expansive desert floor in front of him, various shades of light brown, running between Yerington and Walker Lake. The nearly thousand Skyboats and Skyships spread out for miles across the desert, sometimes interrupted by dried-up rivers leading to nowhere or scattered mesas covered with dirt, sagebrush, and creosote bush. It was an odd sight. Hundreds of Skyboats sitting on the desert floor.

Anyone flying over would think a lake had dried up overnight, leaving these boats stranded. He looked at the Skyboats waiting to launch, all designed by him. That is, after he taught himself sailing, shipbuilding, aeronautics, aerodynamics, propulsion, robotics, nuclear power, miniaturization, the flight of birds, and a hint of interior design. Paige said the last one was a fail.

Along with the Skyboats, there was the massive stage concluding a weeklong concert and thousands of spectators walking around or in front of the stage. A viewing platform built beside the stage was filled with VIPs in their air-conditioned rooms, along with dozens of decked out trailers and RVs behind it. Many had come for the spectacle, less interested in the actual launch. But after of a week of endless promotion, all had become groupies and now awaited the launch with tense excitement. Media from Earth, space stations, the moon, and even Mars (time delayed), watched.

Ben could see the superstructure of *Horizon,* an eleven-hundred-foot-long cruise Skyship that would be the center of Level One and the hub of Sky City. It was the location of Command, as well as thousands of passengers and crew, including Ben's parents. Command was where the captain of his fleet, Roger Sinclair, stood at the wheel, prepared to launch nine-hundred fifteen Skyboats into one cohesive body. The nostalgia of the marine chronometer faded away, replaced with the urgency of the launch. Ben spoke in a tone recognized by his earpiece.

"Here we go. Roger, you ready?" said Ben, using his earpiece, printed with a color match to his skin, sitting below both ears and held in place with a thin support behind his neck. Ben was connected to the captain's earpiece using voice recognition software so familiar no one thought about it anymore, like longitude, electricity, or Wi-Fi. But, for some reason, even in 2070, cell phone coverage was still spotty.

"Yes, sir. Are you ready?" said Roger.

"That's my question to you."

"I was ready hours ago. Just waiting for your signal."

"Right. Well, then, let's,"

"Hey, Dad," said Jason, "are you sure you don't want to make another speech? You've only had three today."

"Jason, this is serious, we're launching," said Ben.

"So rude," said Angie.

"Why are either of you interrupting my launch sequence? We talked about this."

"It's just that it's such a big day," said Jason.

"Such a big day," said Angie.

"I mean, can you ever have enough speeches?" said Jason.

"And you don't want to miss out on memorializing this historical moment for mankind," said Angie.

"Both of you, stop it," said Paige. "This is serious. Roger, ignore them."

"Yes, ma'am, I will," said Roger with no attempt to hide the irritation in his voice at the lack of discipline with the Dawson children. Thousands of people waiting on their signal and Ben Dawson cannot control his kids, again. Roger did not have that problem. Both of his children were well-disciplined. Even though he did not get as much time with them as he liked due to his career choice, the time he had with Steve and Cindy instilled the values of politeness, discipline, and observation. He missed them and his wife Sandy. After this launch, Roger would take a break and get back to Eureka for some quality time with the family.

"Roger, please go ahead with the launch sequence," said Ben.

"Initiating launch," said Roger as he clicked onto the broadcast channel. "Everyone, the launch sequence is now beginning with Level Five."

"Launch the penthouse!" Jason said with a laugh Angie joined.

"It's Level Five," said Ben.

"No one calls it that," said Jason.

"I do," said Ben.

Roger clicked back to Ben. "Sir, at your leisure."

"Thank you, Roger."

Ben clicked onto the broadcast channel, preparing to make another set of comments on the history of the day, and the many firsts being accomplished, and how great it was, and how exciting to have not only the Sky City participants but so many distinguished guests here as well. Then Ben thought about Jason and Angie's comments and how many other people were involved besides him, and how it was getting a little much to hear his own voice. He turned off the broadcast channel.

"Okay, everyone," Ben said to Paige, Jason, Angie, and Daniel as he fired up *Blue Darter's* nuclear engine. "Like we practiced. This is it!"

Ben grabbed his wheel and lifted *Blue Darter* off the dusty ground. The Skyboat rose, clearing the masts around him. From below, when fully extended, Ben's boat would resemble a bird, specifically a cooper's hawk. Growing up, staring at cooper's hawks flying overhead, he was fascinated with their wide wingspans and aerial attacks. Ben placed pine trees in the center of *Horizon's* main deck to nest cooper's hawks, so his invention's inspiration would live and fly among them. The cooper's hawk dimensions outlined his Skyboat design.

After designing the cooper's hawk frame, he placed vertical jets, powered by a sixty-megawatt micro-nuclear reactor, at the location of the hawk's claws. Landing gear was placed in front of the jets. The stern had a single, large jet pointing straight back. Below it was a bird; from above, a sailboat. A sailboat with a sixty-foot mast and eighteen-foot boom, along with a mainsail and Genoa jib furled for takeoff.

Built to mimic the feel of a classic blue water cruiser, Ben built *Blue Darter* with stainless-steel railings and fittings, secured onto a teak deck and white gelcoat polyvinyl chloride (pvc) foam-cored hull, which surrounded an open pushbutton cockpit and oversized steering wheel.

Ben double checked he was clear of any airborne objects and began the wing build out. Beginning ten feet from the bow of the forty foot long hull and extending to five feet from the stern, a six inch slit opened along either side of *Blue Darter*. At the bow end of the slit, on both sides of the Skyboat, a three and a quarter inch long mini robot rolled on its four magnetized ball bearings to the edge of the hull and clamped itself to the side. Another two mini robots rolled over the first pair and clamped themselves down. Then seventeen hundred skeletal mini robots repeated this process forming the wing frames.

Seven thousand quarter sized feather skeleton mini robots rolled out, filling in the wing structure as thirty thousand honeycomb-shaped drones flew over the wing skeletons and attached themselves to the frame and each other using smart hook and loop systems along their edges. A tail wing, twenty-five feet long simultaneously emerged from the back with a thousand skeletal mini robots and four-thousand feather drones, spreading into a fan shape. The entire process was completed in three minutes.

"Okay," said Ben, "come on up."

Paige, Jason, Angie, and Daniel launched their Skyboats, extended their wings, and lined up just as they had sat on the ground, *Firefly* in the center. Paige looked at each Skyboat, checking alignment.

"We're good," Paige said to Ben.

"Level Five connecting," said Ben, initiating the connection protocol. More skeletal mini robots came out of the sides of each Skyboat, rolling to the ends of their wings and clamping together. Once connected, additional skeletal mini robots rolled out creating walkways and increasing stability. The five boats floated together in the shape of a diamond.

"We're up and secured," said Ben over the broadcast channel.

A cheer erupted from the other Skyboats and thousands of spectators. The event was more ceremonial than operational as over ninety-nine percent of Sky City was still on the ground and the other levels were more complex than Level Five. Level Four was made up of one-hundred nine Skyboats with a center Skyboat twice the size of *Firefly*. Each Level's center Skyboat was twice the size of the center Skyboat above it, and those in front or behind the center Skyboat were three-fourths the center. The starboard and port Skyboats ran two-thirds the size of the center. This decline in size continued until the outer boats were at least one percent the size of *Horizon,* the largest Skyship in Sky City.

"Level Four, begin your launch," said Roger.

The Level Four Skyboats fired up. One by one, they launched and aligned themselves. Visual confirmation was not possible to initiate connection protocol. Instead, each Skyboat had a leveling program, adjusting and confirming its position relative to the others. Once the leveling programs all went green, the connecting mini robots rolled out and built the Level Four platform.

"Level Four and Five connect," said Roger after getting confirmation Level Four was stable.

Ben maneuvered Level Five above Level Four positioning *Firefly* directly above *Kapani,* center Skyboat of Level Four and back-up Command for Sky City. Drones flew out to view above, alongside, and below the two levels. The alignment program made minor adjustments, and then mini robots rolled out to secure the two levels with a series of angled struts and ladders. Level Five and Four floated together in the air, a small diamond sitting above a larger diamond.

"We're connected," said Ben.

Another cheer emerged across the desert.

"Level Three, begin your launch," said Roger.

As the one-hundred seventy-seven Level Three Skyboats launched, a small earthquake occurred, which would later be registered as a 4.0 magnitude foreshock. The Sky City launch area between Yerington and Walker Lake had over three hundred earthquakes annually, most less than a 2.0 magnitude. Press coverage focused on the frequency of earthquakes as proof of a careless choice for launching from Ben Dawson's home state of North Nevada instead of a safer location, like the middle of West Kansas.

Ben argued most of the quakes were not perceptible, and the media focused on the wrong point. Also, there were challenges launching anywhere. Tornadoes in the Midwest, hurricanes in the South, New Yorkers in the Northeast. And local and federal governments would not allow Sky City to launch near populated areas, anyway, making the middle of the desert a terrific choice. Thus, all the arguments and mudslinging between the Ben Dawson and the journalists, who never liked Ben and his no-nonsense style, ended with an *agree to disagree* détente, especially once the readership tired of the discussion. The media moved on to how many celebrity sightings they could make during launch week.

"What was that?" said Ben as he saw the masts move on several Skyboats still on the ground.

"Earthquake, sir," said Roger.

"How big?"

Roger spoke to his crew. After a few seconds of waiting, which Roger criticized loud enough to make sure Ben heard, he came back on the line.

"Registering approximately 3.0 magnitude. Correction, 4.0."

"Get everyone up," said Ben. "Now!"

CHAPTER TWO

PASADENA, SOUTH CALIFORNIA

F our hundred miles south of the Sky City launch, the director of the United States Geological Society, Harvey Healy, was preparing to speak on the California Institute of Technology campus.

"How many reporters showed up?" said Harvey.

"Two," said Charles Lindh, director of the Seismological Laboratory at Caltech. "We're getting double the coverage this time."

"No need to be smart about it. Is your entire staff out there?"

"Yes, everyone knows this is mandatory."

"Good, good. Okay, let's go."

Harvey and Charles walked outside the Arms Laboratory and over to Bechtel Mall where a podium, holograph monitor, and twenty-five faculty and graduate students waited. Harvey walked up to the podium with light applause from half the students.

"Thank you. Thank you all for coming. This is a historic day. Today, we will set off the largest earthquake prevention event in history. I'm proud to be a part of this moment as I'm sure all of you are. Ever since the USGS was tasked with active earthquake prevention, experts across the fields of geology, paleontology, geodesy, and topology have worked tirelessly together to create the world's first active earthquake prevention system."

Harvey continued to repeat what these graduate students either learned as an undergrad or were already an active part of. Even the two reporters had written a dozen articles each on the system. But Harvey wanted everyone to understand how they got here. And he hoped the reporters would include this for their readers, some of which would be the backers for the USGS budget, including all three California governors and their six senators.

"Over the past several decades, there have been no major quakes in any part of California. I can confidentially say to you today, that is due to yours and my work, all of our work, to advance the science of earthquake prevention."

A century before Harvey's speech, earthquake prevention began, but had several false starts. Animal warnings, dilatancy (rock expansion before a quake), seismic gaps, and uplift, were all investigated and proved to be unreliable predictive methods. But now the teams used laser-based radar, seismometers, accelerometers, as well as covering Earth with tens of thousands of GPS monitors, called benchmarks, to identify seismic risk. And if they could identify seismic risk, they could prevent it, at least in theory. Initially, no one in the field agreed with that statement. But after the Bay Area suffered a massive 8.5 quake in the fall of 2033, called the Big One, inaction was no longer an option. The president and western governors demanded more from their scientists than just looking back at why an earthquake happened. They also dismissed giving five minutes warning or a range of six months for potential quakes as a form of success. That was when a bold idea came out of a Caltech freshman, why not relieve known stress areas on the

San Andreas Fault by pushing that stress to a less volatile fault line?

The scientific community refused to take the idea seriously; it was laughed out of conferences. But the press loved it and a South California congressman budgeted for the USGS to study the concept. The USGS raced through the study with a goal of appeasing the congressman and stating they did in fact study the ridiculous idea for more than a millisecond. It came back inconclusive, which the South California congressman said was not good enough.

The theory had to work, lives depended on it, his re-election depended on it. Numbers were re-run, a new head of the study brought in, hand-picked by the congressman, and the new study showed there was in fact potential to prevent earthquakes by shifting stress. Success! And the location to move this stress was right next to them, the Walker Lane deformation belt. Much younger at one to ten million years versus the fifty million of the San Andreas, it wasn't even a complete fault line. And it connected to the San Andreas in the Mohave desert. Perfect.

Initial tests were run with extreme caution. One bore hole was drilled in the Mohave at a known protrusion of the San Andreas. The bore hole confirmed the location had built up stress and a small explosive was dropped down the hole and detonated. After the explosion, measurements identified the stress was relieved. A bore hole drilled on the Walker Lane identified a subsequent increase in stress. Maybe it was from the explosion, maybe not, but questions and negative attitudes were unwelcome. What was encouraged was enthusiastic support of an obvious scientific breakthrough.

It became like pushing toothpaste down the tube. Explosions were set off at the northern most part of the San Andreas in Mendocino, across the Bay Area, Los Angeles, and the Mohave. Then the Earthquake Industrial Complex kicked into gear. Specialized measuring equipment, drilling gear, and high-tech explosives were now required for earthquake prevention. All of it needed to be purchased in high volumes. Companies were created specifically for earthquake prevention products and politicians focused campaigns on the success of the program. Once the wheels of earthquake prevention began turning, there was only one direction everyone wanted them to go, and that was faster. Larger budgets, more purchase orders and, yes, more explosions. Twenty years after the start of the program, requirements for determining a high friction point were relaxed. Originally, trenches were dug, lines in the ground studied, movements across fault lines measured, and proximity to populated areas considered. All this was reviewed, reviewed again, and signed off by an entire team of scientists before drilling a hole and blowing up Earth below it. Now, a form could be filled out online and approved in forty-eight hours by automated review software.

The Walker Lane, running from the Mohave toward Reno, and then out to Redding, was expected to become a major fault line in millions of years. Even at that future time, no single seismic event would rupture the entire fault. And it was theoretically impossible for humans to move the primary fault line between the Pacific and North American tectonic plates. Thousands, even tens of thousands of explosions pushing the stress of the San Andreas straight up through the Walker Lane would theoretically do nothing more than create a few low magnitude quakes in the middle of the desert. Except earthquake prevention explosions now approached a million.

"Let's do this," said Harvey as he pulled up the holographic monitor to show a sampling of the ten thousand locations across the San Andreas that would have explosions, all large enough to produce impressive clouds of smoke worthy of sharing online with clever memes. The earthquake prevention explosions were typically fifty to a hundred feet underground and underwhelming. People's attention was starting to drift, and that meant funding might drift. Harvey came up with the idea of a major prevention event, to bring the program back into the public eye. He had to overrule everyone under him to get the project done. It even took a public firing of one of the most senior USGS scientists to finally bring everyone on board. But here they were, with actual reporters present.

"Are you ready to rumble?" said Harvey, laughing by himself as he nodded to Charles.

Charles swiped his tablet and set off the explosions. As expected, small puffs of dust were seen on the screen, one of which was pink.

"Is that a gender reveal?" said Harvey. "People still do that?"

Everyone clapped and wondered how much longer they needed to wait before getting back to their research. Then their watches and tablets started beeping. They looked at them and went pale. The students and faculty went frantic scrolling through the data coming in.

"What's going on?" said Harvey.

"Earthquake!" said one of the graduate students.

"Is it bad?" said Harvey.

Charles scrolled through his tablet as the seismic data came in faster than he could read it.

"Very bad," said Charles. "Valdivia bad."

The Great Chilean Earthquake of 1960 registered a 9.5 magnitude and was the most powerful earthquake ever recorded. Ten times worse than the 8.5 'Big One' suffered by the Bay Area in 2033, the damage not only battered the Chilean coastline but sent Tsunamis across the Pacific.

"Where? Where is it?" said Harvey as the mall emptied while the faculty and students ran back to their desks and laboratories.

"Not on the San Andreas," said Charles.

"That's a relief," said Harvey.

"No, it's not."

*

The earthquake began in the Mohave desert, at the base of the Walker Lane. It ran north through Death Valley up to the east of Bishop. Then it entered North Nevada near Hawthorne heading toward the west of Walker Lake.

The quake ripped through the Sky City launch area as Level Three of Sky City finished launching. The remaining two levels, over six hundred Skyboats, grew twitchy. They had started their engines, and some launched out of sequence. A mob mentality was forming across the desert.

"Everyone needs to follow protocol," Roger announced over the broadcast channel. "We will get everyone up safely, if we follow the plan."

Ben looked around the ground and saw some of the Skyboats begin to shake. He had no idea when the quake would stop or even soften. They had to get all the Skyboats up as fast as possible.

"I said now, Roger! Tell every Skyboat captain to launch. We need them off the ground," said Ben.

"That is not safe, we will have collisions," said Roger.

"Roger, use the emergency launch protocol and let's count on the safety software preventing Skyboats from launching into each other," said Ben. "Do it."

"What about the spectators?" said Paige.

"Let's get the boats up first, starting with *Horizon*," said Ben as he hung up and called his parents. "Mom, Dad, are you okay?"

"We're fine son," said his dad. "We're still on the top floor of *Horizon*. Totally fine. Don't worry about us. Go save everyone else."

"Okay, make sure you have a Skyboat ready to get out of here," said Ben.

"Attention all captains, launch your ships immediately," broadcast Roger. "Follow emergency protocols. Level Four Skyboats head south, Level Three east, Level Two west, and Level One north. Level Five head straight up for now."

Blue Darter, Firefly, Sky Dancer, Freedom, and *Serenity* separated and viewed the unravelling scene below. Level Four separated and began moving south. Some captains panicked and overrode the safety software causing them to ram other Skyboats, sending both to the ground. Ben knew Roger would hold this against him later, and he would have to listen to yet another lecture on protocol. Still, Ben believed sending all the boats up was safer than waiting and losing the entire Level One and maybe Level Two.

The earthquake continued east of Yerington up through Silver Springs, west of Fernley, and then west of Pyramid Lake. After Pyramid Lake, the Walker Lane quake curved west heading south of Honey Lake, south of Susanville, and running through Lassen Volcanic National Park. Back at the Sky City launch, thousands of spectators streamed across the grounds to find somewhere safe, but the entire Earth was shaking, and a rift formed in the ground.

"Roger, we need to start picking up the spectators," said Ben.

"Once we launch the Skyboats, we can begin recovering the spectators," said Roger. "I am not going to add more risk to this situation. You saw those crashes."

"Level Five is going to gather the people in the VIP section now," said Ben. "All the Skyboats are already away from it."

"I don't advise," said Roger.

"Noted. Angie, Jason, start loading VIPs into your boats," Ben said. "Daniel and Paige, follow Angie and Jason. I'll be behind you."

"Alana, you there?" said Ben.

"Ya, why wouldn't I be?" said Alana Noelani, Roger's first Lieutenant and former Air Force fighter pilot.

"How many of Level Four can help out with picking up the spectators?"

"Only me. It's all a bunch of lazy rich people that paid to be close to you."

Ben heard some harumphs over the channel.

"Level Four, stay out of the way but close enough to take on passengers," said Ben. "Alana, go get anyone you can that's in trouble."

"Done."

Alana disengaged *Kapani*. The other Level Four Skyboats moved up in the sky, far away from anything that could harm them, but close enough to gawk at the action. Alana dropped *Kapani,* three times the size of *Blue Darter*, toward the desert floor faster than any of the Level Five Skyboats. She stopped at the center stands next to the VIP section, with the largest crowd. She turned on her megaphone setting.

"People. I'm taking sixty of you. More boats coming and I'll be back."

"But there's hundreds of us," shouted the senator from North California.

"Stay calm; we'll get everyone. Women and children first."

"Keep families together," said the senator.

"No. Women and children first. And stop crying."

Alana lowered her railings, walked onto the stands, and began pushing the women and children closest to her onto the Skyboat while some of the men angled to move with them. She shoved one of them so hard he fell back into others, and they all stumbled onto the ground.

"You're last," she said pointing to him. "Don't break in line."

Alana went back to the wheel and launched, heading up to drop everyone off on the Level Four Skyboats. Ben, Paige, Angie, Jason, and Daniel landed after she launched. Their boats could take about twenty people each, and thanks to Alana, the spectators were more orderly loading onto the five boats, leaving just over half the original group on the ground. They followed Alana up to the Level Four boats, and she headed back down as they dropped off their passengers.

While the quake up north continued to head toward the Pacific Coast, down south it breached the San Andreas and ran through the Joshua Tree National Park, splitting the Salton Sea and going straight through Mexicali, the Colorado river, and then into the Gulf of California where it hit the Cocos Plate and stopped.

Ben raced *Blue Darter* back down passing *Kapani* as Alana went up with another sixty passengers. He landed at the stands and the secretary of the Department of Space pushed himself onto *Blue Darter*. A tall, handsome figure and one of the few in a suit, Kerry Reid had overseen the Department of Space for the past twelve years. While the beginning of his tenure had been marked with success, lately, he had several setbacks, most notably the secession of the moon colonies. Secretary Reid had put much of his political capital on the success of the Sky City launch. Being a private venture, the DOS had given significant leeway to the use of the United State airspace for the many practice runs needed to prepare all the Skyboats to connect as a Sky City.

"What have you done?" said Secretary Reid as he got in Ben's face.

"What are you talking about?" said Ben. "I'm getting you and everyone else out of here."

"Your launch started this," said the secretary. "You have ruined everything. I am getting reports the entire West Coast fell into the ocean. You did this Ben. You and you alone are responsible for everything that is happening."

"Ridiculous," said Ben, "and you know it."

"I never should have supported you and your insane idea. You will pay for this. I will make sure you pay for this. I'm not taking the fall for you."

"We need to get everyone safe before pointing fingers," said Ben.

As Ben flew the secretary and nineteen others to one of the Level Four Skyboats, the remaining spectators on the ground were approaching full panic as the earthquake continued to increase in magnitude. They began running for any Skyboats still on the ground, overloading them. Ben opened the broadcast channel.

"All external Skyboats need to pick up as many people as they can. Start with the other Skyboats on the ground. Use the flying taxi rules to avoid collisions," said Ben.

Up north, the quake continued west, south of the center of Redding and ran through the forests of North California straight into Eureka, splitting the coastal town in half and dropping Broadway and all the land in front into the water. Then the next dozen streets behind Broadway began crumbling. The quake hit the Gorda segment of the Juan de Fuca Plate and stopped. The West Coast from Eureka down to the end of the Baja Peninsula had begun moving northwest, into the Pacific and away from North America. Buildings and houses fell, tunnels collapsed, cables snapped, pipes broke, and the entire world stopped as the tragedy of the quake unfolded.

At Sky City, over two hundred Skyboats flew downward to pick people up. The flying taxi altitude rules, established in 2029 after a series of disastrous crashes, identified specific navigations for personal flying vehicles. Travel must be north at five hundred feet, east at seven hundred, west at nine hundred and east at eleven hundred. Below or in between those altitudes the taxis slowed down to not crash into anyone while changing direction.

Fortunately, pilots only had to look in one direction when changing altitudes to avoid each other. The altitude rules prevented crashes in the air, but slowed down the Skyboats recovery efforts. They continued to pick up passengers as the quake slowed down. A half hour later, the earth stopped moving. Another half hour after that the dust settled. A hundred Skyboats never made it airborne along with hundreds of people either lying on the ground or having fallen into the Earth's newest opening, rapidly filling with seawater.

The remaining Skyboats of Sky City floated above the desert, spread for miles. Staring down at the changed world below, many began flying back to their terrestrial homes. Ben had hoped the launch of Sky City would be spectacular, and it was, but in a way he never imagined.

CHAPTER THREE

LAKE TAHOE, NORTH NEVADA & NORTH CALIFORNIA

AUGUST 18, 2071

"Ben, I'm coming up," said Daniel.

"Why? We're about to launch," said Ben from *Firefly*, floating one-hundred fifty feet above Lake Tahoe along with a hundred other Skyboats displaying various colors on their sails and hulls. A rainbow of gennakers made it appear like a line of hot air balloons in the middle of a boat race.

"Kerry wants to talk," said Daniel.

"What? Now? Haven't we talked enough? The Regatta is going to start," said Ben.

Ben looked over the railing and saw Daniel loading *Serenity* with Kerry Reid and some other members of his Department of Space entourage. He saw a small wiry man, a large man with a buzz cut, and an attractive tightly-wound woman walk onto the deck before Daniel launched.

Ben was exasperated. Eleven months since the quake, and he could not get one day without the government crawling all over his affairs. Since that tragic day last September Ben and Daniel had spent thousands of hours negotiating each step of Skyboat Industries' future. After the government's two-month long damage assessment, which Ben had his team complete in two weeks, he was given a long list of requirements for future operations. They covered the revised Sky City launch, all the updated safety regulations, new flight path rules, even Skyball schedule changes, and an inquiry to review if the annual Skyboat Regatta was even a good idea.

Sky City was allowed to relaunch six months after the quake, but in stages, separated by two weeks, and with no more than two dozen Skyboats at any single physical location prior to launch. Painful was an understatement for the modified launch schedule. Also, Sky City had to remain in position over the desert near Yerington. What was the point of an airborne city if you were stationary? The launch was the least of Ben's concern. Half the Skyboats declined to come back after the quake. The half that did had their own list of requirements for Ben. There were countless concessions to anyone that asked, and Daniel had to be the one putting a stop to it due to the financial burden they placed on the company.

The Department of Space assessed that the Sky City launch was the most likely cause of the quake even though it began hundreds of miles away. Ben argued the ridiculousness of that assessment; a quake of any material size could not have been caused by his Skyboats. Also, there was the minor matter of the ten thousand earthquake prevention explosions. Not to mention the global consensus of the seismologist community that the earthquake prevention program was the cause of the quake and a colossal failure.

However, Ben's personal relationships with leading seismologists, particularly through his father, Dean of the Mackay School of Mining and Metallurgical Engineering at the University of North Nevada, raised eyebrows in the government and the press. The DOS jumped on that and argued the global seismologist community was compromised. No proof was provided, but the media needed readers and printed the scandalous headlines assuming proof would come out later, or not.

Then the DOS negotiated limited flight paths and usage for Skyboats, which crushed Ben's sales pipeline as well as the company's stock price. SBI lost thirty percent of its value once the markets opened back up after the quake and lost fifty percent of what was left after the DOS announced restricted flight path rules for Skyboats. And then as if to rub salt in his wounds, the DOS decided to create a sub-sub-department specific to the regulation of Skyball, the only airborne professional sports league.

They neglected to consider that Skyball games were always held over water or unpopulated areas, and that there had been zero injuries of spectators in its ten-year history as a professional sport, or that the power of the average skyboard was less than that of a typical motorcycle. No, it was another opportunity to regulate something, suck the fun out it, and create dozens of permanent government jobs. Ben's bitterness showed when assuming those last points.

But Ben signed up for all of it thinking each give would be enough. And then they brought up the Regatta. One hundred Skyboats circumnavigating the globe between the thirty and forty-degree parallels over some of the most populated areas on the planet. Kerry Reid always hated the Regatta. Ben expected it had to do with him having flamed out of the first one with a hundred-day voyage. Regatta rules, set by Ben, said you had to get around the world in eighty days to be eligible for next year's contest, and it didn't matter how much money you had, who your parents were, or what title you held.

Kerry Reid was one of many elites snubbed from future Skyboat Regattas. Ben could not care less. The Regatta was a contest for air sailors. A new breed with new skills. He wanted the best to compete. And he knew, but never discussed, that the audience loved seeing underdogs beat out the favorites. Innovative Skyboat modifications and new air sailing techniques brought surprises each year. Even with a nearly three-month long event, the Regatta's viewership continued to climb year after year. Traveling drones videoed the action as well as the cameras placed on each of the Skyboats, making for the ultimate reality show.

And that was one reason Ben pushed to hold the Skyboat Regatta. He wanted a distraction and felt others did too. A break from the stress of rebuilding the West Coast. The new bridges between the mainland and the California/Nevada/Mexico island were still in the pylon stages and more visible progress would not be seen for months. A year seemed like a long time, but not to those grieving loved ones.

People were beginning to move on, and Ben hoped the Regatta could help. Selfishly, he knew it would help him and his family move on as well. So, when the DOS dropped hundreds of pages of regulations to hold the Regatta, Ben agreed. More security, more oversight, faster disqualification for safety infractions, slower speeds, and higher altitudes over metro areas. Yes, yes, fine. Just let the event happen.

In past years, captains chose their team, size of boat and altitudes during the Regatta. Outside of no use of forward power, it was open to the captains' discretion how to win. Now, captains would have to refer to the *Air Sailing Safety Manual* recently published by the Department of Space Air Sailing Safety Sub-Committee (DOSASSSC), to ensure they were not disqualifying themselves during the race. With a twenty-thousand-mile distance, making the eighty-day deadline required ten and a half miles per hour average sailing speed. Always a challenge, but with the new regulations, most boats would find themselves disqualified before finishing.

Only the latitude requirement of traveling inside the thirty- or forty-degree parallels and keeping the start and finish line over America's largest alpine lake remained untouched. The hundred Skyboats waiting to participate in the fifteenth annual Skyboat Regatta were sailing in figure eights or circles just east of the negative one-hundred twenty-degree longitude starting line over Lake Tahoe, also the state line between North Nevada and North California.

As *Serenity* flew up toward *Firefly*, Ben saw the few spectators below split between fans and protesters. He might have made the wrong decision on this one. Then his optimism kicked in, and he told himself once the Regatta was underway, the positive energy of years past would return. He walked across the deck to his team, the same as always, Paige, Jason, Angie, and Ben's senior technical adviser, Ryan Callahan. One of the participating Skyboats, *Wiki Wa`a*, sailed right next to *Firefly*. Alana was behind the wheel while her brother Vali worked the rigging at the mast.

"Hi, Alana!" said Angie.

Alana looked over and nodded, then looked forward again. Vali looked up and saw it was *Firefly* and stopped working.

"Hey, Jason!" said Vali.

Alana was a large Samoan, but her brother Vali was simply huge. He stood to his full six-foot-nine-inches height and smiled, waving at Jason.

"You been practicing your trimming since last time? Or is your dad going to keep you working as rail meat again?"

"That's super helpful Vali, as usual. Hey, make sure you don't get thrown off by the boom this race!" said Jason.

Vali stopped smiling, told one of his crew members his rigging was wrong, and motioned for Alana to keep them moving past *Firefly.*

"We have some visitors coming before things get started," said Ben to the team.

"Just what we need," said Ryan with his black T-shirt, jeans, flip flops, long reddish auburn hair, and a hint of an Irish accent, "they're here to help, aren't they?"

"I'll handle this," said Ben as *Serenity* pulled up alongside. "The rest of you get ready for the Regatta."

The two boats railings lowered into their decks and the mini robots between them connected to form a walkway as the railings of both Skyboats connected. Secretary Reid walked over to Ben's boat followed by his team and Daniel.

"Benjamin."

"Kerry."

"I'd like you to meet my undersecretary, Dr. Martin Myers."

A small, gray-haired man offered Ben his hand, which Ben shook.

"Dr. Myers."

"And this is our lead counsel Robyn Hernandez," said Kerry.

Ben shook the hand of the attractive dark-haired woman who appeared to have a permanent smirk.

"Pleasure," said Ben.

"Mm-hmm," said Robyn, acting distracted, although taking in everything she could while on Ben Dawson's Skyboat.

"And our head of special projects, Dale Dobbs."

"What sort of special projects?" said Ben.

"Security, mostly," said Dale, a large blond-haired, blue-eyed man with what was almost a military haircut, except for the sideburns and stubble. He looked at Ben with a poker face, offering nothing.

"A little early for this sort of event, don't you think?" said Martin as he waved his hands at the other Skyboats.

"Not at all," said Ben. "People need this. A distraction to recharge. It's been nearly a year. Recovery work is well under way. Skyboat Industries has helped with many aspects of recovery hosting people, delivering supplies, and other services. You want everyone to sit around and mope all day?"

"There's always more to do."

"Of course, but people need a break."

"And since we're speaking of more to do, I'd like to schedule time with you after your extravaganza to discuss how you can do more."

Ben looked at Kerry who observed some of the other Skyboats, pretending to ignore the conversation.

"Kerry, when did you want to meet?"

"Oh, this will actually be with the team. We would like to see you in Denver as soon as possible."

"As soon as possible, after the Regatta?" said Ben.

"Isn't this event almost three months long?" said Martin.

"For some even longer than that," said Ben.

"This country cannot wait three months after what you did," said Martin. "There's much more you and your company need to offer the citizens of this country."

"Excuse me? Where do you get off?"

Daniel walked in front of Ben, cutting him off.

"Ben, you're needed on the broadcast," said Daniel. "Kerry, Martin, Robyn, Dale, why don't we head back down? Don't want to be in the way of the launch."

"That's exactly what I want to be in the way of," said Martin.

34

"Can't wait to meet with you," said Ben as the DOS group walked back onto *Serenity*.

Daniel disengaged and headed back down to the ground. He escorted everyone to a viewing table at the Edgewood resort where he had pre-ordered food and drinks. They sat with senators from North Nevada and North California, but the governors refused to be seen anywhere beside their offices since the quake. Not since the Great State Compromise of 2058 had something changed the country so significantly. Of course, the Great State Compromise was after the California compromise of 2044 that split California, Texas, and Alaska into three states apiece and granted Puerto Rico and Washington D.C. statehood.

Who would have thought the biggest fight on splitting three states would be which section of Texas retained the original state name? West Texas went down fast, no surprise. But the Dallas/Fort Worth fight against Houston/Austin/San Antonio almost blew the entire compromise up. In the end, Dallas/Fort Worth capitulated to being called North Texas with a clause that if their population ever exceeded Texas (it hurt them to write that) by more than thirty percent, they would take the name and Houston/Austin/San Antonio would become South Texas.

Originally, the argument for adding more states was around representation for large populations being that Puerto Rico had more people than twenty existing states. That was the main argument until the politicians began negotiating, and then it was about gerrymandering the new senators. Splitting Alaska into three states, with a population the same as Washington D.C., was illogical, but necessary, to even out the expected number of senators for each party.

Once the California Compromise passed, the Eight State Compromise of East Washington, East Oregon, North Michigan, North

New Mexico, North Iowa, North Idaho, North Wyoming, and North Maine passed seven years later. And if you were going to split Wyoming and Maine, then every state was eventually going to split. It continued with the Fourteen State Compromise of 2055, which also agreed to move federal agencies out of Washington D.C. permanently, since it was now a state.

The anticipated conclusion came with the Final State Compromise of 2058 that not only gave the country the fabulously named East North Dakota, West South Dakota, West South Carolina, West North Carolina, and East West Virginia, but granted statehood to the Virgin Islands and the combination of Samoa, Guam, and North Marinara Islands. This resulted in 107 states, 214 senators and 440 voting members in the House of Representatives (statehood granted the five non-voting members voting rights) from the passage of the 28th, 29th, 30th and 31st amendments.

A 32nd amendment passed a year later prohibiting the splitting of any states in the future, and then the rural states moved forward with the lever the big cities never anticipated, control of the money. They squeaked by the 33rd amendment that allowed a state to collect federal money from its citizens, but only for services it deemed necessary. It took just over third of the country's population to pass the 33rd amendment and turned the political power structure on its head.

The rural states created an alliance and combined their funds, allowing them to negotiate with the federal government on funded services. The Rural America Alliance, made up of seventy states, became the most powerful entity in the country almost overnight. Then the rest of the states scrambled to create alliances, like college football conferences, with the Pacific Coast Alliance, NorthEast Alliance, South SouthWest Alliance and, in true form, the Midwest did not even try to make their name cool with the MidWest Metros. Each alliance elected their own super governor, called commissioners, who became the primary contact between the states and the federal government. These commissioners effectively ran the country, with the RAA commissioner leading everything.

When the alliances formed, the federal agencies, seeing the writing on the wall, took the opportunity to grab more day-to-day decision-making responsibilities, pushing the Presidency to a placeholder position. They could change out the president with the vice president and no one would notice. Then the cuts began, and most federal agencies were decimated. Only the military and the newest federal agency, the Department of Space, retained the ability to grow year over year. After all, like the Department of Defense, the Department of Space, along with its many terrestrial responsibilities such as regulating Skyball, was also protecting the entire human race from possible extinction due to outer space threats.

But after the moon colonies secession, the Department of Space was next on the chopping block for the commissioner's funding cuts. Which meant Kerry Reid needed a major win before the next budget review. Major win. And when he sat back down at the table near Edgewood's eighteenth green, with the ten senators from the weakened Pacific Coast Alliance, they were all ears for how his meeting with Ben Dawson went.

"Just as I hoped," said Kerry, picking up his glass. "Sky City, and perhaps Skyboat Industries, are on their way to becoming the newest agencies of the Department of Space."

*

The Commodore's Skyboat, where Ben was supposed to be prior to launch but never was, came over to *Firefly*. The two boats joined via a walkway, and Ben walked onto the Commodore's Skyboat deck where the event's officials and announcers waited. The announcers asked him the standard lines about the state of the Skyboats, the weather, and his predictions.

They kept the conversation light and Ben wrapped it up fast; still thinking about the comments from Kerry and his team. Ben walked back to *Firefly,* the Skyboats separated, and the announcers handed it over to the officials. The Skyboat Regatta president, wearing the event's customary white slacks, light blue polo shirt and Regatta ball cap, took the mike.

"Ladies and Gentlemen," said the president of the Regatta. "It is our pleasure to announce the start of the fifteenth annual Skyboat Regatta."

He was interrupted by boos from protesters down on the ground. Ignoring them, he continued.

"We wish you all the best of luck and will watch you on your journey around the globe."

The Regatta's vice president held up a starting gun and fired. The Skyboats, which were already in motion toward the starting line, crossed seconds after the gun fired. But *Firefly* was not even pointed toward the start when the gun went off. Ben barely knew the race had started.

"Ben, focus!" said Paige from the bow of the boat.

Ben looked at the other boats leaving him over the lake. He got angry at the entire situation.

"Jason, trim the sail!" Ben said. "Ryan, help him out. Turn us around people! Angie, come take the wheel."

Angie took the wheel as Ben walked aft to Paige.

"Something big is about to happen," Ben said.

"With Kerry?" Paige said.

"Him and his team. They want me in Denver as soon as possible."

"After the Regatta? Or during?"

"Let's talk about that."

*

Firefly was having its worst start ever. Ben was distracted, the team felt it, and the entire situation became robotic. After much finger pointing, everyone took a break to eat. Ryan was at the wheel while the rest of the team sat around the cockpit as the California coast disappeared while *Firefly* sailed west over the Pacific.

"We've got a problem," said Ben.

"We've always got problems," said Ryan, looking over the horizon and trying to count the number of Skyboats still in view.

"The DOS is working on something. And it's not just more regulations," said Ben.

"That's good," said Jason. "Because I can't read any more regs like, '*Prior to the start of a Skyball event, the appropriate sub-sub-sub department will provide guidance, including decision criteria and tools, on the range of options for control, including those circumstances where measures, limitations, or authority may be an appropriate intervention.*' It's like they don't actually want you to know what they're saying."

"Or to be able to say anything they want," said Ryan.

"So much cynicism," said Paige. "Maybe they're just bad at their jobs."

Ryan, Angie, and Jason laughed.

"Or they're very good at their jobs," said Jason.

"What are they after?" said Ben.

"Break up Sky City," said Angie.

"Or put us under control of a government agency," said Paige. "Win-win for them; we lose Sky City, and they get everything we built."

"I'm calling Daniel."

Ben put Daniel on speaker.

"Daniel, did you get anything from them after the launch? What's Kerry planning?"

"Too much. They were almost chuckling with excitement. I'm checking with some other contacts to confirm, but what I know now is they plan to file eminent domain lawsuits for Sky City and SBI."

"They'll rue the day," said Ryan, shaking a fist to the sky.

"No one ever rues anything," said Jason. "It's all a legal fight now."

"You know I always have some tricks up my sleeve," said Ryan, "if it comes to it."

"Guys, please," said Ben. "Daniel, what would this look like?"

"First, they would injunction us to stop all our activities. That would squeeze us financially, and then they make the case Sky City is a public good and needs to be in the public domain."

"But what about all the owners of Skyboats?" said Angie. "How can they take away their boats?"

"I don't think they'd do that," said Daniel. "But they would take over the Skyboat Industries' boats and run Sky City like a United States territory."

"And where does that leave us?" said Ben.

"Not in a good place," said Daniel. "They might pretend to pay you out, but it would be nothing."

"I want you to get with your team and formulate a plan to fight this and delay it," said Ben.

"Of course," said Daniel. "And I suggest we begin a cooperation strategy at the same time. We work with them to avoid anything worse."

"Worse?" said Ryan. "What's worse than losing everything?"

"Criminal lawsuits for all of us," said Daniel.

"That's definitely worse," said Jason. "Jail sucks."

"And how would you know that?" said Angie.

"Documentaries and Procedurals. Lots of them," said Jason.

"You're so weird," said Angie.

"Here's what we're going to do," said Ben. "We'll play their game and make it convincing. As of now, no one outside this group talks about our plans unless I give the say so. As far as the rest of Sky City believes, we're handing it over to the DOS. Total confidentiality. I'm losing all my trust in people."

"I never had it," said Ryan.

"Does that mean we do or don't finish the Regatta?" said Paige.

"You will," said Ben. "I'm going to Denver. Daniel, can you come pick me up?"

"Already on my way," said Daniel.

CHAPTER FOUR

DEPARTMENT OF SPACE, DENVER, EAST COLORADO

AUGUST 19, 2071

Ben and Daniel walk into the waiting room of the secretary of Space. It was a nice room as far as government waiting rooms go, meaning it showed only a little bit of concrete. Even after the federal agencies were moved out of D.C., the new offices built across the country retained that stark government aura no matter how much was spent.

Ben and Daniel sat without talking as they waited. There was no point asking questions about where the secretary was or when the administrative assistant thought he might be free. It would be when it would be. After an hour, the assistant stood and unceremoniously walked them to the conference room.

"He'll be in shortly," she said and shut the door, walking back to her desk.

They continued to stare at the walls until thirty minutes later when Martin walked in.

"Gentlemen." He sat across from them. "Let's get started."

"Let's wait for Kerry," said Ben.

"I assure you I speak for him. He's given me every directive for this meeting."

"That's terrific, but let's wait," said Ben.

"That won't be necessary. He's been called into another situation."

"Then by all means, let's get started," said Daniel.

"Well, first, thank you for coming. I know you wanted to finish your little race, but we are still in a state of national emergency."

"It's a Regatta," said Ben.

"Still a race, and ultimately, just entertainment."

"Anyway," said Daniel. "We came to do our part for the restoration of the West."

"And thank you for that. The country thanks you, as do I."

"Uh-huh," said Ben.

"Specifically," said Daniel, "we've prepared a list of additional technology and supplies that Skyboat Industries is prepared to hand off immediately to the Department of Space for this purpose."

Daniel pulled a brief out of his folder and placed it across the table in front of Martin, which he ignored as he folded his hands on the table over the papers.

"While I appreciate you coming with a proposal, we already have a list; actually, it's more than a list. What needs to happen now is the United States Government needs to take control of Sky City and Skyboat Industries immediately in the interest of national security."

"What?" said Ben, getting out of his chair.

Daniel put his hand forcefully on Ben's forearm, and then his shoulder to bring him back down to his seat. Even after Daniel told Ben to be ready for this, he knew it would cause Ben to lose his composure when he actually heard it said to him.

"That's quite the ask," said Daniel. "How did you come up with it?"

"Not important. What matters is we move quickly. Every day, there are more lives ruined because of Sky City's recklessness. And, before we go any further let me be clear, any stalling by the company or, specifically, you, Ben Dawson, will be documented."

"Ben, let's think about how we're going to handle this," said Daniel, which was a pre-arranged code to tell Ben to shut it.

"I know how we're going to handle this. We're not," said Ben and stood. "Meeting's over."

"Ha, ha. Good one Ben," said Daniel. "He's a bit theatrical in his negotiations. Ben, come on, sit back down."

"I assure you this isn't a negotiation," said Martin, "and if you leave here with any hesitation about compliance, I will have the DOJ file criminal charges against you for negligent homicide."

Ben could no longer speak, he was about blow a gasket in his brain, which worked in Daniel's favor.

"Of course, we will agree to the government's wishes," said Daniel. "We are ready to serve our country. It's just a matter of process."

"No, we won't!" said Ben, finally figuring out how to get some words out and looking like he was going to strangle Martin.

"Ben. Sit down and be reasonable," said Daniel. "This can all be worked out."

Now Ben looked like he was going to strangle Daniel. Daniel saw the look in Ben's eyes and decided to end the meeting. He stood.

"Dr. Myers, I'm impressed," said Daniel.

"What?"

"This makes perfect sense, and we agree to it. Agree one hundred percent!"

"You do? I mean, good. No, I mean, of course and you better."

"I just agreed, why are you threatening us?"

"I'm not, just, you better."

"Again, with the threats?" said Daniel "What did you want from us today besides our agreement?"

"That's what I expected. Is he okay?"

Daniel and Martin looked at Ben, breathing like he finished a triathlon. Spittle came out of his mouth like he was also having a stroke. Various shades of red covered his skin.

"He's fine," said Daniel pushing Ben into a chair. "Congratulations all around. Now, how do you want this to be handled, logistically, Dr. Myers?"

"I will have my attorney contact you about specifics, but it needs to be quick."

"Of course. As quick as possible."

"So, you agree to this, right?" said Martin to Ben.

Ben had a wild look in his eyes as he turned to face Martin.

"Breathe, Ben," said Daniel. "Like we practiced. Just nod. That's it. All good. We're good."

Daniel hoisted Ben out of his chair and with firm hands on Ben's shoulder and his back they both exited the conference room. Martin nodded to himself as they left. They saw how this had to go. No one beats the DOS anymore. Not even Benjamin Dawson, who looked a little crazy. That guy built Sky City?

"Let's go home," said Ben as they walked onto *Serenity,* and he regained some of his composure.

"Home? Back to Sky City?"

"No, my actual home, in Verdi. The one I'll probably spend the rest of my time in now."

"Lovely."

CHAPTER FIVE

VERDI, NORTH NEVADA

AUGUST 20, 2071

B en sat in his home office with the lights off and the shutters almost closed, allowing the summer sun to filter in just enough light to make it the right amount of depressing. He tried to read, ended up working on his speed cubing, getting his solve time close to thirty seconds before a corner piece popped off and Ben ripped the entire cube apart. Then he stared at the walls of his office, glazing over the awards, magazine covers and shelves of Skyboat models. He got up to go meditate, which really meant take a nap, when the doorbell rang.

"No visitors," said Ben to himself as he ignored the doorbell and walked to his bedroom.

The doorbell rang again, and then a third time. Ben stomped across the ranch style house excited to let out some of his frustration on whoever dared to ring his doorbell three times, even if it was a kid selling cookies. He opened the door and saw his dad about to ring the doorbell again.

"Oh, good, you haven't killed yourself," said Neal Dawson.

"Funny."

"Can I come in?"

"Sure, why not? Coffee?"

"Okay."

Neal walked into Ben's house with the careful gait of an octogenarian that had multiple knee surgeries. Proud of the fact he walked without a cane, the last thing Neal wanted to do was take a tumble. While Ben went into the kitchen, Neal walked through Ben's living room out onto the back deck overlooking the Sierra Nevada and Truckee River. It was hot, so Neal opened an umbrella over the table and chairs and sat underneath it. Beautiful view from the deck of Ben's historic home next to downtown Verdi. Five acres with five hundred feet of river frontage.

Neal told Ben how smart it was to buy the hundred-year-old home. Not many of those in Verdi, especially with a large lot on the river. After moving in, Paige updated the house, still maintaining the original old west feel of the property. While the town of Verdi built up around them, their property kept the small-town feel. It was an oasis from the frenzy of everything else Ben was going through. When Ben told his dad about launching Sky City, Neal wondered how much time Ben would be spending here. Now, it was the other way around, and Neal hoped he could help Ben spend less time at home. Ben walked onto the deck and handed his dad a cup of coffee, sitting down on the other side of the table. They looked out at the mountains for a few minutes before either spoke.

"Where did I go wrong?" said Ben, still staring at the Sierras. "How did it all fall apart like that?"

"How bad is it?" said Neal.

"Did you know half of the Sky City Skyboats have left?"

"I did."

"And did you know that the DOS is prohibiting SBI from purchasing any more micro nuclear reactors? It's stopped manufacturing. We can't make any more Skyboats. DOS said they need the reactors for the restoration effort, which is a total lie, because I checked, and they're using the army's mobile nuclear reactors, and they have warehouses full of them."

"I knew that too."

"And we're losing tens of millions of dollars a day waiting for approval to re-launch?"

"Figured that."

"The Regatta was supposed to be our re-launch event. I'm running out of time and Reid knows it. He's just waiting for me to hand over Sky City. By the end of the year, I just might have to."

"Sounds desperate."

"Dad, I'm not a whiner, you know that. But I'm up against a wall here. We all are. For only the second time in my life, I don't know what to do."

"That's why I stopped by. I brought you something."

Neal put a book on the table, along with a fat fountain pen.

"What's this?" said Ben as he picked up the book, 'The Future Space Economy', turned it over and looked at the picture of the man smiling on the back.

"That's Robert Stewart. You remember him? Professor in our science department?"

"Planetary Science, right? Advocate for normalizing space travel before it was cool."

"Yes, but more than that. He said our future was out there."

"A bit generic, don't you think? How many space companies had that in their mission statement only to not get *out there*?"

"Yes, but he practiced what he preached. He was a leader at one of those companies that tried. It was acquired before it could get *out there*. After Professor Stewart's company was bought, he tried to go back to the University of Arizona, but they did not want him; said he was damaged goods. He called around, and we ended up speaking. He told me he was done with space travel and Planetary Science. Wanted to forget about all of it and go back to teaching geology. He was even willing to teach undergraduates."

"The horror."

"I offered him a position, and he and his wife, Beth, moved to Reno. Everything was quiet for a few years until he asked me about teaching a course in 'Physics and Chemistry of the Solar System'. Several students had been begging him to tell his theories about space exploration. I agreed, and he started teaching Planetary Science again. Became one of our most popular courses. Then he began doing a series of late-night, off-topic lectures on space economics for manufacturing, mining, and tourism. Wasn't a big deal until he brought up El Dorado. Tremendous riches within our grasp if we weren't too stupid to ignore it. Said he had proof. Said he might publish it, just to see who could get there first."

"Too bad, that would have been fun to watch."

"Maybe, but then he told me he needed to take some time off; felt he was being watched. He and Beth decided to get off the grid. They bought an Airstream and headed to Yosemite. Before he left, he came over and gave me this pen, as a thank you for hiring him when no one else would."

Ben picked up the pen, and it almost slipped out of his hand, surprising him with its weight.

"Heavy."

"And it doesn't write. Never has. Open it."

Ben unscrewed the pen and a metal rod fell out. It hit the table and dented the teak wood. Ben picked it up and looked at it.

"Dull and heavy," said Neal. "You know what that means."

"Valuable."

"Extremely valuable."

"Are you saying this is a sample of El Dorado?"

"That's what I believe," said Neal. "And I got this book in the mail two months after he and his wife left Reno. A month before the police found their trailer with no sign of either Robert or Beth. Trailer was trashed."

Ben opened the book and found the signed title page, inscribed with *'To my friend Neal. Maybe you or your family could do more with this than I could'*. Ben closed the book.

"He had already given me a signed copy of this book," said Neal. "Why would he give me a second copy?"

Ben opened the book again and paged through it. It was filled with highlights and notes in the margins.

"What's all this?"

"A cipher. Highlights, underlines, margin notes. Quite complicated."

"Maybe more than one cipher."

"Actually, yes. I counted three when I was done. And I need you to decode it. Check my answers and all."

Ben closed the book and set it on the table.

"Are you just trying to distract me? Is this a game to keep me occupied until I come out of my funk?"

"Hardly. It's a map."

"To El Dorado?"

"I believe so."

"Then why didn't you bring this over sooner?"

"You were quite busy with your Skyboats. And everything was going well for you. I thought this could be a challenge for your kids. It's not simple; quite dangerous in fact. Something like this will take all your focus. But I don't think it can wait, you need this now."

Ben flipped through the book again. No symbols, probably multiple substitution ciphers. Maybe start with a Caesar or ROT13. He'd also check for a Vigenère square. Quite the challenge. He went into the house and grabbed a pad of paper and pencil. He did not even make it back outside to the deck but set the book and pad down on the counter. Neal came back inside and set the pen down next to him.

"Make sure Angie calculates the coordinates on her own as well. With this sort of thing, we need to be sure."

"Uh-huh."

Ben did not notice his dad had left until he had to turn on the kitchen lights when it got dark.

CHAPTER SIX

PACIFIC OCEAN

AUGUST 21, 2071

The weather changed for the worse with dark clouds forming in front of *Firefly*. Paige, now in command, issued orders for the rest of the team to prepare for it. Main and head sails brought down, storm sails up, wings tightened. Altitude jest set to stabilize. As the storm clouds surrounded them, the Skyboat shook and lost altitude. They worked to get the Skyboat above the storm, increasing the thrust on the jets but not so much as to break the mast. Then they donned air masks and low temperature gear.

Firefly struggled as the wind pushed it off center and rain thrashed the crew. But eventually they broke through the clouds and could see for miles. Only a scattering of other Skyboats in the distance, with full sails. They immediately put theirs out. *Firefly* was on track to miss the eighty-day deadline. As they approached the east coast of Japan, Paige called a team meeting and criticized everyone for losing focus. But she followed up with how well they had performed in the past, that now they had one hundred seventy less pounds of overbearing attitude onboard so they could get back on track and still have a decent finish. Everyone stood in silence for a few minutes knowing Paige was not mad at them, or at Ben, and probably did not care when or even if *Firefly* crossed the finish line.

"Why can't the government just leave us alone?" said Ryan.

"Said everyone in the history of the world," said Paige.

"I'm serious," said Ryan.

"Didn't say you weren't," said Paige, "every government overreaches."

"Ben and Daniel are coming up behind us, fast," said Angie.

"No!" said Jason. "Mom, you have to tell Dad he cannot come back on the boat. No one is allowed on a boat after the race starts. These are his rules."

Serenity came up beside *Firefly*. Daniel had been running the jets at full blast with the sails and mast down.

"I'm back," said Ben as he jumped onto the deck of *Firefly*.

"And, we're disqualified," said Jason. "Now, Vali's team is guaranteed to win, again."

"We've got bigger fish to fry than the Regatta," said Ben. "Let's huddle up."

Daniel secured *Serenity* to *Firefly*, and they settled in the cabin, spread out between the couch and chairs.

"First," said Ben, "what Daniel thought was going on at Space is correct. The DOS is pushing to take control over Sky City and crush SBI."

"So, why are you smiling?" said Paige.

"Because I have a plan. Who wants to be a trillionaire?"

"You know, a trillion's not what it used to be," said Angie.

"Still enough for freedom," said Ben.

"And where would you find a trillion dollars?" said Paige.

"Remember the ocean lithium miners?"

"They crushed the price of lithium," said Jason.

"After collecting their fortunes. But I'm not talking about mining the oceans."

"Then where? the moon?" said Jason. "The cartel would stop you. That's exactly why they're there. And Mars is too far to be practical."

"Neither. Besides, you need to already be mining before the news is out. Both are too late. Something else, something magical, and I don't often use the word magical."

"At least outside of all-hands meetings," said Angie.

"Or earnings calls," said Jason.

"Stop it. Grandpa told me the story about Professor Stewart and his last asteroid probe."

"The one that blew up, melted on the tarmac, and ruined him?" said Ryan. "So many conspiracy theories about how it was more than that. How he was hiding something, and his CEO went crazy trying to find out. They even think he robbed Stewart's home and had Stewart and his wife vanish while camping at Yosemite."

Ben held up the book.

"They were looking for this. Or, what's in it. He sent it to my dad. And there's this little beauty."

Ben set down the book and pulled out the metal rod from his pocket, handing it to Paige. They all leaned in to look at it, then sat back wondering if Ben had lost it.

"Forty thousand dollars," said Ben. "That's what that rod is worth. Imagine what tons would be worth?"

"Tons?" said Paige. "Where?"

Ben pointed to the sky.

"You're not thinking about an asteroid, are you?" said Angie.

"Of course, I'm thinking about an asteroid!" said Ben. "That rod has a density ten times water, which is also ten times the density of any other asteroid samples. It's a full-blown metal asteroid, but its density is higher than iron, nickel, or cobalt. Based on my calculations, that means at least thirty three percent platinum group metals. Thirty three percent! Most samples are lucky to have three percent. Platinum, palladium, osmium, iridium, ruthenium, and rhodium. They could all be present in amounts more than the total mined on Earth. And it's a small asteroid. Not like those kilometer sized rock that need hundreds of people and take months to break down and ship back to Earth. And then once they manage to get it all here, they still have to extract the metals through smelting, electro-refining, and chemical operations. No, this is like picking up a massive golden nugget out of a shallow riverbed. The find of the century. Why wouldn't we go after it?"

"One," said Ryan, "it's impossible. Everyone who's ever tried it, failed, died or both. Two, it's illegal. Three, it's impossible."

"Who says it's illegal?" said Ben.

"Every government on Earth?" said Ryan. "After the 2048 near miss, anyone that tries to mine an asteroid without a global permit gets charged with a NELECA."

"NELECA?" said Jason. "Stop making stuff up. Pretty bad, even for you Ryan."

"Near Extinction Level Event Criminal Activity," said Ryan.

"You read too much," said Jason.

"Ben Dawson, this is crazy," said Paige.

"Well, let's get a permit and avoid the NELECA," said Jason.

"Funny," said Ryan. "That'll take five years, minimum, and an unknown number of bribes. We're talking about the United Nations here, it's not like bribing the Olympic Committee or FIFA. Look, before we waste any more time discussing this, think through it. Even if you could mine an asteroid, which you can't, no one will let you bring it back to Earth. And if you did, who would buy from you and risk their own NELECA charges? It solves nothing."

"Please, stop saying NELECA," said Angie. "Dad, even if we did it, how do you know where to go? There're over sixty thousand NEO asteroids."

"I know exactly where to go," said Ben. "This book has precise calculations, which is good because the asteroid isn't much larger than a storage shed.

"A storage shed is worth a trillion dollars?" said Paige.

"Like I said, thirty three percent platinum group metals," said Ben.

"Still can't sell it," said Ryan.

"There's always the platinum group metals black market," said Jason.

"We're not the mafia," said Paige. "I don't want to be the wife of a kingpin."

"Too late," said Angie.

"But if they did not know it was from an asteroid?" said Daniel. "And we were careful selling each element?"

Daniel tapped his fingers.

"A delicate process, very delicate. And you all need to think long and hard before embarking on it. But should it succeed, we could create a very large and continuous income stream. With careful selling it could secure an independent Sky City."

"Independent?" said Ryan.

"Like a nation, independent?" said Jason.

"Yes, exactly, a Sky Nation," said Daniel.

After everyone stared slack-jawed at Daniel for a few minutes, Ben stood.

"Okay, let's get to the details. Back to Sky City!"

CHAPTER SEVEN

DEPARTMENT OF SPACE

"We have to control this situation," said Martin as he paced across the carpet of Kerry's office. "I don't trust Ben Dawson."

Not only did Martin not trust Ben Dawson, but he also hated him and everything he stood for. Ben Dawson, eccentric entrepreneur, always speaking his mind about government interference. Complaining about how he just wants to be able to create, for the common good. Well Martin actually worked for the common good. And Martin knew what was best for them. Allowing a private individual to run as massive an operation as Sky City was not in the best interest of the common good. And now, after the quake, everyone knew it.

Ben Dawson, the man who literally shook the country, per Martin's press releases. Martin knew, when being honest with himself, which occurred only for a few seconds before he fell asleep at night, that tectonic plate shifts could not be caused by a slew of micro-nuclear jet engines in the desert. Too bad, it made for an emotional story. Martin ran with the story knowing most people don't get past headlines. And those headlines created a crisis allowing un-elected bureaucrats to establish permanent government policies. *Wait, that sounds wrong.*

To make honorable progress toward the Great Reset. Better, but still creepy. How about, Safety and security provided by the Department of Space for the honorable citizen? Ugh, who cares? Martin, like Kerry, needed the Department of Space to become relevant before the commissioners' meeting. They lost the moon, probably losing Mars, and maybe even the Gateway and the brand-new Space Colony. Space Force was so behind, they might not be ready in time to salvage anything. Then, talk about irrelevance. No way Martin is going to lose the very sky above him.

Kerry looked up from his tablet and realized Martin was still in his office. He stood from his desk, walked over to the window, and stared out of it. Kerry wondered why it was viewed as smart, almost prophetic, to stare out a window, yet a sign of insanity to stare at a wall. He guessed staring at a bookshelf would be somewhere in the middle, so long as he kept moving from book to book like he was reading titles.

"Martin, what do you see down there?" said Kerry not actually looking at anything. He was mentally reviewing his toolbox of pithy learning moments. This was how he got to be secretary of Space, his ability to impart wisdom through parables, like other famous people, including that Jesus guy. Kerry's parables were about demonstrating power more than wisdom because what mattered in this world was power and retaining it. And money. Money and power. Oh, and fame. Fame, money, and power; the trifecta that creates a legacy.

And Kerry was a legacy person. And he could continue working on it if he kept the Department intact. It was why he always had his tablet wake himself up with 'Remember, Director Reid, you have great things to do today'. Legacy.

Martin sighed. Another speech he would have to nod through to get Kerry to agree to what Martin had already decided was the plan. Why did someone that went to Stanford, Oxford, was a Rhodes Scholar, and earned a doctorate in 'Government Studies of Regulatory Bodies from the Sixteenth to the Twenty-Second Century' have to report to this clown?

"People?" said Martin.

"Exactly, and they look like ants; fumbling through their day," said Kerry making sure he remembered the lines.

"Of course," said Martin.

Kerry, as usual, made no sense because one thing ants never do is fumble through a day. Martin glanced at his watch.

"So, how do we protect them? That's why we're here right?"

Martin wondered how much faster he could have risen at the DOS if he had Kerry's hair and height, because it was obvious brains were not a requirement.

"Right?" said Kerry, exasperated at having to repeat himself. He was always a little annoyed at Martin because he did not take copious notes during their meetings. But it was Martin's father that hired Kerry into the DOS so he could not fire Martin; at least not while Martin's father checked in with Kerry every quarter.

"Right, of course," said Martin, waving a hand toward the people/ants. "And that is why it is so important we keep an eye on Benjamin. For the people."

"Good point," said Kerry, who was not so selfish as to withhold recognition of his subordinates' realization of his parables, although he was not actually thinking of Sky City, but probably where he was going with this.

"We lost control of the moon by not acting quick enough," said Martin, "and we may have the same fate with the space stations and,

God forbid, Mars. In fact, Space has not had a big win since we won the right from State to be called DOS."

"That was a big win," said Kerry, smiling. "I remember getting the call when they agreed to be forever known as the 'State Department'. Still have the plaque the staff gave me on the wall. Good times."

"So, how can we let Sky City take the very sky above us because we failed to act?" said Martin. "As you say all the time, 'we're responsible for the air above us.'"

Kerry did not recall ever saying that, but he made a lot of speeches, and it sounded prescient.

"Yes, yes. So, what's your recommendation?"

"Eminent domain. The skies are public use, no one person of firm should be able to lay claim to any part of it."

"Of course, you followed my lead perfectly. How quick can this happen?"

"We have to navigate the courts and all that paperwork. But my team can fast track it. Six months."

"And in the meantime? You said we need to control the situation."

"I suggest we monitor Benjamin and anyone working closely with him."

"What sort of monitoring?"

There had been some nasty issues with excessive government monitoring during the period of moon colony independence. Ruined careers.

"Nothing overt, very discreet. But Benjamin is smart and a fighter. We need to know about their plans. I will keep it light unless there's a concrete reason to go deeper."

"Light coverage only, that's an order. Keep me informed if you have to go deep."

"Will do. And as usual, thank you for the nugget of wisdom, always something to chew on after our meetings."

Kerry waved Martin out not realizing Martin had already turned and walked with purpose to his office.

"Get me Robyn and Dale," Martin said to his assistant as marched into his office, half the size of Kerry's, which always felt like an insult. Should be three-fourths at a minimum.

Robyn and Dale walked in seconds later.

"What's up, Boss?" said Dale.

Robyn stood, waiting.

"I've secured approval to move forward with our Sky City project, which includes surveillance. Robyn, secure a warrant for full infiltration of Sky City as a domestic terrorist organization due to the quake. Once you're done with that, prepare the injunctions and eminent domain filings. I told Kerry we'd be done in six months. Get me an updated timeline that shows it happening in half that. Dale, find a way to physically infiltrate Sky City, either you or someone already there. Whatever is happening with Benjamin and his people, I need to know. This is a matter of the highest national security, so get going."

As Robyn and Dale hustled out, Martin wondered what he might be missing. It was going too smoothly.

CHAPTER EIGHT

SKY CITY

AUGUST 22, 2071

After *Firefly* was officially disqualified from the Regatta, *Firefly* and *Serenity* flew back to Sky City. Jason complained, Angie teased him, and Paige told them to stop while asking why she was still having to referee when both of them were in their twenties. Then they all sat silent for hours until Ben could not take it. He set up a video screen between the two Skyboats asking Ryan to set up voice scramblers in and between the two Skyboats.

"Let's talk about the plan," said Ben. "Angie, use the book to locate the asteroid and the shortest path to it before the year is out."

"Didn't you already do that?"

"Yes, and so did Grandpa. But we need to be sure, so you take the book and figure it out yourself."

"You want me to decipher the codes in the book, identify the orbit of an unknown asteroid, locate where it is on the orbit right now, and then how we can intercept it in the shortest time possible, which has to be months from now, not years?" said Angie.

"Good, you know your assignment," said Ben. "Ryan, I need you to come up with a plan to mine the asteroid. And after you decide how to mine it, you also need a plan to get it back to Earth."

"But I said it's impossible," said Ryan.

"Exactly, which means your plan will be realistic. Besides, you are the only person that could come up with the tech for it."

"That's true," said Ryan, looking at the sky and beginning to work through the challenges.

"Jason," said Ben, "you have security. Not only can no one know about our plan, they can never figure out it happened."

"A perfect murder," said Jason.

"Gross," said Angie.

"Ryan, once you decide how to get it here, let's discuss recovery and storage. Daniel, you, and your team will come up with the stall tactics."

"I find the best plan in these situations is to act obtuse," said Daniel. "Ask countless clarifying questions, and since they likely don't know what they want, create many extra cycles."

"Perfect," said Ben. "And, Paige, if you're in, can you run mission control?"

"Why wouldn't I be in?" said Paige.

"You were kind of negative back there over the Pacific."

"Really? And Ryan wasn't?"

"That's just his nature. Anyway, great, you're Project Manager."

"I don't need a title."

"Angie, we need a way to get off the Earth," said Ben. "Probably a multi-hop space run to the asteroid. This is yours as well. That is, once you find the asteroid. Why don't you start with Bobby?"

"Bobby? Bobby Walker?" said Paige.

"Sure, why not?"

"I've got about a hundred reasons why not."

"Well, this is no time for grudges."

*

After everyone returned to Sky City and had a chance to sleep, Ben assembled the team back in the upper conference room at the top of the super structure of *Horizon,* above Command. Half the conference room was floor-to-ceiling windows looking out and up at the hub of Sky City. Much of Sky City was missing, but there were still hundreds of Skyboats around them and just as many personal carriers moving people and cargo. Ben, Paige, Jason, Angie, Daniel, and Ryan sat in the conference room when Alana walked in, wondering why she was invited to this random meeting.

"Where's the captain?" said Alana.

"He's got enough on his plate with Sky City and his personal situation," said Ben.

"Ah, yes, terrible," said Alana. "Sometimes work is a stress relief, though."

"Not this kind of work," said Ben.

The captain called Alana, she clicked him in.

"I'm in a meeting. Ya, I'll ask." She muted him and looked at Ben. "He's wondering how long this will be."

"It will take what it takes," said Ben. "Could be all day."

Alan clicked the captain back on.

"What do you need? Ya, I'll be there in forty-five." She clicked him off. "Okay, I'm ready."

"You always this easy to work with?" said Jason.

"No, sometimes I'm in a bad mood," said Alana.

"I guess we'll start with you?" said Ben to Alana.

"Good idea," said Alana.

Daniel locked the door, Ryan turned on three different noise scramblers and Paige changed the windows to opaque, allowing nothing more than shapes to be visible from outside. Ben pulled up a holographic white board.

"Everybody, here's the plan," said Ben, and he had bullet points and some crude animation show up on the holographic white board as he talked. "Our primary goal is to launch a team into space, build out equipment to mine an asteroid, send the asteroid back to Earth, recover it, and bring everything back to Sky City."

As Ben covered the plan, the whiteboard showed black and white animation of a 1960s rocket leaving Earth, stick figure astronauts leaving the rocket with a rope that they then use to lasso an asteroid and pull it back toward Earth. The crude Earth drawing then magnified showing an oversized rock landing on a Skyboat with smiling stick figure sailors waving and flying it back to an animated Sky City where fireworks shot out above the dome.

"Uh, how long did you spend on that?" said Paige.

"Not long," said Ben, "couple hours at most. Point is, we have a lot of steps. Let's walk through them. Ryan, how about you take this?"

Ryan stood and wiped the holographic board clean with his hand. He pulled out a holographic pen and began writing.

"First, we'll launch from Earth with a LEO Transco rocket. The rocket will clear the Earth's atmosphere and converge on the Gateway station."

"Daniel," said Ben, "I need you to get us access in and through the Gateway."

"Of course," said Daniel.

"Once you pass through the Gateway," continued Ryan, "you'll land at the lunar colony."

"Question," said Angie, "who is this *you*?"

"Good question," said Ben. "It's you, you, you, and you."

He pointed to Angie, Alana, Ryan, and Jason.

"All of you will need to get each other and the equipment safely to the moon. At that point, Jason will come back for the asteroid collection while the three of you will build a spaceship to get out to the asteroid."

"Build what?" said Alana.

"We're going to have to use the parts already on the moon to construct a spaceship to get to the asteroid," said Ryan. "We can't get any new parts up there. No time, space, or money for that."

"You can do that?" said Alana.

"I can do that," said Ryan.

"Okay," said Alana. "Next."

"Ryan, why don't you cover the mining operation?" said Ben.

"As you all know from your pre-reading material,"

"Whoa, when did you send that out?" said Jason.

"Three am. And I'll assume you didn't read it," said Ryan.

"Unnecessary," said Jason.

"The typical methods discussed for asteroid mining and retrieval are solar sailing, cable cutting, or bag capture. All lengthy, expensive, and boring."

"So, what's your plan?" said Alana.

"I'm going to blow it up," said Ryan.

"Of course you are," said Angie.

Ryan clicked on the whiteboard to show his asteroid mining animation, which had enough detail to look like an actual film of an asteroid.

"We'll take micro nuclear reactor silos that will dig into the rock, which will blow it up into equal sized chunks. They will then pulse each rock separately to time them into a row that will re-enter the atmosphere and land over the Pacific, where Ben and Jason will collect them."

"You're going to identify exactly where a boulder is going to re-enter Earth?" said Jason.

"Yes," said Ryan. "I'm good at math. And before it enters Earth's atmosphere, it's called a meteoroid. What you'll be picking up, we hope, are several, very valuable meteorites.

"How heavy are these meteorites?" said Jason.

"About the weight of a 747," said Ryan, "like four-hundred thousand pounds."

"We have to catch an airplane?" said Jason.

"Hey, not a fully loaded one," said Ryan. "That's dry weight. Also, much smaller. Around a five-foot diameter boulder."

Jason stood.

"A five-foot boulder weighs four-hundred thousand pounds and I'm supposed to catch it while it flies down from space?"

"When you put it like that, it does sound pretty hard," said Ryan. "Also, you will need to catch sixteen boulders."

Jason sat.

"This plan sucks."

"Thanks Ryan and Jason for that honest discussion, lots to think about," said Ben. "On that, Angie, tell us more about this asteroid."

Angie stood without the swagger and confidence of Ryan. Although she was the only rocket scientist and the only one in the room Ryan even considered a peer, she was always struggling with poser's dilemma. Perhaps being adopted by the Dawson family from Vietnam or being one of a small number of female Aeronautical Engineers receiving a doctorate at Georgia Tech, or her quiet personality, versus her dad and brother's outgoing style, made her self-conscious. Of course, she was as much a part of the Dawson family as anyone, and they were more excited than even she was to have her. But she looked different, as much as she tried to forget it. Everyone had their issues.

For example, Ryan, a proclaimed permanent bachelor after his second divorce, was terrible at relationships. Jason always had a quip to cover up his insecurities, and her dad, well, there's not enough time in the day for that hairball. Angie took a breath and wiped the holographic board clean with a wave of her hand, and with another wave replaced it with a view of space between Earth and moon. She zoomed in until the white board filled in with a potato-shaped rock rotating in space.

"I went through Professor Stewart's book and identified the asteroid's orbit as an Aten class NEO with a 0.86 to 1.0028 AU."

"That's a lot of decimals on that last number," said Jason.

"Well, Jason, since an astronomical unit is ninety-three million miles, we need to use a lot of decimals."

"Touchy," said Jason.

"Based on that," continued Angie, "and that its orbit is just under a year, I calculated we have an opportunity to reach the asteroid, without detection, during a two-day window where the moon will be full, and the asteroid will be at its aphelion."

Jason opened his mouth.

"That's the farthest point from the sun on its axis," said Angie. "It also will be behind the moon and with a 1.9 inclination angle, meaning, a low angle, so it will be hidden from Earth for two days, November seventh and eighth.

"Two thing," said Jason. "One, was anyone going to point out that November eighth is also my birthday?"

"No, we were not," said Angie.

"November eighth?" said Alana, "makes sense, Scorpio, right?"

"That's right. Thanks Alana," said Jason. "Two, Dr. Dawson, how confident are you that the orbit of this tiny little asteroid is correct?" said Jason.

"Very confident. Over ninety-nine percent confident," said Angie.

"Is that a calculation or are you just spit balling?" said Jason.

"Spit balling?" said Angie.

"It's solid," said Ryan. "The data and the rock. I checked Angie's calcs. She's ninety-nine point nine nine nine percent correct."

"I'm no rocket scientist," said Jason, "but we're attempting to find a dark asteroid the size of a storage shed in the middle of space inside a forty-eight hour window. Seems like we need one-hundred percent."

"I've worked the calculations myself, and so did your grandfather," said Ben. "Professor Stewart was a genius, and he got this right. No one else knows about this asteroid, but it is there, and we can find it. I know we can. This is a chance for true freedom and who gets a shot at that? You can look at the data for yourself if you want to check it for a fifth time."

"I think I will," said Jason.

"Go ahead," said Angie.

"Thanks, I will."

"Do that."

"I'm going to," said Jason, folding his arms. "I've got that latest star-gazing software."

"That's not what I used!" said Angie.

"Enough," said Paige. "Drop it. Jason, you have until tomorrow morning."

"Jason, why don't you focus on recovery instead," said Ben, "you have to be ready to pull down those meteorites after Angie mines them."

"Oh, I will be ready, one-hundred percent ready. But I'm still double checking everything else and looking to add up all our one-percent and point one-percent chances of failure. Hope it's not over fifty percent, but probably is."

"Jerk," said Angie.

"Listen up," said Ben. "Paige is our mission control. She'll set up in *Firefly*, avoiding detection. What she says, goes. And Daniel will continue to run interference between us and the Department of Space."

Ben looked around and saw a mixture of hope, dejection, and anger. But when he looked closely, he saw a spark of excitement.

"Okay, everyone, we have less than three months to save Sky City. Let's go do the impossible."

CHAPTER NINE

PACIFIC OCEAN

SEPTEMBER 8, 2071

"We'll stop here," said Ryan.

Ryan's Skyboat, *Nautilus*, hovered over a turquoise section of the Pacific. Ben pulled *Blue Darter* up next to Ryan, and Jason stopped *Sky Dancer* next to Ben. Jason asked Jesse Taylor, the newly minted Head of Security for Sky City, to join him on *Sky Dancer*. Jesse and Jason played Skyball together in the past. Before that, Jesse play rugby and before that he was in the Marines, or some sub-group of the Marines. He never talked about it. Jesse was average height and build with thick black hair he let grow a bit long in the back now that he was out of the military.

Alabama boys still liked their hair long in the back. But don't call it a mullet, it just looked like a mullet. At least he shaved off the thin mustache. Jesse had a quiet undercurrent of calm about him that gave most people chills when they met him. Nothing rattled him, nothing, and no one. But when he smiled, people relaxed and knew they had nothing to fear from him, so long as they were not a threat. But if they were a threat, they would find out how fast someone could be disarmed and incapacitated, making Jesse perfect for the head of Sky City Security, replacing Jason, who gladly handed it off.

"Beautiful day," said Jesse. "What's the plan?"

"I'm going to teach you guys how to play catch," said Ryan. He undid the two rubber latches of the forty-eight-gallon bear-proof cooler on his deck and pulled out two balls of mini drones, one of which included a nuclear rocket. Ryan loved his coolers. They could be holding iced beverages or tech prototypes, but mostly beverages. Ryan guarded his privacy and used innocuous coolers to carry around cutting-edge technology. He picked up his tablet, expanding it twice to its full size and fired off the canopy drones. They flew a thousand feet above the Skyboats and extended their nano screens across the top of their bodies. The hundreds of drones created four checkered layers with their screens mimicking the ocean. Then he picked up the other drone ball and showed it to Ben, Jason, and Jesse.

"This represents the asteroid chunks that Angie will, hopefully, successfully mine and send back to Earth. I'm going to head up and send it your way, increasing its speed each time until we get close to the actual boulder reentry. The canopy I set up above isn't a perfect cover. One of those satellite viewing geeks at Space is going to figure it out pretty quick and send some of their drones to check it out. I figure we have half an hour before that happens, so this is going to get intense fast. Go ahead and connect, and then use your wings as the net. You will also need to shoot the pneumatic launchers with the grapnels to help stop the rock."

"These things?" said Jesse as he picked up a fifteen-pound launcher that looked like a bloated shotgun with a bag attached underneath.

The pneumatic launcher had an extra wide barrel for the grapnel and large cylindrical fabric bag below the barrel holding the steel cable connected to it.

"Glad you figured that out Jesse," said Ryan.

"Yeah, I've used them before to get into places, never to catch things out of midair."

"Then you're qualified," said Ryan.

"That drone ball has a nuclear rocket in it?" said Jason.

"Sure does," said Ryan.

"You're throwing those things in everything now?" said Jason. "I mean, sure, you figured it out for the Skyboats, but a drone ball?"

"It's the safest thing around," said Ryan. "If you somehow hit it, which you probably will, and break through both steel walls, which you won't, you would be showered with harmless ceramic pellets. But if you want, I can switch it out with those mini jet engines you love, and then if you hit that and it explodes you can be showered with ignited jet fuel. Your choice."

"Just launch the ball," said Jason.

Ryan headed above the other two boats. He stopped *Nautilus*, looked over the side, and they waved at him. Ryan turned back to his drone ball and with his tablet started eight of the mini drones on the outside layer of the ball. They lifted the ball above the deck and Ryan swiped the tablet for the ball to extend its aluminum rods, pushing all thirty-two drones to the exterior of the ball shape with only the nuclear rocket in the center. It went from the size of a basketball to an eight-foot rock, floating in front of Ryan. He turned on all the drones as it headed toward the drone canopy. Once it was just underneath the canopy Ryan had the drones turn the rock over and shut off, sheltering their propellors as the nuclear rocket ignited. Then he sent it down toward the water.

"Here it comes," said Jason as he connected *Sky Dancer*'s wing to *Blue Darter*'s with the mini robots.

"What setting do we want the wings at?" said Jason.

"Let's go with solid," said Ben.

The drone boulder was just above them as the three men shot their grapnels at the drone rock, way too late. Each of the grapnels went over the drone rock as it smashed through the wing barrier, the mini robots flying everywhere and causing both Skyboats to roll hard sending Ben, Jason, and Jesse to their decks. Ryan clicked into their ear pods.

"That's a super F. That boulder fell at one tenth of what I estimate is the actual re-entry force. But there's good news; you can't do any worse. Also, I'm going to initiate the directional sensors on the grapnels."

"Funny guy up there," said Jesse.

"Wanted to see what happened before you had my help," said Ryan as the drone rock shot back up above *Nautilus*. "Let's do this again with more speed."

"Wait, Ryan, give us a sec—," Jason re-loaded a forty-five hundred psi pneumatic cylinder into the launcher and connecting his wings to Ben's when the drone rock turned and headed back toward them.

"Change the wing setting to permeable," said Ben. "Aim the hooks thirty feet above the wings."

Jason clicked in the pneumatic cylinder, picked up the launcher and aimed at the falling rock. He shot a little too early this time, but the directional sensors in the grapnels adjusted the trajectory after ejecting from the pneumatic launcher tube and hit the drone ball flying around the nuclear rocket. Then the grapnel released its own spider-like drones that covered the rock with micro cables.

"Pull in the hooks," Ryan said over their earpieces. "Use the foot pedals."

Jason, Jesse, and Ben pressed the floor pedals next to the winches secured on the decks of *Sky Dancer* and *Blue Darter*. At 3500 rpm they began retracting the hundred sixty feet of steel cables connected to the end of the grapnels. The drone rock fell into the wings as it was pulled back by the retracted cables but still broke through with less mini robots falling into the ocean.

"Release the hooks," said Ryan.

The three of them pressed the release buttons on the launchers and their grapnels let go of the drone rock as it splashed into the ocean. They reloaded the launchers and reset the wings. Ryan brought the drone rock back up above *Nautilus*.

"You ready to start trying?" said Ryan. "We're running out of time here."

Jason, Jesse, and Ben reloaded and heaved the launchers back up to their shoulders. Ben was getting tired. Jason and Jesse were getting annoyed.

"Let's harden the wings up a bit," said Ben as he adjusted the mini robot clamp tension across the two connected wings.

"On my mark," said Jason aiming the launcher at the rock.

"Let's go," said Jesse. "I'm not used to failing."

Ryan launched the drone rock at them with eighty percent speed, four times the prior drop. Ben, Jason, and Jesse could barely see the drone rock, and then it was right above them, like a fastball pitch in the majors.

"Now!" said Jason.

All three hooks headed straight at the drone rock. Before they hit the rock, Jason and Jesse dropped their launchers and were at the winches. As soon as they saw them connect, they hit the foot pedals and began winding in the cable. Ben was a second behind. All the cables became taught as the drone rock fell toward the Skyboats.

"The wires are pulling the rock down faster," said Jesse.

"It'll hold," said Jason.

The drone rock hit the wings. It pushed down into the mini robots and their clamps began breaking and the honeycomb drones splitting in half. The drone rock slowed but fell through the wings. Ben's cable snapped as the droned rock fell toward the water while the two winches on *Sky Dancer* smoked but kept pulling the drone rock back toward the Skyboat. *Sky Dancer* listed, and Jason and Jesse held onto the railings while everything slid to the starboard side. The Skyboat was about to capsize when Ryan turned off the nuclear rocket. The winches snapped the drone rock up, hitting the railing and sending Jason and Jesse back on their heels.

"Come on!" said Jason.

Ryan flew down to them.

"We need to go, I picked up some DOS drones approaching. Bring all that stuff on board and throw me my drone ball. The actual boulders won't be much faster. But they will be heavier."

"I have a few suggestions, for next time," said Jason.

"Send 'em over," said Ryan.

"Good job fellas," said Ben. "Jesse, glad you're on the team."

"Glad to be of service Mr. Dawson."

"Call me Ben."

"Sure thing, Mr. Dawson."

"Okay, let's head," said Ryan as he turned *Nautilus* back toward Sky City.

CHAPTER TEN

LEO TRANSCO, MOUNTAIN VIEW, NORTH CALIFORNIA

Angie and Alana entered the hanger on Moffett Field in Mountain View, North California. While the hanger did not fall into the bay from the quake, the golf course next to it was gone. The pair wore jeans, tennis shoes and T-shirts, attempting to make the meeting as casual as possible. Angie and Alana passed by several short-range passenger carriers, finding themselves drawn to a brand-new rocket ship.

They circled the carrier, admiring the sleek lines as it was a blend of airplane, spaceship, and rocket. They walked up the ladder to look inside at the intuitive cockpit controls, expansive leather passenger seats and massive windows that would allow for spectacular views when airborne above the Earth. Alana saw similarities to the Skyboat controls in the cockpit, which were patented. She had heard about Mr. Dawson's history with Mr. Walker, and those controls seemed to confirm at least part of it.

"A beauty," Alana said to Angie. "This will do."

Bobby Walker made his way to them from across the hanger. He wore a navy suit and white dress shirt, open at the collar. His black leather dress shoes echoed off the fifty foot high ceilings, which were closed now, but opened whenever he wanted to take the ships out for a quick spin into space. A man of average height but unlimited ambition, Bobby prided himself on looking the part of CEO.

Always smiling, even when firing people, which was often, he was first and foremost a salesman. A fanatic about fitness and expensive hair plugs, Bobby maintained the perfect weight for his height and always had a slight tan. Bobby stopped near where the few employees that were in the hanger were working and sent them out so he could have a private conversation with Ben Dawson's adopted daughter and her large lady friend, who looked former military. Once the workers left, he went over to Angie and Alana.

"How wonderful to have you two lovely ladies from Sky City visit my humble workplace," said Bobby as he walked up next to them. "Bobby Walker, CEO and Chairman of the Low Earth Orbit Transportation Company. And while we're at it, former boss of your dad."

Bobby smiled and shook Angie's hand.

"You have good taste," he said, turning to Alana as she stepped off the ladder of the new passenger carrier.

Alana walked over to Bobby and shook his hand, giving a bit more pressure than necessary.

"Alana Noelani, second in command of Sky City."

"Wow, impressive. Congratulations. You like this vehicle?"

"Yes, it's nice. I guess," said Alana taking an instant dislike to Bobby. She did not do slick.

"It's our most advanced short range passenger carrier, the R9. From launch to space station in less than six hours, holding up to a dozen passengers in total comfort along with a half-ton of their cargo. And enough fuel to make a round trip."

"It is definitely what we're looking for," said Angie.

"For what? You don't need this baby to get to Sky City?" said Bobby with a semi-forced, but well-rehearsed chuckle.

"We're planning a lunar mining operation," said Angie. "An exploratory mission to add to the Sky City business portfolio. We need a minimal crew and cargo. This is the size of ship that works for that."

"Fascinating," said Bobby, who was not fascinated, but thinking. "So, Ben wants to mine the moon? That's not a new thing, and he only does new things."

"What we're looking at is new, and confidential," said Angie. "Over seventy-five percent of the moon is still unclaimed and unknown."

"True. But what about the lunar cartel? Doesn't matter if you make a spectacular find on the moon, which I doubt. They won't let you take it off the surface unless it's through them."

"We can work with them," said Alana. "Everyone likes money. Don't you?"

"That's a distasteful way to put it. I don't like money for its own sake. I like what it allows me to do. Look at all the lives my company impacts. We give people a way to pay their bills, raise their kids, pursue their dreams. I think of creating value, not money. That's how we pull people up, by creating value. Ben and I always agreed on that. Too bad, we couldn't agree on more. But these cartel members, I don't get the sense you or your dad have thought through this. They don't play well with others. That's one reason I stick to transportation. LEO Transco is everyone's partner."

"Most people say you are your own cartel," said Angie. "One of the largest conglomerates in the world after you bought up all the other low Earth orbit rocket companies."

"My dear it's called an efficient market. Why would you want two sets of wires across the country for your electricity? Doesn't make sense."

"That's not the same argument," said Angie. "You could have shared launch pads, at least until you bought them all and forced others to pay you to launch off them. Seems very cartelish to me."

"Anyway," said Bobby. "What if you do find something? How do you plan on dealing with them?"

"Not sure why anyone is interested in an exploratory mission," said Angie.

"Oh, they're interested in everything, trust me on that one," said Bobby.

"We didn't come to discuss our mining plans," said Alana. "We need a rocket. How much to rent this one?" said Alana as she slapped the side of the R9.

"Rent? That's not how this works," said Bobby. "I don't scrub the seats and vacuum the carpet after a launch for the next billionaire to use a rocket."

"Okay, how much to buy?" said Angie.

"Well, quite a lot. The problem, however, is this one's sold. As is every rocket in this hanger and every rocket that's going to be manufactured for the next year. We're doing very well if you can't tell from the stock price."

Bobby walked around to the front of the R9 looking at it.

"But I can put you on the waiting list if an order gets cancelled."

"How often does that happen?" said Angie.

"Never. But it makes people feel better."

"So, why did you meet with us if you can't sell us anything?" said Alana, walking over toward Bobby.

"Ben and I don't talk anymore. I wanted to reconnect."

"So, you don't have anything we can use?" said Alana looming over Bobby.

"Well, if you're willing to go a little retro, I might have something."

CHAPTER ELEVEN

DEPARTMENT OF SPACE

SEPTEMBER 9, 2071

"Marty, how's it going?"

"It's Martin, preferably Dr. Myers. I earned at least that much respect."

"Sure, Dr. Myers. Better?"

"Bobby, what can I do for you?"

"Yeah, I'm fine with you calling me Bobby. Anyway, I have information. It's juicy."

Martin sat up in his office chair. He shooed his administrative assistant out of his office and waited for her to shut the door.

"Good, good. What do you have?"

"Turns out your new business partner, Benjamin Dawson, is preparing an exploratory lunar mining operation."

"How do you know that?"

"Because I just sold his team a retro small cargo rocket. Hope he can get it to work, I couldn't. But here's the good news. Even if he can figure out how to get the rocket to work without exploding, there's nowhere to launch it for six months and no way to get clearance to dock at the Gateway or the HOSS 2 station. But even if Ben managed to overcome all those hurdles, I placed a call to let the lunar cartel members know they're coming. So, anyway, that's my gift for you today because we're friends and all."

Bobby clicked off the line. Martin sat back in his chair, put his fingers together and slowly tapped them as he digested the information.

"Robyn, come in here."

Robyn was deposing the CEO of a sky taxi company. She accused him of cheating during the last union vote. Martin ruined her train of thought.

"We're done for today. Don't leave town as I'll be re-scheduling," said Robyn.

"But I've got a business to run on the West Coast," said the CEO. "Especially after the quake."

"Not my problem."

Robyn stood from the conference table and left the CEO, his attorney, and the stenographer to finish up. She rushed down the hall to Martin's office.

"What's going on?" Robyn said as she entered.

"Ben is up to something."

"Of course, he is. People like him always are."

"But this is big. He's bought a rocket to explore lunar mining."

Robyn snorted. "What a waste of money. It will go nowhere."

"Exactly. And Ben knows that. What does he know that we don't?"

Robyn sat.

"He could be trying to negotiate some partnership with the cartel members," said Robyn. "Maybe Sky City will distribute for a lower cost," said Robyn.

"Possibly. He can't sell part of Sky City while we're working through the eminent domain case, can he?"

"I'll look into it. I'm not sure there's a loophole but if one exists, I'll close it."

"Good. Now, what else could he be doing?"

"Maybe he does have some new find on the moon? Something from one of Daniel's contacts? He's going to need a lot of money to restart after you take away his baby."

"True. But you know he's going to fight us. We need to think about the unexpected, the wild card. What are we not considering?"

"I don't know. He's moving to Mars?" Robyn laughed again.

Robyn did not consider Ben Dawson as anything more than another notch for her belt of high-profile wins, like the class-action lawsuits earlier in her career. The bigger the name, the bigger the coverage, that's how Robyn Hernandez always decided which cases to take. Smart, attractive, and ruthless, she was a juggernaut of a lawyer. She knew she would crack into the elites' club, just a matter of time.

"He's not moving to Mars or the moon and he's probably not partnering with any of the cartel members. That's not his style. He's up to something crazy," said Martin.

"Sure, like mine an asteroid," said Robyn.

Martin sat up straight. "That's it! That's what he's doing."

"No way, it's impossible. And Illegal."

"Exactly. That's why he would try it. No regard for the law."

"Well, let him have at it and fail like all those before him. And then we'll arrest him once he's back on Earth based on the 2048 second Artemis Accords, section seven, part three, which states, '*to avoid the possibility of near extinction level events, all contact with asteroids is prohibited without an approved permit from the United Nations. Anyone caught attempting to collect an asteroid within three astronomical units of any point on Earth's orbit will be charged with a global crime against humanity."*

"How do you do that?"

"I pulled it up on my augmented reality contacts. I've configured them to work with hand motions and blinking. You should get some."

"Maybe later. I know who we need to bring into this."

Martin called Don LaRue.

"Don, Martin here. We may have an asteroid hunter."

Don LaRue, deputy director of transportation for the NSA, and a senior advisor to US NORTHCOM, felt his pulse tick up. Not from hearing Martin's voice, that was an immediate buzzkill, namely because Martin always wanted something and promised to repay the favor but never did. No, Don's heart began pumping blood faster through his body because he heard, *asteroid hunter.*

Although Don's title impressed on a holographic business card, he was a glorified traffic cop dealing more and more with LEO Transco complaint escalations. Don was responsible for the sky over the United States and the Pacific. He managed to get that extended up to, but just below the moon's surface. And Don used that to become the pre-eminent asteroid hunter enforcement agent after the 2048 debacle. Two asteroid mining companies competing for the same metal asteroid at 1.04 AU. Idiotic.

Two CEOs fighting to be the first to mine the same rock. They each sent up teams to carve up the half mile diameter metal potato. Mining it as fast as possible, seeing who would beat the other. And then they changed its orbit, sending the asteroid toward Earth. Wasn't the first time two ultra-high egos threatened humanity, but at least in the past they had the decency to be elected. The asteroid missed Earth by thousands of miles, but it never should have happened, and it never would again. Even though dozens of companies had invested hundreds of millions in asteroid mining, it was illegal almost overnight. And Don was tasked with stopping them, no matter what.

For a while Don was a celebrity. Interviewed for expert opinions on identifying rogue miners, extraditing them from the moon or space stations. He even had an agent grab a miner off Mars. Those were the days. He missed the chase, missed going to court as an expert witness, missed the interviews. If this were true, it could be like old times.

"Okay, Martin, what are we looking at? Direct or indirect launch."

"I'm not sure."

"How many AUs, what's the size and any idea on recovery method?"

"No idea what you're talking about."

"How do you know someone is mining an asteroid? Not a hunch I hope."

"What I know is you need to keep an eye on everything Ben Dawson is doing."

"Aren't you already doing that? I got Robyn's note."

"Hi, Don. How are you?" said Robyn.

Martin's earpiece added Robyn's to the call.

"Oh, hi Robyn. I'm doing great now. How are you?"

"Don," said Martin, "Ben Dawson is a criminal and a charlatan. Selling useless flying boats that endanger the DOS' ability to protect the American people. Don't let him fool you with all the speeches and hand-waving."

"You know the official report is the Earthquake Prevention Program and its movement of stress from the San Andreas into the Walker Lane, caused the quake, right?"

"That's from the Seismologist Society of America, and they are all solidly in Ben's back pocket. The report is corrupt."

"Did you read it? It's quite clear and demonstrative of how it began, along with,"

"I'm not going to talk about it."

"Okay," said Don, "either way, you can't hunt asteroids. What do you need?"

"Track his activities. Anything, here, on Earth, or above. Let me know immediately if something happens."

"Will do," said Don.

CHAPTER TWELVE

SKY CITY

SEPTEMBER 10, 2071

The team was back in the *Horizon* conference room. Windows opaque, sound masking on, and doors locked.

"This is the plan as it stands today," said Ben. "Angie and Alana are retrofitting the vintage rocket Bobby Walker agreed to sell to us for a premium."

"Premium?" said Paige.

"Twice what it's worth and he's charging a lot for shipping," said Angie.

"We're assuming Bobby's already told the people at Space we've purchased the rocket. This means even more discretion is critical. Jason, how's our security?"

"As you all know," said Jason, "Jesse Taylor joined us to head security for the mining project, while I will focus on rock retrieval."

"Hi, Jesse," said Angie, like Jesse showed up to his first AA meeting. Jesse stood.

"Hi, everyone. Thanks for your confidence to bring me on board."

"Well, we're probably all going to jail or die, so thank us later," said Ryan.

"Ryan, please!" said Ben. "Jesse, continue."

"That's fine Mr. Dawson, those are the odds I'm used to. For Sky City and SBI, Ryan moved all encryption for any electronic communication devices to photonic chips. While Ryan did that, I upgraded our sound masking systems across Sky City and our SBI offices. We now have multiple layers of white noise to prevent the descrambling of our conversations."

Jesse then turned to face the group, casual, like he was lecturing school kids about walking home safely.

"This is a small team operation, meaning security comes down to individuals. Everyone is going to be equipped with handheld weapons that you will always have on you. I'll hold as many sessions as I can to practice before we ship out. I know there's some fancy gear some of you may want to take, but in a small team setting, where we can only rely on ourselves, reliability is key. Which is why I'm equipping us with mechanical weapons and leaving the light sabers at home."

"They have those now?" said Jason. "Dreams do come true."

"No, that was a joke. I'm talking about handguns, knives,"

"How big a knife?" said Jason.

"Jason, just stop," said Jesse. "Okay, you get the idea. We need to keep our heads on a swivel and be on the lookout for anything that even feels a little off. I'll expect everyone to follow my orders in any situation that either becomes or I believe may become dangerous."

"Sounds good, thanks Jesse." said Ben. "Angie, what's the status on the rocket?"

Jesse sat, and Angie updated the hologram white board to show a picture of an old rocket. As she spoke, she rotated the rocket and zoomed in on it for clarity.

"It was built thirty years ago once the construction of the permanent lunar bases was underway. This was used as a cargo rocket plane with a pilot, co-pilot, and no passengers. The rocket is a fully reusable single stage low Earth orbit cargo transport. Uses methane oxygen propellant, dry mass of a hundred forty tons with a twenty-ton cargo capacity minus any changes we make to accommodate more passengers. Fully loaded weight with propellant of two-thousand one-hundred forty tons."

"Two thousand tons of fuel to send up a hundred forty tons?" said Jesse.

"That's right," said Angie. "To get to low Earth orbit we have to get to 9.4 kilometers per second velocity to escape Earth's gravity and aerodynamic drag. That's over twenty-one thousand miles per hour, and for each pound of payload we add, we need more fuel, but the fuel becomes the payload as well. It becomes a circular calculation as you get a bigger ship."

"Add more fuel and you need even more fuel to lift off," said Ryan.

"Exactly. Most rockets were two-stage in the early days of space travel with the second stage being just fuel tanks to get the first stage off the ground."

"Two stages, of course. Even three or four if that's what it took," said Jason.

Ignoring Jason, Angie continued. "Still use two-stage for Mars' ships that don't refuel in orbit. Now, because of Ryan's cargo requirements, I recommend only four passengers. And heads up, we'll be flying economy class to save weight."

"These four people would be?" said Jason.

"I've decided Angie, Ryan, Alana and Jesse will go," said Ben. "Angie for the asteroid mining, Ryan for the tech, Alana as pilot and Jesse for security. Ryan, can you cover the launch details?"

Ryan stood and reconfigured Angie's hologram to show Earth, then he rotated it to a remote ocean location between South America, New Zealand, and Antarctica. Jason sat smoldering. He did not make the cut. Again. He was smart, but not smart enough when all he worked with was a group of rocket scientists and world-class engineers. He pushed himself in engineering school, even graduated with honors, but he kind of hated it. And it showed.

Whenever the discussions double-clicked into the details, his eyes glazed over. He was given light work, like security, which he was not even going to do since he brought in Jesse. Hard to blame anyone for that decision. Jason was a jock in school, did well in his brief military career, but not like Jesse, no one even knows how deep that guy got. In a normal family, if those exist, he would be seen as a great success, which he was. But as the son of Ben Dawson, he was seen as kind of average.

Jason didn't resent his sister, in fact, he adored her. How great to have such a superstar join the family. But he did resent being second tier sometimes. Jason wondered how it was that they were so amazingly fortunate to be able to adopt a genius baby out of rural Vietnam. He was three at the time, most of what happened back then was fuzzy. After several miscarriages, he was told, his mom and dad discussed adoption. Daniel showed up one day with the paperwork and Jason was sent to stay with his grandparents. After a week-long trip to Hanoi, his mom and dad brought a baby girl back with them.

Years later, Jason realized how many standard deviations Angie was outside of normal intelligence. He asked Daniel how lucky they were to find her. Daniel laughed it off, and Daniel never laughed. Some of his classmates teased him about Angie being the child of scientists captured by communists or university professors killed during an uprising. Jason asked his dad, who pretended not to hear him. He asked his dad and Daniel together once, and they weaved and bobbed like politicians. The question was never answered, and he was told they were lucky to have Angie, of course they were, and he was not allowed to bring it up again.

Jason shrugged and moved on. The two of them grew up close enough to fight like brother and sister, but still create a special bond of children brought together by more than chance. But deep down he still wished he had more gears in his head to compete with the big brains in the room. And that was why he asked questions. At least he could make them explain themselves.

"We'll launch from Point Nemo, said Ryan. "The most remote location on Earth."

"Hold on," said Jason. "You're going to launch a rocket ship over the ocean? On one of our Skyboats?"

"A very special Skyboat," said Ryan.

"This is our edge," said Angie. "No one expects us to launch rockets from the ocean."

"Hmm, why does no one launch a rocket ship over the water I wonder?" said Jason. "Are you going to strap it underneath like Stratolaunch tried to do with their jumbo-sized airplanes?" said Jason. "I mean, talk about lack of creativity. They would have been better off with the world's largest rubber band and sling shot."

"It has to be an old-style rocket launch," said Ben. "That's what we're dealing with. Unfortunately, we can't strap it underneath a Skyboat and ignite it. It would fall to Earth before getting lift off. That's probably what Bobby thought when he sold us this rocket. He knows it needs a launch pad," said Ben.

"All the terrestrial launch pads were booked out for years," said Ryan.

"Point Nemo is over sixteen hundred miles from the closest island, and it is not located in any flight paths, shipping lanes or even spaceship orbits."

"How do you keep a Skyboat from plummeting into the ocean during a rocket launch?" said Daniel.

"I've kitted out one of our cargo Skyboats with rear jets replacing the vertical jets," said Ryan. "It has ten times the vertical power. Also, the deck will be replaced with layers of concrete and fire bricks. We'll take the cargo Skyboat up two thousand feet. That will kick start the rocket launch and allow it to lose altitude while the rocket takes off. We'll probably lose the boat though."

While Ryan spoke, he flicked his wrist and the hologram zoomed into Point Nemo where an animated graphic of the rocket taking off from the cargo Skyboat started. The cargo Skyboat dropped toward the ocean as the rocket took off and hovered just above the water.

"There is another risk post takeoff," said Ryan. "Once the rocket lifts off, we don't know what the DOS will do. And by that, I mean they may try to shoot it down."

"Let's think about that," said Daniel. "Launching a rocket over the ocean is probably not illegal. At a minimum the laws would be silent about ocean launches since no one has done it. We're in a gray area. Angie, is the trajectory avoiding any government airspace?"

"Exactly," said Angie.

"Does it concern anyone else that we need to point out the legality of each step of this plan?' said Jason.

"Assume everything's illegal unless stated otherwise," said Ryan. "Now, once the rocket does not get shot down and clears the Earth's atmosphere, it will converge on the Gateway."

Ryan pointed at the hologram, which shrank Earth as the rocket left it and zoomed in on one of the space stations orbiting the Earth. Multiple smaller manufacturing space stations were visible in the hologram at less than half the size of the Gateway.

"Right," said Daniel stepping up to the hologram. "I've got your contact prepped at the Gateway to manage your transfer through customs and onto the first available lunar carrier after your arrival."

The hologram shrank the Gateway station as a ship left it and headed for the moon, which it zoomed in on one of the lunar mining colonies.

"Once you land on the moon," continued Daniel. "you'll meet with the mayor. His role will be to set you up in town as you prepare for your mining expedition. And that will be all anyone knows; you are exploring the moon for mining."

Ben walked in front of the hologram.

"Let's talk about the spaceship. This one's going to be interesting. The cargo you'll be taking to the moon will be the asteroid mining gear, liquid hydrogen, backup spacesuits and the mining silos. Now, even if we could rent a spaceship on the moon, the rental companies have a very specific clause that won't let renters take their spaceships outside the moon's gravitational pull."

"Like when I off-roaded that rental Jeep in Hawaii," said Jason. "Barely got it back with four wheels on. And they charged extra for cleaning."

"Just like that," said Angie.

"What we do have available to us is the lunar boneyard," said Ben. "Rows of scrapped mining equipment brought to the moon by the first mining expeditions. All that equipment should be in good condition. Ryan's taken aerial pictures of the boneyard and inventoried what's out there."

"It won't be pretty," said Ryan, "but I believe I can get a working spaceship out of it along with a transport vehicle to take it to our exploratory lunar mining operation."

"And where is that?" said Angie.

"Where it has to be, on the far side of the moon, away from the satellites, the cartel members and anyone that might get back to Earth with information," said Ben. "The only thing over there are a few unmanned telescopes and we'll stay away from them."

"And the frontier men. There's a group living out there that survives on their own," said Daniel. "You need to avoid them."

"I'll be ready," said Jesse. "If we do have to engage."

"Everyone needs to be ready," said Ben. "The only thing we know for sure is this won't go according to plan."

CHAPTER THIRTEEN

FIREFLY

OCTOBER 10, 2071

"Did you check the weather over the Antarctic?" Ben said, looking over Paige's shoulder. "There's a storm's brewing."

"No, completely forgot about it. Ben, can you get me some more coffee?" said Paige.

"I'll get it," said Jason.

"Actually, I just want your father to leave me alone," said Paige.

"Do I get that. Dad, you want to take it down a notch?" said Jason.

"That's not how I work," said Ben. "How is it either of you do not know this?"

"Try, Ben, try," said Paige. "And let me do my job."

Paige had mission control set on the dining table of *Firefly*. Two screens, a supercomputer and holograph bases scattered everywhere. It was the least impressive mission control in the history of mission controls, but it was functional. Also, Paige wanted it to look like anything but a mission control. She allowed Ben, Daniel, and Jason to monitor the launch if they behaved, which Ben was not doing, and Paige thought it was only a matter of time before she had to kick him out. She was the Yin to Ben's Yang.

When she met Ben, Paige knew they were a bit of opposites. Her public relations background and natural advertising instincts attracted her to him when she saw how much of blank canvas he was for a marketing company. He needed so much help with his new venture, but she also saw a damaged young man fighting to bring himself back to who he was or thought he was. She sensed the kindness beneath the drive. They became a couple in a matter of weeks, married a year and a half later. Two years after that Jason was born.

When Ben's company was acquired shortly after Jason's birth, they were able to focus on each other and Jason. After Paige suffered three miscarriages, it seemed God was testing them, even though they knew in their hearts that's not how God worked. They had all the money they could ever spend, but what they wanted was a big family. Initially there were arguments and blame between the two of them, but they realized it was neither of their faults; and even if it was, blaming each other only pushed them apart. They accepted their situation and focused on Jason; they still had him.

That was when Daniel suggested adoption. Paige jumped on Daniel's proposal. Ben agreed and Daniel set the wheels in motion. Paige knew Daniel and Ben had late night discussions about the process, probably details she did not want to hear, but she ignored them, she just wanted another baby in the house. And then Angela Marie Dawson arrived. Paige put her entire focus on her kids. She paused her career, even her snowboarding. Her family was everything. And it made her happier than she thought possible. Not because it was a perfect life. She spent many nights worrying about her children, including Ben, and disciplining them at a volume level she would later be embarrassed about. But the struggles of raising Jason and Angie were what she was here for. She was built for it, and she was good at it.

Paige watched the Cargo Skyboat as it reached the point where it needed to divert from its Los Angeles to Auckland trade route and head toward Point Nemo. She initiated the canopies over the cargo Skyboat.

"Starting camo canopies," said Paige out loud, which was picked up by the earpieces of Angie, Ryan, Alana, and Jesse, who were waiting inside the captain's quarters of the cargo Skyboat.

The drones flew upward and formed two canopies above the cargo Skyboat. As the cargo Skyboat left the trade route, a decoy canopy moved across the ocean following the trade route with a picture of a bird's eye view of the cargo Skyboat. The canopy over the cargo Skyboat resembled clear ocean but not a perfect match for where they were heading. This triggered an alert at an NSA air traffic monitor desk, which currently focused on canopy drones per classified orders. The technician saw a note come up on his screen to contact the deputy director of transportation for the NSA and no one else. He called him.

"Mr. LaRue, we have what appears to be a drone canopy."

"Where?"

"Over the South Pacific. And we may have a canopy acting as a sort of decoy. Not a bad rendering."

"Send me the details."

The technician sent a dump of data that would be a wall of numbers to most people, but Don could see through the location coordinates, wind speeds, air quality and other measurements to visualize the scene. What was going on? He needed to get under the canopies. He contacted the technicians' superior.

"I'm authorizing hypersonic drone reconnaissance at the following two locations. Prepare for incoming data. Please confirm."

"Confirmed, hypersonic drones not available."

"What is available?"

"We have two Grumman X-97s in American Samoa that can launch in fifteen minutes."

"Estimated time for intercept?"

"After launch, assuming straight trajectories of the two canopies, the decoy canopy will be in range in two hours."

"And the other?"

"Approximately four hours."

"Get them launched and send me the video links, I want them up on my screen."

"Will do."

Don sat back, hoping this was the beginning of Ben Dawson's asteroid hunt. It was going to be fun.

*

Vali Noelani captained the cargo Skyboat heading toward Point Nemo. More of a sailor than a pilot, but with Skyboats, the two often became interchangeable. Alana suggested Vali to Ben as captain of the cargo Skyboat because, one, he was the best and two, he would never forgive her if she did not use him to make sure the launch was safe. Vali looked up at the drone canopy. It followed the cargo Skyboat as they made their four-hour trek over the two thousand miles of ocean to the launch point. Most cargo Skyboats operated on a slow and steady pace along trade routes. For this trip they increased their travel speed to that of commercial airlines, approximately five hundred miles per hour. That required much different cargo security, installing a tube-like covering over the front of the cargo Skyboat deck and securing all equipment under the tube or in the cabins; essentially making the cargo Skyboat an airplane. Jesse walked up to Vali, who was on the bridge, and looked at the console where the time to arrival was shown via a countdown clock.

"Four hours, huh?" said Jesse.

Vali stared ahead.

"Thanks for doing this," said Jesse.

Vali looked at Jesse.

"You keep Alana safe or don' bother coming back," said Vali.

"That's what I do," said Jesse, staring ahead.

Vali was glad to manage the launch, but mad he was not asked to be security. 'Too much family drama already,' Alana had told him. 'You get me launched okay, that's what you can do.'

Jesse walked into the break room where the team sat. Alana going over the pilot's checklist with Angie. Ryan looking through the cargo inventory. Jesse pulled up the weapons inventory, even though he had checked it a dozen times, just to have something to do. Then he leaned back against the wall and took a nap.

"We're here," said Alana as she nudged Jesse awake.

Jesse shot up, surprised they would have let him sleep for hours. He went to the cargo deck where the crew was building out the launch pad. The rocket, which had been hidden inside empty cargo containers was rolled out to the side of the deck. Jesse saw it differently now that he was about to get in it and shoot up into space. He noticed the worn off paint around the exterior where it had made countless re-entries. There were a few new, shiny, plates scattered around the body where Angie had decided the shell's integrity was no longer trustworthy. It looked like a used car headed for the junkyard after one more weekend road trip.

Bobby Walker had sold them what, to him, was a worthless rocket. But he charged as high a cost as he thought Ben would suffer. What

Bobby did not realize was whatever price Ben Dawson paid for a vintage rocket was immaterial compared to what he had to lose. But then, that's negotiations. Hard to know the true value for the buyer or the seller. Ben agreed to Bobby's price after one counter and a lot of bluster. Ben knew the game.

He had to act like Bobby cheated him, which he probably did. But Ben got his rocket. And then the team spent as much retrofitting the rocket as the purchase price. Still, immaterial in the scheme of what was at stake. With the rocket laid out, the crew opened the rest of the containers to pull out pallets of firebricks and thin layers of concrete. They placed the firebricks on the concrete deck, which had already been retrofitted with extra stability, and then the thin concrete layers. They moved the rocket around as they covered the entire deck with firebricks and concrete, finishing with sloped concrete borders around the edges of the deck to deflect the blast upward. After they unloaded the cargo containers, they dumped them into the ocean.

"Not very environmentally friendly," said Angie, standing on the bridge.

"We'll come back for them," said Vali. "Like this boat."

"I guess there's a price for everything," said Angie.

The crew wheeled the rocket near the center of the deck with half of it stretching over the edge of the stern. Ryan checked the cargo inside the rocket one more time. The crew secured cables to the top of the rocket, and then to the roof of the bridge. After getting the go-ahead, they winched the cables to bring the rocket upright. One of the life Skyboats flew Angie, Ryan, Alana, and Jesse up to the top of the rocket where they entered and awkwardly got into their seats. With everything in place, the crew got into the life Skyboats and flew aft of the cargo Skyboat leaving Vali and the rocket on the boat, alone.

"We're ready," said Vali.

"Okay team, we have a clear signal from your captain. Are you a go for launch?" said Paige.

"Go," said Jesse.

"Go," said Ryan.

"Go," said Angie.

"Go," said Alana.

"Let's do this," said Ben.

"Alana, initiate launch sequence," said Paige.

The screens in the rocket illuminated a sixty second count-down. The screen also scrolled through a checklist highlighting each item green before disappearing.

"Everything's working," said Alana. "We're ready."

"There's a drone approaching," said Paige.

"We expected that," said Ben. "Keep going."

Daniel received a call and clicked into it.

"Yes, Don, we do have a canopy over one of our cargo Skyboats. How is that a violation? Check your regulations. That's right, it's a recommendation not a requirement. The boat is over international waters, as are the canopies. Yes, they're U.S. boats. Fine, we'll bring the canopies down; will take a few minutes to coordinate. No, SBI does not own any rockets."

Daniel clicked off and Ben's earpiece rang. He looked at his wristwatch and saw 'Confidential Caller'. Daniel motioned for him to not answer it. The countdown showed twenty-five seconds to launch. Ben answered it.

"Mr. Dawson?"

"Who is this?"

"Don LaRue of the NSA and advisor to USNORTHCOM. I have

reason to believe you're launching a rocket from one of your carrier ships and are in violation of the space code, section twenty-four."

"Why do you think we're launching rockets?"

Fifteen seconds to launch.

"The big pointy thing sitting on your cargo boat that I'm looking at is a good indication. I'm telling you to stand down, whatever it is you're doing."

Ten seconds to launch.

"Please, walk me through your authority to tell me to not do something you don't know if I'm doing or not?"

"Let me be clear, you do not want to launch anything."

"I don't recall asking for advice, or is this a threat? I've been getting a lot of those lately and it's really beginning to bother me."

"The NSA doesn't make threats. They are highly suggested recommendations in your best interest. Just like I recommend you prepare to be arrested and for anything that lifts off a floating barge will likely be shot out of the sky."

Five seconds.

"You can't just shoot things out of the sky."

"Do it all the time."

"Rockets firing now," Paige said.

Don saw a large heat signature show up on the cargo Skyboat from his satellite video.

"I'll call you back," said Don as he hung up on Ben and called Martin.

CHAPTER FOURTEEN

POINT NEMO, PACIFIC OCEAN

Alana watched the launch countdown reach ten, which was when the oxygen and methane fuel ignited at the base of the rocket. Vali had flown the cargo Skyboat up forty thousand feet into the air, well above the two thousand in the plan. Vali had his air mask and thermal gear on along with a parachute and skyboard nearby. The cargo Skyboat began dropping as soon as the rocket began firing. Vali increased the power of the jet engines, but the cargo Skyboat continued to lose altitude.

The rocket increased firing its propellant, blasting flames all over the deck. The cargo Skyboat dropped thousands of feet as the rocket failed to lift off.

"It's not working!" said Alana.

"I'm going to full power," said Vali as he turned the jets up.

At full power, the cargo Skyboat jets would only last a minute or two. If the rocket did not lift off by then, it would likely fall over into the ocean. As the jets' power increased, the falling decelerated, but did not stop. It was still losing a thousand feet every few seconds. Alana opened the rockets fuel injectors to increase the power. As she increased the power, Vali saw cracks forming across the boat under the rocket.

"It's starting to break up," said Vali. "You need to lift off now."

"I know," said Alana as she considered adding even more power.

She slowly added another increment of fuel, balancing the need to lift off with the fragility of the deck. As the power increased, so did the size of the cracks.

"Ten thousand feet," said Vali. "It's going to fall apart any second now."

"Oh, forget it," said Alana as she maxed out the fuel injectors and filled the combustion chamber. "Now or never."

The rocket blasted out a fire strong enough to begin melting the concrete blocks and the windows on the bridge. Vali covered his eyes and stepped back from the console. At five thousand feet the crack across the deck split the front of the cargo Skyboat, and the bow of the cargo Skyboat fell toward the ocean. It destabilized the rest of the cargo Skyboat, causing it to lean forwards.

"You're out of time," said Vali as he saw the rocket begin to lean along with the cargo Skyboat.

"Almost there," said Alana as she felt the rocket thrust upwards even while leaning.

At four thousand feet Vali threw his skyboard outside the bridge and sent it under the falling deck, but it's twelve lithium powered rotary blades running around the inside edges of the board was nowhere near enough power to move a third of a cargo Skyboat and the front deck dropped into the ocean. Vali lowered the power on the rear jets, which leveled out the Skyboat, but increased the speed of the altitude drop. He looked at his altimeter, which showed three thousand feet and falling. The rocket lifted off at two thousand feet. A second later, at one thousand feet, it cleared what was left of the deck. At five hundred feet

Vali ran out of the bridge to jump over the railing. At one hundred feet his foot was on the railing and as the cargo Skyboat hit the water, he turned mid-leap to watch his sister fly a rocket into space while he fell into the ocean with a huge smile.

Back at *Firefly*, everyone cheered and hugged as the rocket lifted off right before the cargo Skyboat fell into the ocean. Everyone, but Daniel. Reserved as always, Daniel nodded and shook Ben's hand, but he was also keeping track of the running costs for Ben's crazy project. He knew Ben had decided this was all or none, but Daniel always calculated return on investment. It was like breathing to him. Daniel did not expect the costs could get anywhere near the potential return, but if everything went south, he wanted a backup plan to salvage SBI, even if Ben did not have one.

Daniel had started working with Ben after Ben moved back to Reno. Ben's father, Neal, connected them, asking Daniel for a favor to get Ben back on his feet. Bankrupt, after having lost the patent lawsuit to Bobby Walker, and humiliated throughout Silicon Valley, Ben was in a dark place. Neal was concerned Ben might throw his life away. Daniel Nguyen had recently retired after selling his semi-conductor company. Coming up the ranks of the technology industry, Daniel had been general counsel, chief strategy officer, chief operational officer and at his last company, chief executive officer. Tall, thin, and handsome, he looked like the quintessential executive. And he talked like one; slow, deliberate, and pithy. Second generation Vietnamese, Daniel remembered his roots but grew up all-American in Fremont, North California. His parents instilled in him a strong work ethic, which translated into top grades, top schools and top job offers. He married his high school sweetheart after college and started his rapid rise in technology, specifically semi-conductors. They had three kids in five years and Daniel was on top of the world. He took the next step and founded his own company. Using his reputation for success, Daniel raised millions with a few phone calls. His connections landed him multi-year contracts even before his company had a working product. Hiring, growing, and keeping up the press coverage kept him one hundred percent focused on the company, even after his wife was diagnosed with breast cancer. He tried to take time off, but there was always the next emergency at work. And when he came home to a crying wife and crying kids, it became easier to say he had to be at work than deal with his family issues. After all, Daniel did this for them, right?

When his wife took a downward turn, Daniel's parents intervened to demand he stop working, and only then did Daniel realize his mistake. His wife told him it was okay, but he knew it was not. Six months later she passed away. He sold his company and moved the kids to Incline Village on Lake Tahoe. They were not old enough at the time to understand, but when they went away to college on the East Coast, they never came back. Daniel sat in his empty house on the lake wondering how it all happened to him. He busied himself with guest lecturing in the College of Business at the University of North Nevada Reno. The students were fascinated with his stories of starting, running and selling companies. If only his kids thought he was that interesting. Then he ran into Neal Dawson. They became friends and their friendship gave Daniel a way to engage with someone that did not remind him of his past. When Neal asked for help with his son, Daniel hoped working with Ben would allow him to process through his own dark memories and find a new approach to life. One that did not include waking up with regret each morning.

When Daniel first met with Ben, he realized how easy someone could get themselves into a funk, ignoring anything positive, focusing only on what went wrong. Yes, Ben had gone through a rough patch, and it was not a fair outcome, but he was young, smart, and now more experienced, which some would call hardened. Daniel saw Ben as lucky. Of course, Ben saw the opposite. Daniel started by making Ben get a new daily routine of exercise, reading and writing. Then he had Ben start making plans.

"It's a blank slate," said Daniel, "your future, that is. Who gets a blank slate in life?"

"Newborns," said Ben, like a brat.

Daniel was used to this and did not tell Ben to go ahead and live in that dark cave. He had learned patience.

"That's not what I meant. You're ready to move on and have nothing holding you down."

"I'm bankrupt."

"That's a state of mind. You're broke, not poor."

"What if someone steals my idea again?"

"Don't let them. I can help with that. You have an idea?"

"No, maybe. It's a device. I don't know. It always bothered me at Bobby's company, but we never took the time to fix it. It would combine some new applications with hardware. Not sure it will scale. Probably not worth the time to work on."

"Anyone else working on it?"

"I doubt it. Such a boutique problem. Only happens when you push a network to its limit. We were hitting the limit but didn't hear anyone else talking about it."

"Don't these sort of problems end up growing as more companies push their limits?"

"Maybe in a few years."

"Then why not ride that wave?"

ALAN PRIEST

Ben decided to tinker with his idea. Once he began hitting problems, his attitude perked up. And before he knew it, he was back to living with purpose. He woke up thinking about how to solve the next set of technical issues. After he got his prototype working, it was time to start his company. That forced him back out into the world where he had to deal with fundraising, paperwork and finding office space. Then he met Paige. He put up a good front, but eventually she found the hurt man underneath. Fortunately for him, Paige found his ability to overcome hardship more attractive than his attempt to act like a big shot.

Over the next two years, as Ben got married, grew his new company, and left his ugly past behind him, Daniel stayed close. He joined the new company as advisor, then board member, and when Jason was born two years later, godfather. Daniel still hurt every day, and he knew the pain would always be with him. But working with Ben kept him distracted. And every now and then, he found himself living in the moment, which freed him from his past. That kept Daniel working with Ben and his Skyboats. Not his first choice of how to spend the rest of his life, but it beat the alternative of staring at a lake from his living room.

"Daniel, how do we stop them from shooting down the rockets?" said Ben.

"How fast until they're in orbit?" said Daniel turning back toward Paige's screen.

"Eight minutes," said Paige.

Daniel thought through the process to authorize a missile launch with the NSA. Multiple people and multiple approvals before anything would finally launch. He just needed to interrupt one step of the process for five minutes. He called his NSA contact to tell him that any rockets over the oceans could have human passengers and shooting them down required additional authorization and will absolutely result in a long

110

and drawn out forensic investigation focusing on his department. His contact said he would make sure they knew what they were getting into before firing any missiles.

"I bought us time on the missiles Ben," Daniel said. "Should be enough to get everyone into orbit."

"Thank God, great job Daniel."

"Missiles?" said Paige. "They were going to shoot them down?"

"They threatened," said Ben. "Nothing happened."

"Ben, if one of my children is in danger, you better tell me immediately. Got it?" said Paige as she pointed a finger in his face.

"Got it," Ben said, stepping back. "I got it. Besides they don't even know who owns the rocket."

"Ben, I know you think your Cayman Islands Rocket Company is very clever," said Daniel, "but the NSA is going to follow the paper trail, and it will all come back to us. You still own that rocket. It's just a matter of time before they work it back."

"Yes, but it's going to take them awhile. We're fine."

Ben got a call from Don five minutes later and added on Daniel to advise him real time.

"Mr. Dawson, we've identified that the rocket belongs to you, personally. That means you are wholly responsible for the launch."

Ben muted Don.

"I did not expect that," said Ben.

Daniel raised an eyebrow. Ben unmuted Don.

"Well, Don," said Ben, "if you were correct, which I'm not saying you are, what do you recommend?"

"I recommend you turn yourself in."

"What other recommendations do you have?"

"Mr. Dawson, I'm done with recommendations. I'm assuming your rockets are headed toward the Gateway. Once they reach there, any people and cargo will be subject to detainment and extradition back to the United States. This was foolish on your part. We'll be in touch. By the way, big fan of Sky City."

Don clicked off. Paige and Daniel stared at Ben.

"I think that went pretty well, all things considering." said Ben. "He's a fan, right? And everyone's about to be in orbit with only lost one cargo Skyboat. Phase one is complete!"

"Don't oversell it," said Paige. "Daniel, how good is your contact at the Gateway?"

"We're about to find out," said Daniel.

PART II

Most people thought space would be the final frontier, until the Great Setback. It came as a surprise then, that most of mankind's growth would occur just above them.

SkyWorld, Jubilee Celebration (2150)

CHAPTER FIFTEEN

ABOVE EARTH

The rocket entered the mesosphere, thirty-one miles above the Earth's surface. The fuel Alana burned to lift it off the cargo Skyboat accelerated the rocket to one-hundred sixty feet per second squared, placing 5Gs of pressure on the passengers and with that, the potential to lose consciousness, which Angie and Ryan did. Jesse just threw up. The plan was to keep their acceleration to one hundred feet per second squared, around 3Gs of pressure and more like a roller coaster than a fighter jet. But liftoff was more important than a few minutes of discomfort, at least that was Alana's take. The rocket crossed the Kármán line, sixty-two miles above the Earth's surface, and they were in free space. As the pressure of gravity left the spacecraft, Angie and Ryan woke up and everyone paused to look down at the Earth.

"Does it concern any of you how much debris we just dropped into the ocean?" said Angie as she stared at the blue waters of Earth.

The three of them stared at Angie then looked at each other.

"Uh, ya," said Alana.

"Oh yes," said Ryan.

"Absolutely," said Jesse.

"In fact," said Ryan, "when this is over, I'm sending your dad a strongly worded letter on the matter."

"I'm signing it," said Alana.

"Me too," said Jesse. "Do you want to sign it, Angie?"

Angie looked at each of them.

"No thanks," said Angie as she turned to look back out the window.

A few minutes later Alana fired the first burn to change the rocket's current orbit as part of the Hohmann transfer that would eventually match the Gateway orbit. Three hours later she fired the second burn to transfer into the Gateway's orbit, ten miles in front of the Gateway. Alana rotated the rocket to do a braking burn, then continued to rotate the rocket several times to perform correction burns and line them up with the Gateway.

The Gateway, a joint effort of the United States, European Space Agency, Canada, Japan, Australia, and New Zealand, was built in 2037 as part of the Artemis Project after the repurposing of the failed lunar orbital station. The lunar orbital station ended up being too far from Earth for use as a productive transfer station and repurposed for manufacturing of lunar mining materials. The new Gateway was positioned three-hundred ten miles above the Earth, which allowed for reusable rockets to be launched between Earth and the Gateway and reusable spacecraft to be launched from the Gateway into space, making low Earth orbit passenger and cargo transfers an economic reality. Two years after the Gateway went into regular use, China and Russia partnered to launch their version of the Gateway, the High Orbit Space Station II (HOSS 2). India followed with a smaller space station, but it did not gain the traction of the two larger stations and ended up primarily being used for zero gravity experiments.

Gateway 2.0, like previous space stations, was modular in construction using a simple block structure (i.e., ugly) that morphed into what it was today. The center line was a series of various-sized blocks, like the habitat modules, service modules, hangers, and docking tunnels. Large solar arrays and communications antennas were placed at the ends of the center line. After travel to and from the Gateway increased, a hundred-foot cylindrical docking station was added to the middle of the center line. Opposite the docking station, still in the middle of the center line, a two-hundred-foot tube was added and then a two-hundred-foot diameter sphere installed. The sphere was not pressurized and held industrial operations and material storage. The layout worked great for the first year and a half until the long-term Gateway residents complained about the lack of gravity. So, between the solar arrays and the docking station/industrial sphere, four rotating tubes with cylinders on their ends were added. They looked like two barbells rotating in opposite directions. They maintained one rotation per minute to create gravity inside the four cylinders at the end of each tube. The rotation created less than one standard Earth gravity, but the space station occupants did not care, they had gravity! They placed their living spaces, offices, recreation facilities, shopping, and the famous StarGazer restaurant inside the cylinders.

Daily flights to and from Earth began and the space economy was born, creating a need for real space manufacturing facilities. Curiously, one of the major holdups for the space economy were the spacesuits. Designed by committee for decades, they were amazingly safe and just as impractical. No one got excited about space travel when it meant becoming the Michelin Man, or woman, and having to carry a backpack large enough to tour Europe for the summer. During New York's fashion week of 2035, a top designer remarked that people were not going to live in space until they looked good doing it. That sparked a contest amongst the world's top designers to create a new space suit, one designed for living. Two years later, the contest ended with the winner creating an athleisure design that hid the safety equipment all around the body and retained a recognizable human shape, all while avoiding looking like a superhero costume. The revolutionary helmet design resembled a hoodie with a faceplate. When inside atmosphere, the back of the hoodie helmet would fold down like a hood and the faceplate folded into what appeared like glasses hanging on the wearer's neck. After the new space line was made available, people decided to make space their home, and it was not long after that when the first babies were born in space. And some of them grew up there, identifying more with their space habitats than Earth.

Earth's manufacturing and launch capabilities could not keep up with the demands of a successful, growing Gateway. That drove the first separate space manufacturing station, placed near the Gateway for ease of delivering product, but far enough away to avoid potential collisions. Built with a double keel structure, it consisted of two long parallel metal trusses connected using shorter trusses at the top, bottom, and middle. It was a large rectangular shape with a center support. The center support extended out on either side of the longer parallel trusses and had solar arrays and communication antennas built on them. Between the parallel trusses were the manufacturing facilities along with limited habitat, service, and storage modules. Most workers chose to live on the Gateway and commute to the manufacturing facility, allowing them to enjoy their non-work time in gravity. Once up and running the manufacturing facility focused on taking material mined from the moon and manufacturing 3D printed and molded products for both the Gateway and HOSS 2. It was able to manufacture at a fraction of the cost of sending the same materials up from Earth. With the economics proved out, another space manufacturing facility was built on the other side of the Gateway in a triangular, or delta, shape. This facility focused on zero gravity processes for Earth, including ultrapure and container free material manufacturing. Space manufacturing created a space ecosystem that developed partnerships and contracts outside the Earth's legal system. The Gateway, HOSS 2, and manufacturing stations realized the leverage they were gaining on Earth, like the moon miners, years earlier.

Then on January 1, 2050, the Space Colony was announced. A monumental step in space colonization, to be built in medium Earth orbit that moved between one-hundred thousand and two-hundred thousand miles above the Earth, it would house ten thousand people when completed twenty years later, or 2070. Following the Space Colony announcement, in 2051, the Space Station Government Collective was established, creating an independent entity for citizenship outside Earth. At the same time, the United States was going through its statehood civil war, which distracted the United States from fully engaging in the process. The collective clarified space and Earth economic partnerships as well as propositions for dual-citizenship. Taxes would still be paid, property rights respected, and business could expand. However, the problem of space station independence was intentionally not debated, allowing everyone to return to their internal countries' problems. Twenty years later, the newest chancellor of the Space Station Collective, Niko Genji, per his campaign promise, restarted those independence discussions with the major governments on Earth. It was not going well.

As Alana approached the Gateway for docking, space traffic control identified her and pointed out that their rocket was not capable of docking at the Gateway's docking station due to its outdated structure.

Instead, they guided her toward the landing platform at the sphere and informed the crew to keep their helmets on until they passed through the airlock, which would be inside the sphere past a ladder on the platform. Alana's rocket was supposed to land standing up, but the small entry to the sphere would not allow it. Because they were still traveling in front of the Gateway, Alana rotated the rocket to enter the sphere backward and fire braking burns to stop inside. The last five hundred feet to reach the sphere took an hour to travel, and Angie and Ryan raced through the math to tell Alana exactly how long and how much to fire once they entered the sphere. The rocket was fifteen feet outside the sphere when they stopped writing on their tablets, giving them another two minutes before entering the sphere for the final landing thrust.

"Okay," said Angie as she read off her tablet, "you need to thrust for exactly 1.2 seconds when we cross the threshold, and then you might need another 0.7 seconds if we don't stop. So many factors, the formulas are crazy complicated."

"Ya, I'm going to eyeball it," said Alana.

"You can't do that," said Ryan. "It's very complicated."

He held up his tablet, full of calculations.

"Is this all in your head to eyeball?"

"It is, but less messy."

The rocket crossed the threshold of the sphere and Alana waited.

"Now," said Angie.

Alana waited. They crossed over the platform for them to land on.

"Alana," said Ryan gripping his seat.

Once the rocket's tip passed over the platform Alana hit the thrusters for half a second. Ryan, Angie, and Jesse stopped breathing. Then she aimed the rocket down toward the platform where it tapped, leveled out, and slid to a stop twenty feet from the entrance. Alana went through the controls and shut down the rocket. Then she put her helmet, faceplate, and gloves back on and turned on her air. She unbuckled and got out of her seat. No one moved as she walked by them to the door. She turned around.

"You comin'?" said Alana.

Angie, Ryan, and Jesse shook themselves, pulled their helmets and faceplates up, put on their gloves, and followed Alana out of the rocket. Fortunately, or unfortunately, it seemed everyone at the Gateway knew of the teams' arrival and there were a dozen spacesuits waiting for them when they got onto the platform. One of the spacesuits came up to them and reached out a hand to Alana.

"I'm Dutch Gordon, United States Ambassador to the Gateway. Do you need assistance with your cargo?"

"Yes, that would be appreciated," said Alana.

"Quite a landing, by the way," said Dutch. "I'll have my team get your cargo out of the rocket and secure it. Now, if you please, we have some paperwork to fill out."

Dutch started toward the ladder leading down to the tram that would take them to the rotating modules of the Gateway.

"Hold on," said another spacesuit coming up to them. "Where do you think you're taking these people? I have orders to arrest them."

"Really?" said Dutch. "From whom?"

"The deputy director of transportation for the NSA."

"Oh, well, in that case, of course. But can you do it after they meet with the chancellor? He's requested their presence."

"The chancellor wants to see them?"

The other spacesuit walked over to his team, they huddled for a moment, one checked a tablet, and then they all went down the ladder and disappeared. Dutch waited for the loading dock to empty before talking.

"Sorry about that," Dutch said. "Even up here people get territorial. Let's head down."

Dutch led the team down the ladder through the airlocks to the tram platform. They watched the screen that showed the location of each tram across the Gateway. There were four trams, all traveling in the same direction.

"Only goes in one direction?" said Angie.

"It's a small place," said Dutch. "And space is tight."

Two minutes later an eight seat tram appeared, and four workers got out to head into the manufacturing sphere above them.

"Please, after you," said Dutch.

The four of them got in, followed by Dutch, and the tram roof closed overhead. The tram ran on magnetic rails and curved down to the center line of the Gateway, across to one of the rotating tubes, curved up into it, and then curved to a stop on the second floor of a rotating cylinder.

"StarGazer Restaurant, Chancellor Offices, Gateway Boutiques," said the automated female tram voice.

"We'll get out here," said Dutch as he exited the tram.

The tram had stopped in the middle floor of the cylinder. Dutch walked over to the ladders, one heading up to the top floor and the other down to the lower of the three floors in the rotating cylinder, with 'lower' and 'top' only relative due to the artificial gravity. They followed him up, into the StarGazer restaurant. Each floor of the two cylinders was a seventy foot diameter circle with the tube taking fourteen feet out of the center of the top two floors. In the restaurant, they walked up beside the tube to the hostess' desk. The restaurant buzzed with excited tourists, important business meetings, and no empty tables. With less than a hundred seats, a reservation at the Star Gazer restaurant was more difficult to secure than a trip to the moon.

"Hello Dutch," said the hostess.

"Hello Mandy," said Dutch. "These are guests of the chancellor."

"Of course," said Mandy, and she spoke at a whisper only heard by her earpiece.

The floor shifted, and the tables moved closer together, creating enough space at the back for one more table, which came up out of the floor. The diners noticed, then ignored the movement since they were not told to get up from their tables. Three waiters appeared from an elevator at the back of the center tube carrying six chairs to the new table along with place settings.

"Right this way," said Mandy.

Angie, Ryan, Alana, and Jesse sat at the table. It was difficult to not stare at the glass ceiling with the view above their heads that rotated between the Earth, moon, and the stars, along with the manufacturing stations on either side. Jesse was the first to crane his neck straight up and stare. He realized if he did not look at the other rotating tubes, he avoided any sense of nausea.

"Amazing," said Jesse.

"Chancellor Genji will be right with you," said Dutch. "I've ordered food while you wait."

Two waiters came out from the elevator that led to the kitchen on the floor below and placed several plates on the table. They brought drinks and left the four to themselves, who were now all staring at the windows in the ceiling. As they finished their meals, a hush came over the restaurant. Chancellor Genji walked in and went straight to their table without looking sideways. He pulled out a chair and sat. The conversation continued in the restaurant with more hushed tones.

A short man of Japanese descent, Niko Genji observed the group before speaking. He wore his Gateway whites, the universal outfit of the space station, which allowed for easy movement but not so loose as to flap around in the minimal gravity. As he sat the two waiters for their table came out to clear the plates. Not looking at them, Niko put his hand up, and they turned around and disappeared in the elevator. At the same time, two noise-cancelling drones dropped out of the ceiling and hovered between them and the other tables. At that point the other patrons went back to their normal level of conversations.

"I received an interesting call before your arrival," he said with an accent common to people raised on the space station and similar to BBC English. "The United States government is not pleased with you and your travels here. I wonder why?"

"Us too," said Ryan putting down his coffee. "Since when did prospecting become a crime?"

"Prospectors?" said the chancellor, with deliberate pacing of his words. "For Sky City to send it's best off to space for prospecting seems a bit risky, don't you think?"

"Not risky," said Alana. "There's me, Tech guy. That's the Security guy. Neurotic family member there."

"I'd like to think of myself as the one that's actually going to be mining on this mining expedition," said Angie.

Alana shrugged.

"And what is your specialty?" said the chancellor to Alana.

"I'm a pilot."

He sat back and stared at the four of them.

"This is an interesting situation, don't you think?" said the chancellor.

"Yes, ha, ha," said Angie. "Interesting."

The chancellor looked at Angie, and she realized she did not need to answer his rhetorical questions.

"I ask you to look at this from my perspective. Here I am, minding my own business, and there's a lot of business, when a rogue team of prospectors appears on my landing platform. Then I get a call saying you're to be extradited back to Earth immediately. What do I know about this new situation that has been thrust upon me and the people of the Space Collective?"

Niko knew all about the situation, which was why he was chancellor.

"We have our own issues with the terrestrial governments," continued Niko. "As you know, the Space Colony is nearing completion, there are already a thousand inhabitants preparing for the official launch next year. But who does the Space Colony belong to? It has supplies from Earth, the moon, our manufacturing plants, as well as its own manufacturing plants. It is built to be self-sufficient, in fact it must be, to survive. So why would it be part of another government's jurisdiction, or worse, multiple governments?"

"Is that the Space Colony?" said Jesse pointing at the massive triangular truss above their heads, visible through the glass dome.

"No, that is a manufacturing station," said the chancellor. "The Space Colony is located over a hundred thousand miles away, toward the moon. Best location for collecting the material mined off the moon in the mass catchers located at L2."

"L2?" said Jesse.

"It's a Lagrange point," said Angie. "One of five spots where the gravitational pull between the moon and Earth cancel out. One point is in between the moon and the Earth. One is behind the moon; I know, crazy, right? One is on the other side of Earth opposite the moon, and two are at sixty-degree angles from Earth to the moon but still on the moon's orbit."

Angie waited for a response.

"Fun fact, they originally wanted to put the Space Colony at L5, which is one of the sixty degree spots, but turns out you can move mass easier from both the L2 point and Earth to a resonant orbit instead of the L5 location."

"That was a fun fact, Professor Dawson," said Alana. "Thanks."

"I know, and the original wheel Space Colony design, which is technically called the Stanford Torus, came from a NASA study done back in 1975," said Angie.

"Fascinating," said Alana.

"Right, and do you know what a resonant orbit is?" said Angie.

"Angie," said Ryan.

"What?" said Angie.

"No one cares. We just want to get to the moon," said Ryan who turned toward the chancellor. "Chancellor, we understand you have many problems and we're a new one you did not ask for. What do you want to do?"

"Well, life is a series of problems, isn't it?" said Niko. "And as chancellor I am responsible for dealing with the Gateway's problems, of which your four are now one of those problems. And what are my choices in this matter? I could send you back as asked and curry favor with the United States government, which happens to be negotiating new colonial terms, along with the alliances. Not a bad idea. Also, I could ignore these requests as a show of our strength and independence. Let you go on your way and tell them their problems are not our problems, and we do not have to jump when they ask us. Or I could put all of you in jail here. We do have a jail on the space station if you did not know.

Now, if these are my choices, what do the four of you think I should do?"

"You could tell us who it is asking to send us back to Earth," said Angie.

"Not relevant," said the chancellor. "I asked which of the choices I should make. What do you think, and why?"

"Here's what I think," said Ryan. "You could ask how much it's worth to send us back, and then squeeze hard for your negotiations. Maybe it's significant, but we all know we're small fry compared to what you're negotiating. Or, you could have us cool our heels in space jail for a week and see who makes the most noise. Do you have space court too? Because you're going to need it if you arrest us. Or, and this is my final answer, you could let us continue our mission, ignore the NSA, see what happens, which is going to be awesome, and why are we discussing this when you know we just want to get out of here?"

"We're really missing that Daniel guy right about now, aren't we?" said Jesse.

"Thank you, Mr. Callahan. I appreciate your forthrightness," said the chancellor. "But the other nuance you neglected to mention is letting you continue your mission assumes you will be coming back here. And there's the matter of rocket storage. Are you suggesting we dump your rocket into space for a truly clean sweep of your presence? I doubt that. No, in the real world, you do not get to wash your hands when something affects you. Serious people deal with it. And smart people use it to create leverage. I will rephrase my rhetorical question. What should I do to create the most leverage for the Space Collective?"

"Governments suck," said Ryan, then caught himself. "Sorry, this one seems nice. Very clean."

"No offense taken. I understand, believe me."

"To answer your question," said Angie. "I believe your greatest leverage is to let us through and create an ally with Sky City."

"But Sky City is about to become a part of the federal government, like the TSA, is it not?"

"That's where you come in," said Angie. "By letting us through, we have a shot to keep our independence. And if we do, and you helped us, we will remember that."

"And if you don't, I lose nothing because it wasn't my problem to begin with."

"Exactly."

The chancellor scratched his chin and observed Angie, then the rest of the group.

"So, we can go?" said Jesse.

"Of course, you can. And you go with my hope for your great success on your exploratory mission. I look forward to hearing about your adventures."

"Great," said Angie and the four of them stood to leave.

The chancellor stood with them.

"One more thing," the chancellor said. "A small item. Regarding your proposal of becoming allies in our mutual quest for independence. In return for my allowing you passage through the Gateway, would you consider allowing me to ask your father for a favor?"

"Name it," said Angie. "You got it."

"Oh, not today. In the future, when it would be more beneficial. Could you relay that request to your father?"

"What type of favor are you talking about?" said Angie.

"Nothing immoral, I assure you. As I discussed, leverage is most valuable in negotiations. And leverage at the right time is often the difference between success and failure. That is what I am looking for with Benjamin Dawson. Leverage in the future. This is my ask in return for your safe passage through the Gateway and back. Do you agree to my request?"

Angie hesitated.

"Done," said Ryan. "Let's go."

And he led the team out of the restaurant.

CHAPTER SIXTEEN

SKY CITY

Jason walked into Vali's shop, a large, covered space on the deck of one of the cargo Skyboats. Vali had gone back to work as soon as he returned to Sky City. No sense worrying about Alana, it was out of his hands. At least that's what he told himself. He worked to keep from worrying. Vali was welding something large; helmet on and sparks flying. Jason waited, but Vali did not stop welding. Either he did not know Jason was there or did not care.

"Hey!" Jason said as loud as he could.

Vali shut off the blow torch and looked over at Jason. He set it down and raised his welding helmet.

"Ya, what? You want to talk about where I keep the Regatta trophy?"

"I need to talk about some cargo boats."

"My sister okay?"

"Yup, spacesuit app shows her and the rest of them are still breathing."

"Has to do with that rocket launch?"

"You think I would need it for something else?"

"How many?"

"How many you got?"

"You ask me more questions I won't help you."

"I need sixteen."

"That's half my fleet."

"And we need to retro-fit them."

"Ah, that's the best part, right? Tell me what you need. It'll be done."

Vali pulled down his helmet and turned the blow torch back on. Jason left Vali to his welding.

CHAPTER SEVENTEEN

ALLIED GATEWAY SPACE STATION

D utch met them outside the restaurant.

"He's very polite, isn't he?"

"Sure, if you do what he wants," said Jesse. "Where's the exit?"

"At the docking station. We'll use the tram. I had your cargo pulled off the rocket. It's waiting for you."

"Terrific, thanks," said Angie.

They went down the ladder and a tram waited for them. After they got in with the canopy closed, Dutch entered an override code, and they went through the next stop without slowing down. It must be a common occurrence because the dozen people waiting did not appear to notice. Then they found themselves at the docking station and Dutch swiped his wrist band to open the automatic doors. The docking station was a medium-sized room with passengers waiting and a passenger ship connected at the end of the room. Dutch handed each of them a metal card with their name and a barcode etched on it.

"These are your passes on the passenger ship to the moon. Good for a return trip anytime in the next ninety days. You don't plan on staying more than that, right?"

"Depends on how much we like it," said Ryan. "I hear the moon is nice this time of year."

"Well, good luck anyway," said Dutch as he shut the door.

They walked toward the passenger ship and saw their cargo trunks, unopened, lying next to it along with all the other luggage headed for the moon. The porter placed the luggage into the loading bay located under the seating area like a three-dimensional puzzle. He had the luggage pieces spread out across the floor and looked through each one before deciding how to pack it underneath. Above the loading bay was the door to the seating area, which loaded from the rear. There were another two dozen passengers preparing to get on board when the luggage was loaded. After a painful thirty-minute loading process, the passengers began sitting down.

The seating resembled an expensive tour bus with jet engines on either side. Every seat was taken. The passengers were all worker types starting a tour or returning after a break. Tourism on the moon was not a thing yet. Too rugged and nothing to do but work. The four of them kept to themselves during the six-hour flight, which was easy because no one wanted to talk to the dandies in the fancy space suits.

The passenger spacecraft approached the northeast hemisphere of the near side of the moon to land at Galileonia, the mining and manufacturing lunar capital. The original lunar colony, New Washington, was based at the south pole to mine the ice sitting beneath the mountains at the polar caps in constant darkness. However, for moon mining and transportation off the moon, a second colony was created between the Maskelyne and Censorinus craters on the south end of Mare Tranquilitatis.

Of course, no one on the moon used such pretentious language to talk about their planet. For them it was the Sea of Tranquility. There are no seas on the moon, but back in the seventeenth century astronomers were busy naming everything they saw in a telescope before the other guy could. And they made things up as they went along, like seas on the moon. As Galileonia began growing, the China/Russia partnership founded New Shanghai in the northwestern region of the northern hemisphere.

New Shanghai was in the crescent of the Bay of Rainbows (Sinus Iridum), near the Sea of Showers (Mare Imbrium) and quickly became a mining town for structural materials to expand the HOSS 2 and the Gateway. Although New Washington at the south pole was economically successful mining water for use on the moon and as space craft propellant, the tremendous amounts of money made at Galileonia and New Shanghai brought out the major investors, and ultimately, created the lunar cartel.

As the shuttle approached the moon there was no sign of any construction. During the two-week lunar night, lights could be seen on the surface as far away as Earth, but when the sun was shining on the moon's surface, only at the final hundred miles above the moon could passengers make out the colonial domes, mining sites, and rough roads with occasional vehicles riding on them. They approached the middle of a plain where a glass and steel dome structure, like a sea turtle shell, sat. The dome had five steel stripes running across the long end with glass in between.

They landed near a smaller dome made of pure steel attached to the larger dome. The landing was smooth, smoother than any airplane landing on Earth. The passenger ship rolled over to the steel dome and two wide doors opened. After the passenger ship rolled into the dome, the doors closed behind it. It then rolled to the end of the dome through two smaller doors and into a room just larger than the spacecraft. Once inside, the doors shut behind the passenger ship and they heard a hiss of air entering the chamber for several minutes.

"Welcome to Galileonia," said the automated flight attendant. "Be sure to have your documentation on your tablets for customs as you exit the ship. And please pick up your luggage before going to customs."

The rest of the passengers stood and pulled down small bags from the storage above their seats. Then a bell rang in the hanger, and a red sign turned to green. The seat belt sign and choking icon turned off and the doors opened. As they exited the ship, it was a tight fit around the other passengers and their luggage. Everyone else was already in line for customs, and they had to wait in the doorway until the line shortened to get out and reach their trunks. They grabbed the cargo trunks, pressed the wheels button on each of them while Ryan pulled out his tablet to tell the trunks to follow him as they stood at the back of the customs queue. The queue ended at a small table with one customs officer. Anyone could physically run past the customs area. There were no barriers set up to prevent running or walking by it. But there was nowhere to go.

The doors to the lunar habitat would not open without the customs officers' signal. Of course, there was the emergency exit. But there had not been an incident involving that door in a decade. The last runner that tried to leave via the emergency exit, found it would not open if the doors sensors identified even one person inside the room without a space suit, which customs officers intentionally did not wear for that purpose, and the runner was tasered while pushing on the door. He woke up in a prison cell on Earth. The advances in sedatives, which were developed for space travel to Mars, allowed for comas to be induced for weeks, which was especially useful for transporting criminals.

As they approached the table, Angie held up her tablet with her passport on it while the guard stared at it through his augmented reality glasses, downloading her background information. After a full minute, the guard looked at her and the rest of the team.

"Passports, please."

Ryan, Alana, and Jesse each hold up their tablets. He scanned them with the same deliberate manner as Angie's.

"This is everyone in your group?"

"Yes, the four of us," said Angie.

The guard looked away, staring into his glasses. He nodded a few times, up, up, then down. He blinked and stared into his glasses for another minute. Angie tried to breathe normally. She looked at Ryan, Alana, and Jesse. They were so calm. How? This could be the end of their mission, right here in lunar customs.

"Please, follow me."

The guard stood and walked them to another door. The four of them followed with Ryan shushing Angie as she tried to ask several panicked questions at once. The guard opened the door to a small room with a table and chairs, all white, like the walls, floor, and ceiling.

"Please, wait here," he said and closed the door, leaving them inside the room alone.

They stood around the table staring at each other.

"What now?" said Angie.

"We sit," said Alana as she took a seat.

The others followed. They sat for an hour with Angie trying to talk every few minutes. The other three took turns shushing her. Eventually Jesse told her the room was bugged, and she kept quiet, mumbling something about how everything had been bugged for decades so who cares? The door opened, and a tall black man entered in western gear with a Stetson hat, boots, shoulder holster and tin star on his chest.

"No way," said Jesse. "Sheriff Steele."

"Who?" said Angie.

The man walked over to Angie and took off his hat.

"Joaquim Steele, ma'am. Head of the Vigilance Committee of Galileonia. But most call me Sheriff Steele."

"Is that an elected position?" said Ryan.

"Appointed. For as long as I see the need to keep it," said Sheriff Steele taking a seat and putting his hat on the table. He leaned back and stared at them.

"So much staring," said Alana. "It's tiring."

"You four are what I call trouble-makers," said Sheriff Steele. "And I don't want your type in my town."

"Why do you think we're trouble-makers?" said Angie.

"Because I don't know how it would be possible to get more people giving me a heads up on your arrival."

"Good point," said Jesse, nodding.

"We're here to prospect, like thousands of others before us," said Ryan. "What's the trouble in that?"

"Oh, so, Sky City is broke now, eh?" said Steele.

"Ever since the quake, Sky City is under pressure to hand over its' intellectual property and who knows what else to the United States Department of Space," said Angie.

"They asking for Ben's first born now?" said Ryan.

"Well, we wouldn't care about that," said Angie.

"Sounds like a heap of trouble for you," said Steele. "Still, why bring this problem up here?"

"We've got a limited window to shore up our business before

everything is gone," said Ryan. "I put my life into that place. I don't want to hand it over to anyone."

"Didn't exactly answer my question," said Steele.

He put his hat on like he was going to take a nap.

"When you all are done with your rants, I'll begin listening again."

"We're done," said Jesse looking at the other three. "Right? No more complaining."

"I don't complain," said Alana. "It's these two. Always uptight about something."

"And you're always uptight," said Ryan.

"Cuz, you got that right," said Alana as she laughed. "But it's different."

"Sheriff," said Angie, "we have a plan to get control of our city and company back. It's high stakes and a bit crazy, but with a little support from you and the mayor, we'll be out of your hair."

Steele stood.

"You don't want the mayor's help, too expensive," said Steele. "He just left for Earth, anyway. Preparing for the summit. My guess is he's figuring out how much of the moon he can give away to stay in charge up here."

Steele opened the door to the interior.

"Let's go."

They followed him as he walked back into the room with the passenger ship, loading up for a return trip to the Gateway.

"Now, you will need a place to stay. I'll walk you over to O'Flannigan's. Make sure you get two rooms, they're small for Earth standards. Leave your projectile weapons with me; they're not allowed in town."

"What if we need to defend ourselves?" said Angie.

"Unlikely, but if you do, use something that doesn't shoot; I suggest you have a knife or two at the ready. Where you headed for your prospecting?"

"The far side of the moon," said Alana.

Steele's gait hesitated.

"You know what you're getting into? Heading to the far side?"

"We got a tip there's some big veins just waiting to be dug into," said Ryan.

"Better double check that tip."

They walked past the customs table, through the door and into the large dome. The team found themselves at the corner of Fifth and Codependence streets. Buildings made of steel and rock went for four blocks in one direction and three in the other. Steele walked them two blocks to First Street and took a right.

"O'Flannigans is right on the corner of the next block. Can't miss it."

"What's with Codependence Street?" said Ryan.

"The miners labeled it Independence Street, but the mayor called it Colonial Parkway. Vigilance Committee started calling it Codependence, and it stuck. Next street is Main, then Fortnight and last is Crescent. We're on First Street, Second is east, then Fourth. West is Third, then Fifth is where you came in. Based on when they were built. Expansion comes slow here."

Steele looked down the street, which was busy with pedestrians, but not packed.

"And get out of those space suits. It's bad form to wear anything but street clothes in town. Just carry your emergency air. Those suits make you stick out like tourists waiting to be taken advantage of. O'Flannigan can point out the shops. Good luck."

Steele turned back toward the landing dome and disappeared down Third Street, leaving the team with their cargo trunks. They stared down the oldest, newest looking western town they could imagine.

CHAPTER EIGHTEEN

GALILEONIA LUNAR MINING COLONY, SEA OF TRANQUILITY

While Angie, Alana and Jesse headed toward O'Flannigans, Ryan walked the other direction, donned his helmet, faceplate, and gloves, and exited the dome at the Codependence Street airlock heading toward the bone yard. The bone yard sat about a mile outside of town, past the hills. Ryan wore his foot weights, so the walk took about ten minutes. There were no official markings or signs identifying the bone yard, but it was easy to find. After heading north for a while, he saw a dozen rows of loaders, motor graders, draglines, and mining shovels. These machines were sent to the moon at great expense to mine for copper, manganese, nickel, cobalt, lithium, and rare Earth metals.

Profitable mining became harder every year on Earth in the 2040s. Environmentalists succeeded in shutting down land-based mining near any living creature, leaving only the most remote deserts available. Then the International Seabed Authority outlawed all sea mining and the Human Rights Council stopped third world mining unless countries could prove conditions were humane and not involving children, which proved impossible for the mining companies and their corrupt leaders.

Miners then looked upwards, and the moon no longer seemed like an unreasonable location to search for the non-stop demand of metals making up all the batteries and electronic components covering the Earth. The miners had to fight opposition to lunar mining before they even got their plans in writing. 'It could change the moon's orbit!' 'What about the tides?' 'You could bring back alien life!' The objections went on and on.

Turned out those making the objections only had leverage to stop the companies that incorporated inside the countries with lunar agreements. And there were plenty of countries that had no interest in participating in the self-limiting agreements of the U.S., European Union, and Canada. The Cayman Islands was the first to offer investors a fast-track to lunar mining incorporation. They identified rocket and launch pad schedules, booked slots in advance, and created a brokerage marketplace to facilitate selling any lunar materials making their way back to Earth. Other countries followed and when the U.S. dropped out of the lunar mining pact, it all fell apart.

Then the lunar mining race was on. Billions committed by large conglomerates to be first. Bigger was considered better. In hindsight, that thinking was a bit upside down. But at the time, like any business craze, thinking was backseat to action! Either you're first or don't bother. Carve-outs of the mining conglomerates went public, and everyone wanted in. Because the new companies had not sold anything, their financial reporting focused on metrics self-created to demonstrate what they believed to be progress. How much equipment they shipped to the moon, how much land they claimed for mining, and all the lunar rock assays.

Public financial metrics are a lot like dividends, always in place once started. It forced these new companies to double down even when they knew the metrics were wrong. And the partnerships between the lunar mining companies, space travel companies, and the investment banks forced the farce to continue long after even the least knowledgeable spectator saw the jig was up.

Mining on the moon was a new experience and, like anything new, had unforeseen complications. The large machines had too many failure points and needed frequent maintenance. The change in gravity and lack of air affected the mechanisms behind the machines' designs, and they continuously broke down. One example of moon mining was that dust took eight times longer to settle than on Earth. And much of the dust was fine particles that not only covered the machines but got inside them. This required replacement parts to be shuttled to the moon constantly, which required mechanics to be stationed on the moon.

Each person on the lunar surface required expensive habitat, food, and gear, all of which drove down future profits. Even with the mechanics on-site, the machines were down more than they were operational. One analyst mentioned that machine uptime seemed more important than other metrics and should become a standard reported metric. After a near lynching, he dug in harder. Then he announced to the public that moon machines had less than fifty percent uptime. Questions arose around when exactly did these companies expect to be profitable? The CEOs and CFOs gave soft answers involving a lot of platitudes, but when cornered they answered in a roundabout way with, *we don't know*. Support for large lunar mining operations stopped. Suddenly it became too expensive to justify the metals being mined.

Most of the original companies went bankrupt, selling out at pennies on the dollar to the remaining three. Those three, Moon Mineral Mining, Original Lunar Mining Company, and the Chussia

Lunar Mining Company, reorganized and moved in a smaller direction. Lunar sluice boxes were built, individual miners hired, and simple tools used to work the mines. Open pits were the common method at first as digging tunnels required support posts, which had to be shipped in from over two-hundred thousand miles away until the space manufacturing factories were built and could supply steel posts, much of which was manufactured with mined moon rock. Tunnels were dug and deeper mines resulted in more valuable metal finds. The three mining companies became profitable, very profitable. That was when they agreed to keep the moon's business amongst themselves. A partnership was formed, and small scale mining continued. The large machines never came back into use. With no financial justification for shipping them back to Earth, they sat on the moon's surface gathering dust, but without an atmosphere, no rust.

Ryan had looked over the boneyard layout from pictures before leaving Earth. He checked the accuracy of those pictures and yes, the machines were there, just as he hoped. But what state were each of them in? Many were stripped down more than he expected. He took out his tablet and walked around the bone yard, logging which machines had usable parts. He climbed out of a bulldozer when a small spacesuit jumped out from behind one of the two-story high Caterpillar lunar dump trucks.

"Hallo, you lost?" the spacesuit said with a Bavarian accent.

"No," said Ryan.

"Then why are you here? These machines are private property, just like the land you're on. You're trespassing."

"No one said I couldn't walk around."

"I just did."

"Who are you?"

"A concerned lunar citizen."

"Not helpful. Who are you and why are you bothering me?"

"I'm Max Schwarz. Owner of Schwarz's Equipment Rentals."

"So, all this is yours?"

"Oh, no. These are the property of the cartel members. But they barely even know what is here anymore. No one comes out to this area. Why are you here?"

"Field trip. I'm going to the national park next."

Max walked closer to Ryan to see the writing in his tablet. Ryan closed it.

"Why are you really here?"

"Maybe I need to borrow some of these items. What's it to you?"

"Oh, this is exciting. Are you building a machine out of spare parts? Like the old MacGyver show? So good. I can help."

"No thanks."

Ryan started to walk away; he decided to come back later when Max was gone.

"Oh, but you need my help. Or at least my discretion."

Ryan turned around and walked up to Max.

"Is that a threat?"

"No, well, yes. But it doesn't have to be. Why not let me help? I am the best on the moon with old equipment."

"Are you? Why do you want to help a stranger? Business slow?"

"Maybe, but If I help you, you could help me."

"With what?"

"A favor. Between new friends."

"What is it with people asking for favors?"

"Favors make the world go round, that's an old German saying."

"No, it's not."

"There is nothing more dangerous than solitude. That's Goethe. The moon gets lonely."

"I could go for some solitude right now."

Max looked hard at Ryan.

"This project seems like a big deal to you. I think it's worth any favor I or my descendants need in the future."

"Descendants? Like medieval times?"

"No, like the moon. Perhaps it should be two favors?"

"Fine, a favor for you or your kids."

"Or grandkids. Or their kids."

"Sure, except I won't live that long, and I don't have kids."

"But there's medical breakthroughs every day. In fact, some think lunar gravity extends life. Maybe you live forever? Tomorrow I bring you a bracelet. Inside will be a token torn in half. Wear it always and when someone brings you the other half token, then you will know the favor is due. Do whatever is asked."

"Maybe I refuse, who knows?"

"*Nein! das können Sie nicht!*"

Max took a breath.

"Don't do that Ryan Callahan. You do not want to do that."

Ryan looked at Max. This now seemed to be a lot less coincidental meeting than it originally appeared. He also realized why Angie hesitated with the chancellor on the Gateway.

"Deal."

"Great. Now we are friends, what machine do you want to start with?"

Ryan pointed to a massive hydraulic mining shovel.

"That big one behind you. We'll need the cockpit."

CHAPTER NINETEEN

ngie, Alana, and Jesse walked down First Street to O'Flannigans, which sat on the corner of Main and First, right in the center of town. A single-story structure that could not be more than a small restaurant or bar. They looked around for any other buildings that might be a hotel, but nothing larger was on the street. There was a tiny porch with seats in front of the double doors heading inside. The double doors had an airlock since each lunar building had to be one hundred percent contained in case of a dome breach. They opened the doors and went straight through the airlock. The airlock was open but would automatically engage if a breach alarm sounded.

Inside, they found a small lobby with chairs. At the back of the room sat a stairway on the left and elevator on the right, both going down. Angie and Alana took the spiral stairway down a level while Jesse put all the trunks in the elevator and met them down on the lower level. Beneath the surface, O'Flannigan's opened up. The room appeared to be a half block long. Bright LED lights lit up the center of the room, but the sides were more dimly lit where the bar and restaurant sat. On the right, a mountain style restaurant with tables and chairs, and open kitchen in the center. On the left, a bar with drinks on steel shelves and a large mirror behind them running the length of the bar. A half-dozen stools sat in front of the bar and four high tables sat in front of them with three stools apiece.

Everything in the bar was metal, but much of it had been finished to look like wood. While the town's forest had been growing for a dozen years, only the bamboo had been harvested, and in small amounts. Steel, leftover from the mining operations, was readily available, while wood was more valuable than gold on the moon. Construction in Galileonia consisted of steel and more steel. Also, steel could withstand a breach, which meant life or death in an emergency. Wood was for decoration, if you could afford it.

A small crowd sat in the bar talking amongst themselves. When the three of them walked by, they stopped talking, glanced at them with indifference, and went back to their conversations. Newcomers showed up every day. Ninety percent of them were gone in a week and ninety-nine percent in a month. The three of them walked to the check-in desk at the back of the lobby. The desk was a massive steel table with an inch thick wood top, the most wood they had seen since landing. A broad shouldered, red-haired, middle-aged woman stood behind the desk wearing an untucked flannel shirt and jeans. Her hair was held up with a long pin.

"I'm looking for O'Flannigan," Angie said. "Sherriff Steele said we could find him here."

"He's out," said the red-haired woman. "But you can talk to me."

"You're O'Flannigan, aren't you?" said Jesse.

"How'd you guess? Steele likes to play games. You wouldn't think it with that slow draw and slower gait. Like he's fooling anyone. I'm Bridget O'Flannigan and this is my establishment. The first hotel on the moon. Second bar, after the cosmonauts. Go figure they'd have a bar open before a hotel."

"Is the entire hotel underground?" said Jesse.

"That and more," said Bridget. "Gym's down the hall after the rooms. First set of colonists built out these caves as living quarters. Kept them safe from the solar flares, cosmic radiation, and meteoroids. Dome does a decent job since it's been built, but you still want to be underground most of the time. If you plan on living here, that is. You plan on living here? Don't look the type, but this here's a mental place, not physical. I reckon he'd make it."

Bridget nodded at Jesse.

"Could we get some rooms? Steele said you would have some available," said Angie.

"Joaquin likes giving out orders," said Bridget. "This your group?"

"And one more."

"What brings you here?"

"Prospecting."

She laughed. "Okay. You want to keep your business to yourselves. That's fine. Doesn't matter to me so long as you pay your bills."

Leaning over the table, she said, "I can give you two rooms. Pay in advance a week at a time. How long you think you'll need them?"

"Hard to say," said Angie, "but we're good to pay each week in advance."

Angie handed over her card, which Bridget scanned. Then she pointed the scanner at Angie.

"Let me see your hands."

Angie held out her hands.

"Palms up."

Angie turned her hands palms up and Bridget scanned them.

"You two as well."

Jesse and Alana put their hands up to be scanned.

"Who's the other one?" said Bridget.

"Ryan. Irish looking guy."

"I'll decide how Irish he looks. Your hands will open the doors to each of your rooms, eleven and twelve at the end of the floor. Tell him to see me when he gets in. Now, where are you prospecting?"

"The far side," said Angie.

"Ha, stupidest thing I've heard all week. I may need you to pay two weeks in advance. How are you going to handle the LTs?"

"Pardon?" said Angie.

"Lunar Tongs. They've been living on the far side for years. You're not going to sneak into their territory and mine a fortune without them stopping by for a chat."

"You have some suggestions?" said Angie.

"No. I'm not in the advice business," said Bridget. "Besides, I'm sure the daughter of the founder of Sky City has a few resources available to her."

She winked and motioned for them to head to their rooms. They walked across the lobby to a cave-like hall with doors on either side, which continued to shrink as they walked down it. They came to the end of the hall with the gym door in front and the doors to their rooms on either side, eleven and twelve. Someone exited the gym and had to climb over them and their trunks to get by but appeared nonchalant about the situation.

"Only a little claustrophobic," said Jesse as he put his palm up to the door, hearing it click open.

As Jesse opened room eleven's door it hit the end of one of the two single beds in each of the rooms. The beds in each room were lined up along one of the side walls. They looked like army grade barracks with white sheets. A pillow sat at one end of each bed along with a scratchy looking gray blanket. The other side of the room had a small closet, a sink and toilet with a removable tank to be emptied by guests as needed, per the note above the sink. It also had a logarithmic scale for the water rates if you went over two gallons a day. A floor to ceiling mural of a window looking at the lunar sky with Earth in the distance was on the wall at the end of the room, slightly reducing the cave feel.

"I take back my comment," said Jesse. "The hallway is very spacious."

"Will the trunks fit?" said Angie.

"Maybe one of them. We'll have to store the rest. I suggest we leave the solenoids in the room and the rest of the equipment in storage."

"Sounds good," said Angie.

Jesse pushed the solenoid trunk to the door, and it stopped, hitting the edges of the doorway.

"Let's open the lid and angle it in," said Jesse as he opened the trunk.

"Maybe just pick them up and take them inside first," said Angie.

"That'll take too long. Alana, here, grab this end."

Jesse picked up the end of the trunk and held the lid next to the door as Alana picked up the other end. He turned the trunk to make it fit through the doorway.

"Okay, just tilt it a little," said Jesse.

"Why not try to," said Angie moving her hands as they kept tilting the trunk. "No, wait, no!"

Jesse turned the trunk too far and the nuclear solenoids fell out bouncing in and outside the room.

"Put it down," said Alana, lowering her side of the trunk.

Jesse put down the trunk and picked up the solenoids in the room, putting them on the cot near the door. Alana handed him the ones that fell into the hall. Jesse maneuvered the trunk into the room, stepped over it and back into the hall.

"Well, it's in the room," said Jesse.

"Men," said Angie, shaking her head and walking back toward the lobby with the other trunks following her.

"Not sure how Ryan's going to sleep with all that stuff on his bed," said Jesse as he shut the door.

CHAPTER TWENTY

ngie, Alana, and Jesse headed back out onto First Street. They walked across the street and into a clothing store labeled Outpost.

"Welcome Angela Dawson. Welcome Alana Noelani. Welcome Jesse Taylor," said the automated sensors as they passed through the doorway.

The door in the back slammed open and a middle-aged lady ran out, disbelief in her eyes.

"Ladies!" she said. "What can I do for you today?"

"We're here for some outfits," said Jesse.

"Men's clothing in that corner," the shopkeeper said while walking over to Angie and Alana.

"What brings you two lovely ladies to our corner of the moon? No, wait, I'll guess. You look all business; business trip. Right?"

"Yes, we're here on business," said Angie.

"Then you'll need some business outfits. Ha, ha, I'm kidding; no one wear's business outfits here."

"Is this all the men's items?" said Jesse looking at four outfits.

"Gray or blue, that's what I've got," the shopkeeper said without turning her head. "Oh, isn't that darling? Yes, I think it will fit you."

Jesse took a gray outfit, went into the changing booth, and waited for an hour while the three ladies tried on every piece of clothing and accompanying accessories in the store. The shopkeeper refused to let Angie and Alana out of the store until they each had a minimum of six complete outfits. She gently wrapped each of their outfits and placed them in bags with more care than parents show to newborn children.

"Okay, our night line will be coming out next month and I want to see you two back here, no excuses!"

"Sounds good," said Angie as she and Alana carried their bags outside the store and were instantly charged for their purchases.

"Bye now!"

The shopkeeper teared up as the three of them left and walked across the street.

"Why don't you give me those bags and I'll put them and our suits back in the room," said Jesse.

Angie and Alana handed Jesse their bags and looked down the Main Street.

"I'll get the food over there at Morton's," said Angie.

"I'll be down there," said Alana pointing to a Mining Tools and Supplies sign.

"Great, I'll head to The Ammunition Depot, and we'll meet back here," said Jesse.

As Jesse went back into O'Flannigan's, Angie and Alana walked down Main Street in the direction of the landing dome, to the heart of the retail shopping district, only a block long. Angie entered Morton's General Store while Alana continued walking toward Mining Tools and Supplies. Angie walked down the one of the two aisles in the general store, filling up her bag with vacuum packed prepared meals. She dropped hundreds of energy bars into the bag, got a second bag and looked for the beverage section when a slim, attractive, older Chinese women entered the store, which caused the checkout clerk to flinch, then stand very still. Angie looked over her shoulder, the women caught Angie's eye, and headed straight for her.

"Angie Dawson, I'm Wei Shi," she said as she bowed.

"Hello, Ms. Shi. It is nice to meet you."

"Please, call me Wei."

Angie knew Wei Shi ran the Chussia Lunar Mining Company. She also knew no one ever called her Wei.

"So, what do you have here?" Ms. Shi looked at Angie's bags of food, putting her hand in and moving items around to see what was at the bottom. "I don't recommend the vegetable lasagna. The eggplant never comes out right."

She removed her hand in a slow deliberate manner that sent a chill down Angie's spine.

"Heading out for a while?"

"We're prospecting."

"I've heard. You know, Chussia would be happy to assist and potentially partner with you. I am an admirer of what Sky City is trying to accomplish."

"Did accomplish."

"Remains to be seen. I understand there are problems remaining independent."

"We are here to make sure Sky City remains independent."

"As independent as a company can be. All those regulations can be so annoying."

"They're not all bad. Most of them are to protect the individual."

"Yes, well sometimes individuals need to protect themselves. Here, on the frontier, life is rugged. Takes a more self-reliant person to survive. Regulations are useless. Most partner with others to smooth the path. Why not rely on the experiences of those that came before you? No need to go through the same struggles we already figured out."

"That is very generous, thank you Ms. Shi. I will keep it in mind."

Angie began walking down the aisle to continue her shopping when Wei Shi grabbed her arm, just above the elbow. A gentle touch, but this time, the chill covered Angie's entire body.

"Timing is important Ms. Dawson. My offer will not be available for long. It is much better to partner early, before things get out of hand."

"What do you mean?"

While Angie and Wei Shi were talking, Alana dumped tools into multiple baskets and taking them to the checkout counter of Mining Tools and Supplies. She cleared entire shelves of the limited inventory in the store.

"Watch these for me," she said to the clerk.

Alana picked up another basket and walked to the middle of the hand-tools section. She grabbed several hammers when she heard a voice behind her.

"You need all those?" said an Australian accented voice.

Alana turned and saw a blond haired, blue-eyed middle-aged man that looked like he popped out of an African Safari.

"Why? You need some?"

"Ha, no. Just seems like a lot of tools. You a prospector?"

"No, I'm a pilot." Alana turned back to the hand tools.

"A pilot? Fascinating. I'm Aiden Wolfe, by the way."

"Okay. Have a nice day."

Alana grabbed some crowbars, then levels, screwdrivers, paper cutters, razor blades for the paper cutters, zip ties, hook-and-loop ties, and all the duct tape in the store, dumping everything into another basket. She walked the fourth basket to the counter and gently placed it on the counter even though it came in at over fifty pounds. Aiden Wolfe walked up beside her and put his elbow on the counter, admiring her tool selection. He looked at the clerk, whose brow was sweating.

"Do you think she should care about knowing me?"

"Yes, sir."

Aiden turned to Alana.

"You see, everyone thinks I'm a good person to know in this town."

Alana looked at the store clerk.

"This normal? People get harassed in your store?"

The clerk avoided both parties' eyes and began waving the infrared gun over the baskets to ring them up.

"Look, I know why you and your friends are here. I run OLMCO, the Original Lunar Mining Company."

"My partners and me. Not friends."

"Whatever. The scuttlebutt is you're prospecting for Sky City. Some new vein running down in the ground. That you would know about a vein in the ground that I wouldn't is, well, ridiculous. But maybe you have some information I don't. Unlikely, but you made the trip here. I also heard you weren't supposed to come. That true?"

Alana showed her payment card to the clerk who scanned it and began bagging the tools as fast as possible. Supply stores did not allow for automated purchasing since too many items managed to disappear inside lead coated bags. Moon men liked to steal tools. Aidan kept talking, as was his nature.

"You will probably be approached by others. I suggest you pick wisely, go with success, and that's me. I can be your partner too."

Alana turned to Aidan.

"Why do I need another partner? You don't even look like you belong here."

"Oh, but I do. My company founded the MMP with a mission to

maintain a fair market for lunar mining materials. It's an important role in keeping market prices stable."

Alana rolled her eyes, picked up her bags of equipment, and started walking out. Aiden followed her.

"We supervise the distribution of Lunar mining for the good of humanity. You have to go through us to take anything larger than souvenirs off the surface."

"The Tongs ship material to HOSS 2 all the time," said Alana as she stopped to look at Aidan.

Aidan stopped smiling for a moment.

"Conjecture," he said, back to smiling. "I like your chutzpah, it's refreshing, unlike most of the scared little children that show up her thinking they're conquering the final frontier, which it isn't anymore. Seventy degrees and sunny, even during the two week-long night. All those 'adventurers' getting dejected when the gold or lithium or helium-3 isn't lying on the ground to pick up off the sidewalks. Sure, you can sweep up some valuable dust at the dance hall, but even in the beginning, it was random prospectors finding the veins. Way before the news stories. I was one of them. Up here when mining was getting figured out; working harder than I thought I could, day after day, month after month. All while big machines were breaking down, grown men crying like babies, fogging up their face masks, and crying some more. I brought my safari outfit for when I hit it big. Kept it vacuum sealed for a year. Ridiculous? Yes, but true frontier man are odd ducks. Who else leaves everything behind? Not the guy that freaks out when a coffee shop is more than two blocks away. As if that guy even knows the working end of a shovel. Most of them make the trip here, look around, and book a seat home, like that was the journey, just getting here. These days, if you want to make money mining on the moon you need a partner. OLMCO has the best distribution channels. You'll get better equipment, less delays and faster payment."

"You should work on that pitch, especially the last part. Boring."

Alana walked out the store. Standing outside the door were two larger versions of Aidan. Aidan followed Alana out and circled around her to stand between his two men. While Aidan circled Alana, Jesse exited The Ammunition Depot at the corner of First and Fortnight carrying two heavy duffel bags down the block to the corner of First and Main. As he turned onto Main Street looking for Angie and Alana, three Americans were waiting for him kitty-corner to O'Flannigan's, in front of the Lunar Mart, a small convenience store.

"Full load you have there," said the older of the three, a brown-haired wiry man in his fifties wearing jeans and an untucked plaid shirt. He took a step toward Jesse. Jesse looked straight at him, set down his duffel bags and scanned Main Street, seeing Alana surrounded by three safari hunters, Angie exiting the general store with a Chinese woman and that no one else was on the street. Then, two blocks away, at the end of Main Street, Ryan came around the corner with Max, who stopped short when he saw the scene.

"*Ah, nicht gut,*" said Max to himself.

Ryan looked down the street.

"Who are those people?"

"The three tigers. They're never in the same place together. See you tomorrow."

"No, wait," Ryan said, but Max had already skipped down Fifth Street to Fortnight and vanished between buildings. Ryan decided to jog down to the scene. As he started running, everyone pulled out weapons and pointed them at him. He stopped running but not being used to the lower gravity, he tumbled to the ground, skidding to Third Street, next to Alana. Jesse had his hand on his knife, waiting to pull it out if things escalated. Alana dropped her bags and grabbed a hammer and a long screwdriver out of them. Angie stepped back toward the doorway of Morton's still holding her bags. Ryan got on his knees and sneezed. That caused Wolfe's men to take a step toward him with weapons pointed at his head. Ryan froze, hands and knees on the ground.

"What's going on here?" said Steele from behind Jesse with a voice loud enough to echo off the bubble.

Everyone watched Steele as he walked down Main Street without pulling any weapons, but they were visible all over his body. Almost ridiculous, really, how many gun handles, knives, tasers, stun grenades and mace spray cans were visible. Jesse wondered, one, how the weapons did not impede his movement and, two, how he could load up like that. He needed a lot more hook and loop straps. Once everyone heard Steele's voice, the weapons disappeared. When Steele stopped in the middle of the street an uneven circle formed around them.

"I see we're all getting to know each other," said Steele. "Quite the welcoming party. Wei, Aidan, and Al."

Steele nodded at the MMP Directors who were a step closer to Steele than the rest of the group.

Ryan raised a hand.

"I don't know anyone."

He stood, dusted himself off and joined the circle.

"Well," said Steele, "you have the pleasure of meeting each of the company heads for the lunar cartel."

"Such a dirty phrase," said Aiden.

"That's Aiden Wolfe of OLMCO; Wei Shi who runs Chussia Mining, and Albert Jackson, Moon Mineral Mining CEO."

"Pleasure," said Ryan, lying.

"Let's just stop this right here," said Steele. "No one draws guns in town."

"These are short range tasers Steele," said Albert Jackson. "You know that. No one's pulling out guns."

"You drew a weapon on newcomers. I don't care what it is. What did they do to provoke you besides show up? I guess that's enough these days. They're here to prospect, which is still legal. Leave them be. Once they come back, they can decide whether or not to stake claims or quit."

"We're not quitters," said Alana.

"We'll see," said Steele.

Wei Shi turned and walked away.

"Good luck," said Aiden motioning to his men. "Let's go."

"Nice job keeping the peace, Steele. As usual," said Albert Jackson. He looked at the team and motioned them away. "Talk to you later."

After the directors left the street, other people appeared on the sidewalks as if nothing had happened.

CHAPTER TWENTY-ONE

WASHINGTON D.C.

OCTOBER 15, 2071

D on put his water glass down and looked around the Old Ebbitt Grill, filling up with diners. He tried to relax and act like this was a casual lunch, no big deal. His hands shook a bit, and he let go of the water glass. Daniel slid into the other side of his green upholstered booth.

"Not waiting long, I hope?" said Daniel.

"Oh no," said Don. "Just sat." At least the booth provided decent coverage from other seated patrons.

"Can you believe this place is over two hundred years old? Not in this location, but still a good track record for any business. You up for oysters?"

"Never really been into them but could give it another try."

"Well, if you don't like them here, you'll never like them. Think of it as a litmus test for you and oysters."

Daniel waved at a smartly dressed waiter who stood just outside of earshot and came right over.

"Yes, Mr. Nguyen?"

"A dozen oysters, chef's selection, and a bottle of champagne."

"Your usual?"

"That would be terrific, thank you."

The waiter headed straight into the kitchen.

"I can't drink while I'm working."

"Of course. Maybe just a sip with the oysters; makes for a wonderful pairing."

Daniel sat back.

"I must say, I was surprised to hear you're a fan of Sky City."

"It's an impressive accomplishment."

Don took a breath. What was he doing? Acting like a Sky City groupie? He worked at the NSA. He was good at it, and he liked it; he sort of liked it. Okay, it paid the bills. Also, he had gathered enough connections through his career to get his two sons into decent prep schools with scholarships, the only way they could attend. His wife had never been thrilled with all the D.C. politics, but she put up with it for the sake of the family. It was hard for her and Don to admit they were settling, with his career, their house, the future; but after rejections from several private companies over the years, he put his energy into the NSA.

They treated him reasonably well. One of the few agencies still headquartered in D.C., and they liked the area. Predictable. Start in an analyst role and move up the ladder, promotions like clockwork every three years of service, and now director. Don's resentment toward the private sector, particularly technology, came out in his oversight efforts. But it was more like an overlay hiding his desire to be a part of it. The NSA did allow him to research technology solutions for the department, one way to scratch his itch. Ultimately, though, he worked at a federal agency and his limited political skills held him back from the best positions.

"Look, Don, I don't want to overstep here, but we need some help."

Don knew it, a bribe most likely. He put both hands on the edge of the table to prepare.

"With the revised launch of Sky City, there's a need for improved security. It's a much more complex organization now. Thousands of people in and out daily."

"Uh-huh."

"We need to improve security in ways never contemplated before. I'll be blunt, we would like to have you consult with us on our security."

Don leaned forward, relaxed his grip on the edge of the table. No way.

"Before you object," said Daniel, "it would not be a conflict of interest. In fact, with the plan for the DOS to take over operations of Sky City, a full security review has to happen sooner rather than later. We're not going to ask you about confidential government protocols. And we would request you bring nothing but your thoughts and suggestions on what we have in place today and where we need to go tomorrow."

Don thought about what areas he would look at first. Communications, of course, but then physical security would take a while. He had many ideas the NSA had shelved that he could look at.

"I'd need clearance to be a consultant."

"Of course. I'm already working through the approvals. It would be all up front and papered correctly. And we won't insult you with a nickel and dime rate."

Daniel slid a piece of paper over to Don. The rate was five times his effective hourly rate at the NSA. He put his hands under the table before they started shaking and nodded.

"Because it would have to be done on your off-time, we want to make sure you're compensated for that. If you have to take vacation time to consult, the rate will be doubled. You will also be reimbursed for travel time and expenses, any expenses we don't pay directly, that is."

"But if you're about to hand the place off to the DOS, why are you worried about security now? Might as well wait and save the money, right?"

Daniel leaned forward.

"You and I know that could take months, even years. Every day is a risk for exposure. This cannot wait."

The oysters arrived with the champagne. The waiter opened the bottle, the popped cork caused Don to flinch, still concerned people were going to see him with Daniel Nguyen, General Counsel and Vice Chairman for Sky City. But no one looked. As usual, the other patrons were much more interested in themselves.

"I don't know. This sort of thing is frowned upon."

"Is it? By whom? All the other consultants? I suspect it's because they don't want anyone else elbowing in on their gigs. I'm talking to you Don specifically because you are hesitating. Anyone that jumps at this opportunity is not the person for the job. I've hired too many consultants that focus on billings and not solutions. And to be clear, we do not want you to come in and pat our backs telling us what a great job we're doing on security. Ben is expecting you to break us, show us our vulnerabilities, everywhere."

"Ben Dawson requested me?"

"Of course. Nothing matters more to him than the security of Sky City and he's not too proud to bring in the best. If it is going to make Sky City better, he will take whatever criticism he gets."

Don reached over and tried an oyster. Still slimy, but had a different, more enjoyable, briny taste as he sat with Daniel discussing Sky City consulting.

"Cheers," said Daniel, raising his glass.

"Cheers," said Don as he also raised his glass and took a long drink of the champagne. Creamy and crisp in his mouth. Smoother going down than he expected. Not at all sharp, like what he normally experienced. He looked at the bottle sitting in the ice bucket and thought about buying some.

"Don, in order to better orient you with Sky City security. We need you on-site for as long as we can get you. Our preference is you stay at Sky City for a week before the conference."

"Uh, well, I have vacation, but…"

"Totally understand. We don't want to take you away from family on your vacation time. When you come, you and your family would be our guests. Along with full access to the recreational facilities."

"Including Skyball?"

"Absolutely, we have beginner classes scheduled every day."

Don finished his glass and almost broke it setting it down on the table.

"Sounds great."

CHAPTER TWENTY-TWO

PACIFIC OCEAN

OCTOBER 16, 2071

P aige was crying again. She felt it coming today. Sometimes, it hit her and the tears just started flowing out of nowhere.

"Paige are you ready?" said Ben into her earpiece.

Paige wiped her eyes and swiped down on her tablet. The drone rock screamed down past *Firefly*, through the connected wings of *Sky Dancer* and *Blue Darter* sending mini robots flying onto the decks of the two Skyboats and into the ocean.

"Paige!" Ben said from the deck of *Blue Darter*. "What's going on?"

Paige leaned over the railing of *Firefly* looking down at *Sky Dancer* and *Blue Darter*. A drizzly, overcast day on the water. Ben wanted to practice retrieval under as many weather conditions as possible and picked a dreary day to take Paige and Jason out for yet another session.

"What's going on?" Paige said in a voice that made Ben and Jason wince. "What's going on is my daughter is up there, Ben!"

Paige pointed to the sky.

"We all know that," said Ben. "C'mon Paige, we need to practice."

"Do you? Fine."

Paige swiped the drone rock back up to *Firefly*, and then swiped it down at full speed. The mini robots had just finished reconnecting the wings when it shot through them and blasted both wings completely off their Skyboats. Paige swiped the drone rock back up and was about to swipe it down on Ben's head when she began crying and dropped the tablet.

"I blame you, Ben! This is all on you. If something happens to our daughter, I'll never forgive you."

"Paige, listen,"

"No, I won't listen. You always do this. You get an idea in your head and get everyone on board without asking me, and then it's too late and I have to agree or I'm not the cool parent. And now our daughter is up there alone."

"She's not alone Mom."

"Are you up there? Am I? Is he?" Paige pointed at Ben like he was guilty of a crime, which in Paige's mind, he was.

Ben got a call from Daniel, which he happily answered.

"Ben, you free?" said Daniel.

"I'm here with Paige and Jason."

"I'll add them on. Hey, guys, how we doing?"

"Not good Daniel," said Paige.

"Oh, sorry to hear. This is a stressful time. I'll get right to it. Don's on board but Martin's filed an injunction against Sky City."

"What does that mean?" said Ben.

"He's trying to shut us down until he takes over."

"He can't do that," said Jason.

"It just takes one judge," said Daniel, "and he's shopping it."

"Even just a few days of a shutdown would be a disaster," said Ben. "We wouldn't recover. We're already losing Skyboats every day. People are losing faith in Sky City."

"I know I have," said Paige. "Next time I see that Myers guy I don't know what I might do."

"Can you get him off our back?" said Ben.

"Send him some tech Dad, some useless prototype he'll think is cool," said Jason.

"What tech would Martin possibly think is cool?" said Ben.

"Give him your stupid fusion cannon," said Paige.

"That's a joke Mom," said Jason. "It's just jet fuel in a hyper compression chamber. Fusion is always twenty years and a couple hundred billion dollars away."

"Real fusion has never been tried," said Daniel.

"Not tech," said Ben. "He's all about politics and getting a seat at the table."

"Then put him in charge of something and get it over with," said Paige as she lowered *Firefly* to the same altitude as Ben and Jason.

"Why not give him a seat at the table?" said Daniel. "Offer him an SBI board seat."

"What?" said Jason. "No way. That guy on the board? Then I'll stop believing in Sky City. *Mr. Dawson, aren't you dedicated to the cause? And by cause, I mean communism.*"

"That might work," said Ben, ignoring his son. "He would love that; SBI Board Director. You can do a press release, maybe even hold a press conference. Make it happen."

"Sounds good," said Daniel, hanging up.

Paige looked at Ben.

"Until Angie is back on Earth, this is all your responsibility. Understand?"

"Yes, I understand," said Ben as he set down the launcher.

"Get her back!" said Paige as she pushed the throttle on *Firefly* and flew back to Sky City. The canopy drones chased after her.

"We will," said Ben in a whisper not at all believable.

"Guess we'll try out the fishing poles next time," said Jason packing up the nine-foot carbon fiber rod with motorized reel. "Don't worry Dad, it's going to work out. That's just how Mom is."

They headed back to Sky City at a much slower pace than Paige. Ben was not looking forward to facing her anytime soon.

"Yeah, but she's also right," said Ben.

CHAPTER TWENTY-THREE

BONE YARD OUTSIDE GALILEONIA

OCTOBER 18, 2071

"This is it?" said Alana. "You expect us to risk our lives, get off the ground and fly into space in this? What a pile of junk."

"That was the point," said Ryan. "If it looked like a sleek spaceship, how could you tell anyone you're using it to mine the moon? Did you really expect me to give it a paint job?"

"Maybe you could have used less primer?" said Jesse.

Alana walked around the pieces Ryan and Max had pulled from the abandoned machines. They were in the middle of the bone yard to avoid detection. Ryan created his open workshop by moving some of the dozers around. As Ryan and Max worked, they would fit two pieces together then take them apart. Ryan never put the entire spaceship together at any one time. The transport was another matter. He finished it early. Nothing suspicious about a transport, except maybe for how heavy duty it was. Ryan and Max had impressed the team creating such a military grade vehicle from spare parts. But the spaceship was another matter.

"So, how does it all come together?" said Alana.

"Let me show you," said Max.

He walked over to small cabin lifted from an excavator.

"Here's your cockpit. Seats two uncomfortably. We modified the control panel for the ship's controls."

He picked up a large wire coming out of the bottom.

"This will connect to the other parts, starting with this cargo hold."

He walked over to a what looked like a cargo van compartment, which it was.

"Very high tech," said Angie.

"It'll work," said Ryan. "The doors will be connected to the control panel. And it can open on both sides. I retrofitted the doors for airtight seals. Installed an airlock seal at the front to secure the cockpit."

"This the engines?" said Jesse looking at another pile of equipment.

"Stay with the tour," said Ryan.

Max looked a little put out that Jesse walked away from the group. This was his moment.

"*Ja, die Motoren*," said Max walking between Jesse and the engines. "Hardest part of the job," said Max. "Pulling parts from dozens of machines to make them. Very complex you know, chemical engines, nuclear engines, propellant decisions. But I am happy to announce we used only a tiny small amount of duct tape on the final rockets."

"What?" said Alana.

"Max," said Ryan. "It will work. They're single propellant rocket engines. Classic."

"Guaranteed?" said Angie.

"Absolutely," said Ryan.

"You sure?" said Angie.

Ryan looked at Angie, and Angie looked back at Ryan.

"Fine," said Ryan. "I'll work on them some more. Give me a day."

Jesse walked closer to Max.

"I'm confused. Why are you so helpful?" said Jesse.

"Friendship," said Max.

"I don't buy it," said Jesse. "What's your angle?"

"My angle is relationships," said Max. "Relationships are most important. Right, Ryan?"

"I guess," said Ryan, now annoyed at everyone and digging into the engine.

Angie looked at her watch.

"We need to go. Steele asked to meet with us before we head out, which sounds like tomorrow now," said Angie. "Alana, can you get all our gear ready while Jesse and go see what Steele wants?"

"Fine," said Alana, "then I'm coming back to ask our technician some technical questions."

Max saluted Alana as she walked away. Angie and Jesse went over to Steele's office, the Vigilance Committee Headquarters, located on First Street between Codependence and Main. Two men walked out as they entered, the last holding the door for them. They walked into a small room with holographic whiteboards where Steele erased a name from the Most Wanted list and wrote it under the No Longer Wanted list. He looked over at them when they walked in.

"I need to know where you plan on mining," said Steele. "For safety purposes."

Angie went over to his desk and pulled up the holographic globe of the moon on her tablet. She centered on the Eastern Sea (Mare

Orientale). She pointed to a spot one hundred miles west of it and stretched the image to zoom in.

"Here is where we are headed. The plan is to explore this area for rare Earth metals mining."

"That's not safe. Not safe at all. In fact, where you plan on going might be the most dangerous place for human beings in existence. The only thing you'll find out there are criminals."

"It's where our data tells us a big find could be."

"One, I do not believe that. That's no different than any other place on the moon. Two, you will be attacked multiple times before you get there, then attacked while you are there, and if you do find something, which you won't, you can count on the same coming back."

"So, you don't recommend it?" said Angie.

"Look, I'm not your ward, and having you all here is creating problems for me, so I prefer you gone. But in good conscience, you need to come up with another plan or just head back to Earth. What you're planning right now is suicide."

"We appreciate your openness, and if we could do something else, we would," said Angie. "But not going out there is suicide for Sky City."

"In that case, what firepower are your brining?"

Jesse took the duffel bag off his back, the one he always had with him since the lunar cartel's welcoming party incident. He dropped it on the desk and opened it. Jesse began placing the guns and ammunition on the table from the bag. "I've got a second one too."

"It's a start, but you'll want these," said Steele as he walked over to a locker at the back of the room. He opened the door and pulled out two large laser rifles, a dart gun, a crossbow, and what appeared to be a bazooka. He then dragged a trunk from the bottom of the locker out and opened it to reveal ammunition for the weapons.

"This is my personal stash, saved for special occasions. This seems like one. I'll put together an invoice, that is, if you want them."

"Pay the man," Jesse said to Angie as he picked up the bazooka, put it on his shoulder, and looked through the sights.

CHAPTER TWENTY-FOUR

SKY CITY

OCTOBER 19, 2071

D r. Martin Myers, Robyn Hernandez, Dale Dobbs, and Don LaRue stepped off the Skyboat transport onto the deck of *Horizon*. Ben, Daniel, Paige, and Roger were there to meet them. Ben walked up to Martin.

"Martin, so nice to have you and your team visit Sky City before the conference," said Ben. "We appreciate your taking the time to learn more about how this operations works so you will have a better understanding when we agree on oversight."

"This isn't a pleasure visit," said Martin. "And if it were up to me, you'd already be shut down."

"Well, thankfully, it's not up to you and that's why we're all here." Ben said as he waved his arm around to show off his city, which was enormous and impressive, especially when you looked at it from the *Horizon* deck. Everyone but Martin was taken back by the size of Sky City, even with only half the Skyboats from the original launch. All the renderings and partial builds did not do justice to its actual presence. They marveled at the hundreds of individual Skyboats connected to each other, creating a flying city. The group walked up to their hosts and shook hands, introducing themselves. It was very pleasant, cordial, and fake.

"Welcome to Sky City," said Roger, taking charge after a glance at Dale. "It is our pleasure to host you. I have taken the liberty of having your itineraries sent to your tablets. We will start with a tour of Sky City followed by a light meal, and then a reception this evening with our Level Four members. Tomorrow you will be our guests of honor at the Skyball game where you can ride the skyboards with some of the players during warm-ups. Following the game will be a reception with our lead scientists and engineers. We will then begin the conference bright and early Wednesday morning."

"Lovely," said Martin, furious at Kerry for forcing this diplomatic meeting ahead of the conference. Apparently, there are more approvals required for blowing up a rocket ship besides yelling 'I said blow it up!' on an NSA conference call. This glad-handing day was Martin's penance. Kerry told him to mend fences with the Dawsons. Unlikely. While Martin would never say it out loud, it was better that the rocket did not get blown out of the sky. Now he could say nothing happened, all good, while they lined up their eminent domain lawsuits after the injunction failure. That judge would regret not granting it.

Roger walked them onto a waiting Sky City transporter, which looked like a large white raft floating in the air, except the transporter had four gimbaled micro-nuclear powered engines mounted underneath, autonomous collision prevention sensors, a half dozen self-leveling gyroscopes, and communication software that kept the transporter in contact with all other airborne transporters. Once they were all on board, Roger pulled out his tablet, raised the stainless-steel railings around the edges and smoothly lifted them off the deck at a feeling of near zero acceleration. The passengers were able to stand without holding onto anything and just enjoy the view, which was the point. Robyn, Dale, and Don looked around again, enjoying the sight while Martin had his arms folded. Apparently, he had a goal of zero enjoyment for the entire trip. He would likely succeed because he only found enjoyment in life's simple pleasures of self-recognition, criticism, and taking complete control of other people's accomplishments.

"Sky City is a closer to an Asian boat harbor than a land-based city," Roger said as he went through the tour script he used to love to give, but now felt hollow since the quake that ruined his life.

When the earthquake hit Eureka, everyone followed the guidelines and ran out of the buildings, heading to open ground. But then the town crumbled into the Pacific and did not stop. Ninety five percent fatalities. Eureka was gone. Roger took his Skyboat out to Eureka the day after. He flew over what remained, turned the boat around and flew back. He saw no point in walking through the destruction. A military man, Roger knew a lost cause when he saw it.

His family's location tags in their watches, earpieces and tablets showed their location, like thousands of other Eureka residents, at the bottom of the ocean. Tragic was an insufficient description. Roger returned to Sky City and resumed his duties. Ben told him he could do whatever he wanted for as long as he wanted. Roger said work was what he wanted. It was all he could do to stay sane. But inside him, he fell apart. And Roger looked for someone to blame.

"More like a three-dimensional harbor," Roger continued. "Nine-hundred fifteen Skyboats making up five levels and as you can see, they are each spread out by the distance of their wing spans, which along with the nuclear jets creates the elevation technology. Wing sizes are as wide on each side as the ship is long making Sky City almost two miles wide. Being airborne, geographic boundaries don't come into play, so long as we stay above the mountain tops. The wings, along with the connecting walkways and trusses, are made up of the three mini robot types that vary in strength. The Skyboats are closer front to back than side to side and the tail wing tensile strength is doubled that of the side wings, allowing the Skyboats themselves to act as a skeleton for the city. Of course, weight is always a primary consideration and each Skyboat has strict weight limits."

"Why did you stop at nine-hundred fifteen Skyboats," said Don, who unlike Martin, was unable to avoid getting wrapped up in the majesty of this technological marvel. Even after a week in Sky City, he was still fascinated.

"It was based on how we spread out the weight, the edges of Sky City are lighter than the center, acting as wings to the center boats," said Ben, who could not help going over his design.

"Can you make a larger Sky City?" said Robyn, also now fascinated and getting the stink eye from Martin, which she ignored.

"Once we prove out this one, why not?" said Ben. "Since we launched last year, we've captured thousands of small improvements for the next Sky City."

"Next Sky City?" said Martin.

The transport was between Levels Three and Four. Roger began flying toward the edge of Sky City. He took advantage of Martin's interruption to take over the tour.

"As I mentioned before, Sky City's horizontal and vertical footprint is approximately two miles long by two miles wide with a diamond shape.

It's five levels are nearly fifteen hundred feet high giving the appearance of a squashed pyramid."

Roger reached the edge of Level Four and stopped within arm's reach of the Sky City canopy. It was a weave of honeycombs with a slight hum from the drones supporting it. Don and Dale, being guys, reached out and touched the canopy, not knowing if it would electrocute them, stick to them, or had some other creative way of being harmful. It was in fact, safe to touch and sponge-like.

"The canopy is semi-permeable, similar technology to the wing drones," said Roger. "The mini drones each have a six-inch diameter multi-walled polycarbonate honeycomb sheet with smart hook and loop edges. The honeycomb sheet can be secured to the underside of the drone or released to hang by one edge at the bottom of the drone. The honeycombs then attach to the other drones to form the canopy. The drones adjust their positions based on wind and external elements, like birds or approaching Skyboats.

The polycarbonate honeycomb contains silver chips that create a mirrored effect when the drones shine a light into them, allowing for an opaque view if it becomes too bright for any section of the city. Some, or all, of the sections can open up to allow wind or rain in as well as the ability to manage through storms; allowing the canopy to bend but not break. When we need to move, the canopy collapses and the drones fly into each level's center Skyboat in a matter of minutes. And because they are solar powered, their fight time can be unlimited. But spares switch out with other canopy drones if some do need recharging."

"Who came up with this?" said Don, seriously considering buying a Skyboat and quitting the NSA.

"Our Chief Architect, Ryan Callahan," said Ben. "Genius, isn't it?"

"I guess," said Don, looking up at the height of the canopy with his mouth open. The canopy rose a few hundred feet over Level Five.

"It also helps with atmosphere and temperature control, which allows Sky City to hover at higher elevations," Roger said.

"Yes, thank you," said Martin. "All remarkably interesting to school children on a field trip, which we are not. Now, can we sit down and discuss why we are actually here? That is, the transfer of Sky City to the Department of Space."

"But that's exactly what we're doing," said Daniel. "You need to know about Sky City if you're going to run it."

"Do I?" said Martin. "Roger, you run this City?"

"I am the captain of Sky City flight operations, but Ben manages Skyboat Incorporated, which handles hospitality."

"Well, then Roger can keep doing what he's doing, reporting to me, while Ben can tell Robyn how to fold towels, if that's even necessary. I think we're done here."

"What about the hydroponic gardens?" Don said as he looked at the Sky City brochure on his tablet. He had saved that visit for the tour.

"I said we're done," said Martin and motioned Roger to return them to the big ship where they started.

Don looked hurt as Roger turned the transporter back to the top deck of *Horizon*. No one spoke for a minute until Don asked Daniel a question about how fast they were able to grow the food. Daniel went over the hydroponic garden technology as well as the small farm boats that raised chicken, goats, and fish. He talked about how they shipped larger livestock in from farms across the globe. As Daniel spoke, Dale began asking Roger about security, making Roger uncomfortable. Paige started small talk with Robyn to avoid telling Martin what she thought of him, while Ben looked up at the top of the canopy, thinking. The transport landed back on the deck of *Horizon* and Roger escorted them into a small café where they took a private room in the back where lunch was laid out on a table. Everyone sat down except for Ben.

"As Roger said, the management of Sky City Inc. is my purview as CEO and Chairman. There are, in fact, significant logistics to discuss. Although Roger was correct in that our focus is hospitality, this is much more than a hotel or cruise ship. We are a real live City with utilities, training requirements, and rules, among other things."

"I suggest you document them and give it to Robyn," said Martin between bites.

"Of course, we have documentation. And if Robyn wants to set aside the next two years, she could get through all of it. The point of this discussion is to identify where to focus your team's time during the conference. As an example, we have thousands of contracts with vendors both on and off Sky City. Most have clauses that allow them to terminate the contract under a change of control. I suggest we avoid that problem with proper wording that the DOS is providing oversight and not an actual change of control."

"Except it is a change of control," said Robyn. "We're not concerned about your vendors. My team will review the contracts and send out modifications assigning the contract to the DOS."

"What if they refuse?" said Ben.

"Why would they? Most companies spend millions to get a contract with the DOS. I'll sweeten the deal by approving them as a credentialed DOS vendor. Who's going to give up that?"

"We have already thought through all of this Ben," said Martin as he continued to eat his food and talk. "This isn't a merger with another company. Tell them they'll be working for the DOS. It's called a memo. And speaking of memos, I had asked for one before we got here. Why haven't you provided it to me yet?"

Ben wondered how long it had been since Martin had last read something longer than a memo or been punched in the face. He pointed his finger at Martin, opened his mouth, and Daniel stood. The meeting could not derail into a yelling match.

"Dr. Myers," said Daniel, "there are unique features about Sky City and Skyboat Industries. For one, the city is airborne. Second, it's a combination of privately owned vessels and company owned ships. Perhaps Robyn's plan with the vendor contracts would work. But the private Skyboat owners don't care about a contract with the Department of Space. Are you going to force them to stay a part of Sky City? No, but you need them, they pay the bills. And what of the hundreds of employees? How have you considered their reaction to becoming a government employee?"

"Well, they'll get more vacation time," said Don.

"I'm talking about morale as much as logistics. This may not be a merger, but the lessons are the same. Most mergers fail. To begin with, there's no such thing as a merger. One company buys another and pretends they're equals. Everyone knows that's not true, but they all repeat the corporate talking points because during a merger, budgets get cut and people get fired. It's hugely disruptive and people get scared. We are trying to avoid that situation. Service, supplies, and security. They all need consistency. This is a very autonomous place. It's one of the principles Ben started with. If we aren't careful, that will be in jeopardy. Robyn, do you agree?"

"Of course," said Robyn, frustrated at Daniel's mansplaining speech, even if it was right. "This process should be handled delicately."

"As if Space could organize its way out of a paper bag," said Ben. "I mean when's the last time someone said, *I've got a logistics problem and need to call in the Department of Space*? Do we want to talk about the failed lunar orbiting gateway? How many billions were wasted?"

"That's out of line! Even if I don't understand your paper bag reference," said Martin, wiping his mouth and throwing down his napkin.

"Oh, well do you understand budgeting, forecasting, or supply chains?" said Ben, throwing down his napkin. "But to be fair, you are world class at wasting money, wasting time, and killing dreams. Congratulations."

Ben put his hands on the edge of the table and very nearly tossed it over except for the fact Paige pulled him back into his seat and grabbed his thigh until Ben's eyes watered. Daniel shook his head. Ben was not helping his case, again. Martin smiled. He crossed his fingers, hoping the next outburst would include physical harm, maybe to him, if he was extra lucky.

"You know," said Daniel, "we're getting off topic. Let's get back to timing. Robyn, what is your opinion on how long the team needs to update these contracts?"

"Realistically, three months."

"Three months?" said Martin. "First, we agreed to six weeks. Second, Ben might leave the planet in that time."

"Okay, that makes no sense," said Ben. "Leave Sky City? And go where?"

"I don't know, the moon, Mars, an asteroid? Anything to avoid having to face what you did. I'm not even talking about the illegal rocket launch. Robyn, four weeks. You have four weeks, or you're fired. That's what I'm announcing at the conference. Does everyone understand this or am I going to have to repeat myself?"

Daniel and Paige looked at Ben. He smiled but it had no joy in it. An uncomfortable silence fell over the table.

"Challenge accepted," Robyn said, diffusing the tension. "Ben, can we meet in an hour to go over this?"

"You and Daniel should connect," said Ben standing up and no longer smiling. "He knows the contracts. I will see the rest of you tonight."

Paige stood, and the two of them left the room before anyone else had stood.

"Okay," said Daniel lightly slapping his hands on the table. "Roger?"

"Let me have the porter show you to your rooms," said Roger.

CHAPTER TWENTY-FIVE

GALILEONIA

Angie, Ryan, Alana, and Jesse had their spacesuits on, trunks loaded, and transport warmed up as they stood at the edge of the boneyard. Steele, Max, and Bridget joined them for their departure. It was not often they got to send off a group into the wild of the moonscape, especially because it was not a wise thing to do. As the team packed the transport, Ryan declared the engine to be version 2.0 and ready for flight. Alana pulled Max over and interrogated him. Max answered her questions, looked to Ryan for help, she told him not to look around, and after much back and forth, Alana left him and climbed onto the transport, minimally satisfied with the state of the rocket engines.

The fastest way to get to the Eastern Sea would have been to take a rocket transport to New Shanghai and drive from there. But they had too much gear and too high a profile to get on any transport requiring identification. Instead, they would take the road to New Shanghai for about a thousand miles until they reached the Eratosthenes Crater, just north of Copernicus Crater. Then they would head west taking a path forged by the telescopers. It was likely to have highwaymen on it, but the other option of traveling over the raw lunar surface would extend the trip by a week or more, which they couldn't afford.

"Okay, let's roll," said Angie.

The transport was an open carrier with two seats in the front and a flat platform behind it. They had strapped all the equipment onto the platform. Angie took the wheel, Ryan sat shotgun with Jesse and Alana in back between the equipment.

"Keep your eyes open at all times," said Bridget.

"Good luck!" said Max.

"You'll need it," said Steele.

Angie, Ryan, Alana, and Jesse headed out. They drove away from Galileonia straight toward the Armstrong and Aldrin National Park where Apollo 11 landed. Angie paid the entrance toll at the automated booth while Ryan downloaded the overview brochure and park map onto his tablet.

"You guys want me to point out the sights?" said Ryan.

"Sounds great," said Jesse. "What are they?"

"Way over there, where you can't see, is the Apollo landing site. And, we're done. Did you enjoy your visit?" said Ryan. "Only fifteen more miles of untouched regolith awaits us"

"Why is there a park here?" said Jesse.

"Stopped the mining near town. The original colonists didn't want anyone mining to close to their home. The park pushed them out," said Angie. "Read that in *Moon Miners – The Last Frontier.*"

"Interesting," said Alana. "That you read that book."

The only sounds came from their wheels on the road as they drove through the park and got onto the main road.

"So, what would we be looking for that might be a threat?" said Ryan.

"Here, on the moon, I'd say any movement or light," said Jesse. "If it moves it's a threat."

"Got it," said Ryan clutching his rifle.

Two transports passed them on the main road the first day. Both cargo carriers moving goods between the colonies. As the transports passed them, the dust the tires spit up obscured their view for minutes afterward. It took forever to settle with the low gravity.

"Okay everyone," said Jesse. "Be on the lookout for a truck spitting up dust followed by an attack. Any dust in your face, get your heat sensor visors up."

They finished driving the first day without seeing another vehicle. It was agreed they would drive fourteen hours a day to keep the trip under ten days and arrive before the fourteen day night. Days were an arbitrary construct on the moon with its twenty-nine-and-a-half-day rotation period. But talking in two-week periods was useless, so they continued to refer to Earth days with the moon day and night overlayed on top. The trip called for an Earth day-and-a-half on the main road with eight Earth days on the trail. Fourteen hours on a bumpy transport with almost the same view all the time. Ryan found it difficult to stay on low alert; he drifted off more than once the first day, and then was out early after they got started on the second day.

"Lights approaching," said Angie.

Ryan woke up and saw the oncoming lights. Jesse turned and stood from the back to look around the transport, watching the approaching vehicle. The truck approaching them was smaller than the two previous ones, it was not a cargo truck. Angie had driven them through the Sea of Vapours (Mare Vaporum) and entered a section of road carved through hills of moon rock. No way to go off road until they made it to the Sea of Showers, which was miles ahead.

"Get ready, this looks wrong," said Jesse. "Ryan and Alana turn the heat seekers on your guns. Angie, stay on the road. Don't let this truck push you off."

When the truck approached them, it turned on high beam lights to blind Angie. She looked to the side of the road to avoid the headlights. The truck made a slight move toward the transport as it approached and bumped them as it went by. Angie held the wheel tight to keep the transport on the road. As soon as the truck passed them, it stopped.

"Here we go," shouted Jesse.

He and Alana stood and aimed their guns at the stopped truck, waiting for any bodies to appear, but it just sat there. The dust from the truck passing them rolled over the transport.

"Someone's coming," said Ryan. "I see bodies walking toward us."

"Guarantee there armed," said Jesse. "Alana, you got this truck?"

"I got it," she said with her gun aimed at it.

Jesse jumped down and ran to the front of the transport as the figures closed in through the dust.

"Stop right there," he shouted through his amplified speaker. "Don't come any closer."

The spacesuits kept walking toward them.

"Okay, everyone," said Jesse, "these people mean us harm. Take them out or they take us out. Alana, that includes the truck."

"Got it," said Alana.

*

Andre sat in the driver's seat of the truck. His four teammates in the truck climbed out. He looked in the rearview mirror, wondering how quick this job would be. Four miners on a transport, very stupid. He had received the call from a cargo driver that some small mining team was driving solo across Colony Road. His team assembled and left New Shanghai at a normal pace, like they were delivering goods to Galileonia, until they were outside the colony lights.

Then, to make sure they intercepted the team in the middle of nowhere, Andre used the jet propulsion installed in the bed of the truck and reached them right where they wanted. His team was based out of New Shanghai because Steele would have had them followed if they left from his town. Not that New Shanghai did not believe in law and order. In fact, inside the town, it was quite a bit stricter than Galileonia. They just stopped caring once you left. And these sort of opportunities were not common anymore. Most small operations had stopped coming to the moon years ago. Andre wondered how much this operation would turn out to be worth. Ransoms were the norm. Most of the equipment could barely be resold. Bored children of the ultra-wealthy coming to the moon for adventure was the best. Like the Moscow kidnappings when he was young. Easy money. Well, easier than this.

*

Jesse ran around the side of the transport to the front and began shooting. At first, he could not see the spacesuits, but his sensors picked them up, and then he saw the six approaching him illuminated as red figures on his face plate. Ryan shot wildly and, to no one's surprise, hit nothing. It did have the positive effect of sending three spacesuits to the ground, leaving Jesse with three approaching the transport. He took a knee, let out his breath and focused on the closest one, who was firing at the transport. Jesse fired off a series of shots and the spacesuit fell. He then looked for the next closest and repeated, taking one more out. The other one dropped to the ground for cover as the transport got close.

Alana saw four spacesuits exit the truck from the back.

"Nuts," she said under her breath while firing a sweep of bullets at the four spacesuits and the truck's tires. Hitting two, she saw the other two run to opposite sides of the road. Then suddenly the truck fired up a jet engine underneath the bed.

"What is this?" said Alana.

*

Andre hit the red switch as soon as he heard the gunfire. He would circle back once everything died down, literally. From his rearview mirror he saw the person in the back of the transport throw her gun down, and he smiled. She was looking for something and pulled up what appeared to be a bazooka. Andre pushed the power to full on the jet. She fired straight at him. He looked at his speed, looked in the mirror and banged on the steering wheel with his fists expecting it to speed up the jet engine. He then sat mesmerized looking in the mirror as the brightly lit missile appeared to approach in slow motion, remembering he should turn off the road, but then he was hit.

*

The truck blew up and a smile came across Alana's face until the two remaining spacesuits jumped up from the side of the road and began running after the transport. They were falling behind and stopped to press their boots. They then began jumping in the air toward the transport, closing in.

"The two behind us dropped their foot weights," said Alana.

"Good idea," said Jesse, doing the same. He then jumped toward the third spacesuit on the left side and shot him from ten feet in the air in the middle of a dust cloud. After seeing him go down, his sensors went off.

"I'm hit," he said. "Keep driving, don't stop."

Jesse's suit identified the holes caused by the bullet and immediately filled the space between the outer and inner suits with expandable foam. Jesse's arm was grazed, but he shook it and decided he was good to go. Steele had told him the only way to put someone down for good was to fire all over their face shield. Also, if you shot into someone's space suit multiple times, it would go into emergency mode and limit their movement, effectively incapacitating them. Either way got them out of the fight.

The transport drove past the three moving spacesuits that Ryan kept firing at and missing. They stood as the transport passed them and jumped on board. Ryan jumped back onto the platform and knocked one off with the butt of his gun. The second grabbed Ryan's gun out of his hands and the third pointed his gun at Ryan.

"Hold onto something," Angie said through the earpiece.

Ryan looked down and grabbed a strap. Angie swung the transport to the right, and then the left. The spacesuit pointing the gun at Ryan fell off the transport, firing into the air. The one with Ryan's gun charged him. Ryan ducked and began moving around the spaceship parts attached to the platform, keeping out of the line of fire.

*

The two spacesuits leaping toward the transport were getting close. Alana put down the bazooka and picked up the gun. They were almost simultaneous with their leaping, so she focused on the one on the right and shot. The spacesuit fell to the ground and rolled, not getting up. The other landed next to her and tried to grab her gun. She stood, yanked her gun back and hit the spacesuit's helmet, one, two, three times with the butt of her gun until it cracked. Then she pushed the spacesuit off the transport while the cracked helmet filled with opaque sealant.

Jesse looked around through the dust for the last person on the ground. He heard a noise behind and turned to see a spacesuit rushing him, gun firing. Jesse dropped and the spacesuit stopped, also dropping. Jesse reached back for a grenade, pulled the pin, counted to two and lobbed it toward the spacesuit. It blew up and Jesse went face down to protect his face shield from the debris. Once the rocks stopped falling, he got up and walked over, seeing a figure laying in the dirt, spacesuit torn open. Then Jesse launched himself toward the transport, leaping twenty feet in the air with each step.

Ryan was in the middle of the platform, crawling around the cargo hold. Each time he looked up, shots were fired at him, and he ducked back down. The direction of the shots was across from him on the other side of the cargo hold. He decided to unhook the cargo hold off the platform. Leaning down, he released the first belt. Ryan jumped around to the other side of the platform, reaching the second belt. He could hear the spacesuit moving toward him, almost at the side of the cargo hold. He released the second belt and the cargo hold slid off the side of the transport dragging the scrambling spacesuit with it. It landed on top of the spacesuit's legs and rolled off. The spacesuit rolled over but was unable to get up.

"What was that?" said Alana holding a handgun and standing on the other side of the cargo hold just beyond where it rolled off the platform. "You almost rolled that onto me. Besides, I had him."

"How was I supposed to know that?" said Ryan. "Angie, we need to go back and get our cargo hold."

CHAPTER TWENTY-SIX

SKY CITY

OCTOBER 21, 2071

B en felt violated. He, Paige, and Daniel stood on the upper balcony over the atrium watching the guests pick up their meeting packets and look for their conference rooms. Sky City was overrun with bureaucrats, opportunists, and looky-loos. The DOS team, the NSA team, both team's contractors, and everyone's spouses and partners had all shown up for the Sky City Transfer Conference. After a wild first day with the visitors flying around each level, stopping anyone at any time to ask them their business, Ben sequestered them on *Horizon* unless escorted. That left hundreds of conference attendees and their guests roaming the decks and halls of *Horizon* making requests most people would consider embarrassing.

"Did you label Martin's opening meeting as I requested?" said Ben.

"No, I did not title it *The Big Cluster* if that's what you're asking," said Daniel.

"Shame," said Ben. "How did we get into this mess?"

"It's less than optimal," said Daniel.

"Right, less than optimal. How do we get rid of these people as soon as possible?"

Ben got a tap on his shoulder.

"Ben Dawson, how long has it been?" said Bobby Walker.

"You're here too?" Ben said. "Daniel, we're going to have a talk later."

"Of course, I was invited," said Bobby. "Don't blame Daniel. I secured the contract to ferry supplies to Sky City post take-over; I mean transfer. Both here on Earth and from the space stations."

"Bobby Walker," said Paige. "How long has it been since you sued Ben?"

"Paige, hello," said Bobby. "You look terrific, as ever."

"You look tired, Bobby. Do you need to lie down?" said Paige.

"Never felt better, excited to be here. What an amazing accomplishment. You don't have any of my IP hiding in here do you Ben? I'm sure my team will find out during the diligence process," Bobby winked as he nudged Ben with his elbow.

A short, squat bald man walked up to Bobby, pushing his glasses back onto his nose bridge.

"Boss, everything checks out, like you said. Plenty of spots for transit. Probably will need to use the current transport vehicles, at least for now. Also, I took all those pictures you asked for."

"Everyone, this is Caleb Browne, my Chief Operating Officer. Best in the business."

Caleb looked at Ben.

"You know, it's a serious safety hazard to have the large cargo transports come in at the top levels," said Caleb. "They should only come in at the lowest level and have their cargo off loaded there."

"We're saving trips by having them come in at various levels," said Ben. "Why did you take pictures?"

"If one were to fail, many people could be injured or even killed," said Caleb.

"Our boats don't fail," said Ben. "And there's no reason for you to perform any diligence if you're just a supplier."

"Caleb isn't known for his tact," said Bobby.

"Ha, ha, sure, Bobby," said Paige. "Ben, relax. Everyone's entitled to their opinion, and who cares about photos?"

"Also, I don't like the colors," said Caleb.

"What?" said Paige as she put her face into Caleb's. "You don't have any idea what you're talking about. These color patterns have received design awards world-wide. Inspirational is the most common phrase used. And that outfit you're wearing, by the way, is a thrifting disaster."

"Hey, everyone. The meeting is going to start soon," said Daniel, moving between Paige and Caleb. "Let's head down to the theater. See you two later."

Daniel moved Ben and Paige away from Bobby and Caleb and toward the auditorium as everyone else entered. The attendees looked for their names on the placards. Robyn made sure they followed DOS protocol with highest-ranking government officials closest to the stage, their staff immediately behind them, followed by lower ranking officials and finally the contractors in the back, who never cared about where they sat. Instead, they lived by the philosophy of 'you take the credit, I'll take the cash'.

Roger Sinclair walked on stage across from Ben, Paige, and Daniel, who were on the other side of the stage.

"Why is Roger kicking this off?" said Ben to Daniel.

"He asked, and it seemed appropriate him being captain," said Daniel.

"Not to me, but it's too late now."

Roger clicked into the speaker system.

"Ladies and gentlemen, thank you for coming. As we are all aware, the agenda is quite full."

Roger went through the initial speaker list, the breakout teams, the breakout sessions, re-grouping, dinner, evening tours, morning tours, breakfast on the veranda, morning sessions, lunch with a show, main theater session summarizing prior sessions, afternoon on your own, dinner, break (also known as when the actual work of the conference got done), then breakfast with summary of accomplishments and action items for the staff.

"I think I'm going to barf," said Ben.

"I agree," said Paige.

"Trust me," said Daniel. "This conference will create a mountain of paperwork these teams will get bogged down in and suddenly the timeline will grind to a halt."

Martin walked up to the podium as Roger finished.

"Thank you, Captain Sinclair. We appreciate your openness to this difficult process. I only wish everyone at Sky City was as helpful in moving things along. That being said, let me make it perfectly clear that Secretary Kerry has tasked us all with a four-week timeframe. Four weeks to take over. This means transition complete. So, tear up whatever nonsense you were thinking of and come out of this conference with a four-week plan. There's an old saying you can choose time, resources, or quality, but not all three. Well, I'm here to tell you that old saying is garbage. I choose all three because I believe in the power of 'and'. You can give me time, resources, AND quality. Right? Of course that's right.

Be positive people. Also, I have agreed to become a board member of Skyboat Industries, so resources are not going to be a factor. Sky City will pay for everything you need. It has plenty of resources to offer us that did not get affected by the quake that the rest of us felt so dearly, starting with Captain Sinclair."

Martin put a hand on Roger's shoulder, which was almost above Martin's head. Roger stiffened, the loss of his family in Eureka was still raw and the awkwardness of Martin's hand did not help.

"I challenge each of you, make this happen for Roger and the others who suffered immeasurable loss. They deserve our best, the country's best. Sky City can be part of the country's best with the work of everyone in this room. Now before you get started, let me remind you, anyone in this room that doesn't personally give me a heads up on a delay will be fired immediately, along with their team. Also, if you discuss any of this with anyone, you will be fired immediately and charged with treason."

"You can't fire me," said Bobby Walker to nervous laughter.

"I can fire your contract and charge you with many, many indictments, some actually real," said Martin, not looking up from his notes. "Got it? Thank you everyone."

Everyone stood and applauded. Daniel started applauding, looked at Ben, who folded his arms. Paige nudged him as she applauded, and Ben started a slow clap that he sped up while his anger increased. Robyn and Martin walked over to Ben, Paige, and Daniel as everyone else hurried out before being charged with treason.

"Have a seat," said Martin. "Robyn, do you have those papers?"

The group moved to a table and sat as Robyn pushed a stack of documents in front of each of them with 'sign here' tabs along the sides, and then dropped several black ballpoint pens on the table.

"I'm going to need you to sign these NDAs," said Martin.

"How about I agree to not talk?" said Ben.

"No, you need to sign whatever I put in front of you."

"Why is that?"

Martin leaned into Ben, who noticed his halitosis and leaned back.

"Think of your family," said Martin, turning to Paige. "Paige, you as well. This is about your children's future. You want them to have a clean slate, every parent does. Robyn, tell them about the press releases."

"With your cooperation," said Robyn, "the DOS will publicly state that Sky City officially had nothing to do with the quake."

"Which it didn't," said Ben.

"Yes, but the public thinks it did," said Martin.

"Only because you told them that," said Ben getting agitated.

"We had good reason, at the time. Anyway, that's water under the bridge," said Martin. "I'm trying to help you and your family today. Not to mention all the employees at Sky City, like your friend Mr. Nguyen here. I'm sure his children don't care, but he probably wants to retain his squeaky clean reputation."

"Leave me out of your discussion," said Daniel.

"Tch, tch," said Martin. "Atypical for you to lose that icy veneer Daniel. Hit a sore spot?"

No one spoke.

"Either way, Benjamin," said Martin, "we have the leverage, like always, and this is my personal gift to you for your cooperation in the hand-off of Sky City. It could just as easily go the other way. What sort of future lies ahead for Jason and Angie if their dad is in jail? Who would hire them or want anything to do with them? Could they even get married and keep the family line going? Paige, talk to him. I know you would do what's right for your kids and any future grandkids, right?"

"I would do anything for my children, Marty. Anything," said Paige.

"It's undersecretary or Dr. Myers or both," said Martin.

"Is it?" said Paige. "Where do we sign?"

As they were signing the documents Don LaRue walked back into the auditorium. His excitement made him unaware of the tension in the room. He had a sheaf of papers in his hands that he motioned to Daniel with a smile.

"What's that?" said Martin.

"My preliminary report," said Don.

"For what?"

"A review on physical security. There're several areas to improve the efficiency of the systems already in use."

"I didn't ask for that."

"I did," said Daniel.

Martin looked at Don.

"If I don't ask for it, you don't do it, understand?"

"But what's the difference?" said Don. "This is an improvement and we're taking over anyway."

"I'm ordering you, don't do anything except what I tell you to do. And then, do that immediately. Understand?"

Don nodded. He left gripping the papers.

"Robyn, handle this," said Martin as he stood. "I've got to see Captain Sinclair."

CHAPTER TWENTY-SEVEN

COLONY ROAD BETWEEN GALILEONIA AND NEW SHANGHAI

The team got the cargo hold back on the transport and checked for cracks. There were some dents, but the integrity of the cargo hold remained intact. They headed out as quick as the transport would take them. After three more hours of driving, they pulled off the road into a crater and switched off the lights. Twenty minutes later the dust settled, and it would be difficult for anyone to know they were there.

"We're going to need to assume that when that team doesn't show back up, someone's coming to check on them," said Jesse. "And whoever follows that team will be at least twice as strong and much more cautious."

"Let's get off this road then," said Ryan.

"I agree," said Alana. "Can't stay on the main road anymore. Where's that trail?"

Angie pulled up the map, and it showed them as a red dot, about one hundred and fifty miles from the trail head.

"We can get there in three hours. Can we risk it?"

"Have to," said Jesse. "But I want to make some adjustments to prepare for our next altercation."

Jesse had them reconfigure the transport placing the spaceship cockpit behind but above the front seats. Ryan adjusted the connections to allow the spaceship cockpit to control the driving, holding two of them while the other two would stay in the cargo hold. Also, Ryan copied the idea of the truck that attacked them and hooked the jets up to the driving controls in the cockpit.

"If we use the rockets, will it hold?" said Jesse.

"Not for long," said Ryan.

They loaded up with Angie and Ryan in the cockpit. Alana and Jesse sat in the cargo hold where Ryan had cut out windows on each side. He said they could solder them back on later, probably. Once Angie got the hand of driving from the cockpit, they made it to the telescoper trailhead in a little over three hours. Turning onto the trail, not even as wide as their transport in spots, slowed them down. They had been traveling fifty miles an hour on average and slowed down to about twenty.

The trail was used in the 2050s by astronomers to place radio telescopes on the far side of the moon, free of the Earth's radio noise. Without an atmosphere, the moon allowed them to place telescopes that covered the frequency spectrum. The excitement for what could be found with telescopes on the moon created a frenzy across the astronomy community. They brought out their infrared, ultraviolet, x-ray, gamma ray and cosmic-ray telescopes. Then they mounted them, tested them, left them, and waited for the results to come in. Of course, some of them failed, but not all. New discoveries were being made each month. Papers written. Doctorates earned. A new age of discovery dawned. And then they all went offline. No one could find out the cause for the power failures.

A team was sent out, never returned. Another team sent out,

flying over the telescopes in a low orbit rocket, never returned. A small military band took one more group out. Before their communications were cut off the home base heard about a group of bikers approaching. Nothing else. The telescopes were abandoned. A full scale military force would be able to put down whatever group was out there, but a full-scale military force was two-hundred forty thousand miles and several billion dollars away. Space Force focused on protecting the space station and had virtually no presence on the moon or Mars. And the small presence they did have on the moon focused on the colonies, where mining took priority. Astronomy was a nice-to-have, and for now, no one was having it, at least not on the far side.

They drove on the trail for days covering more than two thousand miles. Slow but steady progress as they traveled west through the Sea of Islands (Mare Insularum). Once they left the Sea of Islands, the path consisted of going in and out of shallow craters or around deep ones until they hit the Eastern Sea (Mare Orientale) and the path flattened for a bit. They had sunlight for another five days and needed to be in position to camp before it turned to night. Traveling during the two week lunar night would require them to use their lights, and in the pitch black of the lunar night, those lights would be seen for hundreds of miles, begging for danger. At least in a campsite they would be able to set up their defense systems. Fortunately, once they approached the western edge of the Eastern Sea, they were on the final hundred miles to go on their three-thousand-mile trip.

"Angie, you missed a bump back there, you want to circle back and hit it just to be one hundred percent?" said Jesse.

"You sure you were a Marine with that complaining?" said Alana. "All that diversity training made you soft."

"Something like that," said Jesse. "Hey, how about using those engines Ryan attached for the final leg?"

"Ya, could use some of these ridges as ramps and pop the engines," said Alana.

"Interesting," said Ryan. "Could be a test run as well."

He pulled out his binoculars and looked ahead, then to the sides.

"Alana, can you look at the crater beyond the ridge in front of us?"

She pulled out her binoculars and leaned out the cargo hold.

"The one with the broken crust on the right?"

"Yes, what do you think about trying to launch off an edge like that?"

"Launching is easy, we need to be able to land."

"What do we need to land? Flat area?"

"Downward slope, like a ski jumper would be easiest. Flat might not keep this thing together if it isn't soft. Can't land on a boulder or small rocks. Would break us in two."

"How do we know where we'll land?" said Angie.

"I have to calc it," said Ryan.

He sat to think. The angle of departure, the speed of departure, the gravity, the jet engine propulsion, strength of velocity and length of flight from using the propellant. And the angle coming down for impact. Too many variables, and he would be making assumptions on all of them. Might as well wing it. Wait, he still had that space flight simulator on his tablet. Great game, really hard, particularly the Jupiter gravity assist to the Oort Cloud. He pulled it up and looked at the settings.

"What are you doing?" said Angie. "Is that a game?"

"No, but yes," said Ryan. "I am playing a game."

"Me, too," said Jesse. "Helps me focus."

Jesse smiled and showed Alana his high score on Mega Maze Breakout.

"We might be coming up on someone," Angie said. "I saw something flash out there on the left. Ryan, if this is going to work, now would be a great time."

"We are crossing over to the far side," said Jesse. "Terrain is much rougher."

Ryan entered their coordinates and started the spaceship simulator by launching a low orbit ship on the moon from near zero velocity. He kept crashing until firing the fuel for less than three seconds. Then it flew for only nine miles, but the ship did not explode when landing on his screen like in the other simulations. Angie saw another flash on her left, but closer. Like something going over a crater.

"Everyone get ready, I expect we'll have visitors soon," said Angie.

Jesse put away his tablet and pulled out his gun, as did Alana. Ryan looked up.

"Okay, let's do this," said Ryan. "We're going to use the jet fuel for three seconds, no more."

"You sure?" said Alana.

"I'm sure we're going to do this," said Ryan. "Angie, head over to that ridge on the right. I'll get the engines ready to fire."

Ryan paged through the menus on the control panel screen. He came to his jet engine page, which now seemed way too complicated considering the amount of time he had to launch the engines. Angie saw several flashes now, almost in a line, continuing to get closer to them.

"Ryan, time to go," said Angie.

"Almost there, can you speed up?"

"Doing it," said Angie pushing the throttle forward.

The transport began bumping along forcing Jesse and Alana to use one hand to hold on.

"Going to be hard to defend us like this," said Jesse.

"Hopefully, we won't have to," said Ryan.

The flashes had turned into shapes. Angie could see bikers coming toward them. Looked like a dozen.

"Incoming," said Angie. "Less than a minute."

"Punch it," said Ryan. "I'm going to fire the engines as soon as this thing has a clear path upward."

Jesse leaned outside the cargo hold but could not see ahead of the crater rim they raced toward.

"We're blind back here," said Jesse.

"Hold on with both hands," said Ryan.

Jesse and Alana slung the guns over their shoulders and grabbed bars in the cargo hold. Ryan strapped himself into the passenger chair then hit the button on the control panel that started the jet engines. The transport was three quarters of the way up the crater edge, aimed at the sky when the left lower jet engine ignited. The other three did nothing. The transport lurched right. Angie turned the steering wheel hard left and the transport skidded sideways toward the top of the crater rim.

"Ryan!" Angie said as she gripped the steering wheel trying to keep the transport from turning in circles.

"Working on it," said Ryan. He overrode his own protections to ignite the engines. Two seconds later the other three engines ignited, and the transport began fishtailing up to the crater rim, and Angie overcompensated with the steering wheel. She had it semi-straight when the transport cleared the rim. The transport lifted at a sixty-degree angle over the crater. Ryan cut the engines. It continued to lift for several seconds and leveled out. They looked below them as the transport, nearly three hundred feet in the air, passed over a line of lunar motorcycles, which had entered the crater floor, stopped to stare at them, turned toward where they were going to land, and raced after them. The transport angle began dropping.

"Where we going to land?" said Alana.

"Inside the crater," said Ryan. "It's a flat surface approximately nine, no eight miles away."

"We'll be sitting ducks," said Jesse from the back. "We can't land in the crater, get us past it!"

"Can we go further?" Angie said. "Outside the crater?"

"That's too rocky," said Ryan. "We'd have to get outside the Eastern Sea rim, another twenty miles."

"Do it!" said Jesse as he saw the motorcycles pacing them on the ground.

"These engines are not built for bursting!" said Ryan.

"Ryan!" said Angie. "We're going to tilt down!"

"Fine," said Ryan.

He pressed a button on his tablet's screen and fired the engines for nine seconds. One of the engines kept firing for a half second after the others shut off, turning the ship south. Angie looked down for the end of the rim.

"There," she said pointing. "I'll aim for the outside of the rim."

Angie then realized there was no aiming the transport.

"Alana and Jesse, can you pull out something to use as wings and guide us down?"

"There's no atmosphere, you can't use wings," said Alana.

"Right," said Angie, dejected.

Jesse grabbed his gun and pointed it to the side of the transport.

"How about this?"

"Ya, that might work."

Alana picked up her gun and motioned Jesse to the other side of the cargo hold.

"We're going to shoot our guns."

"Uh, okay," said Angie.

Alana shot her gun straight out the side of the cargo hold, and the transport overcorrected to the right.

"Jesse," said Alana.

"Got it," said Jesse as he shot an entire clip from his gun, overcorrecting the transport to the left.

"Guys," said Angie, "we need to be straight for landing."

"Ya, we know."

Alana shot a few bullets and almost got the transport straight.

"Jesse, less is more."

"Okay."

Jesse fired off a few shots and the transport still went too far.

"We're landing," said Angie.

Alana shot a dozen more bullets, and the transport went just a bit right. Jesse started firing, the transport began turning left, then Alana started firing as the transport headed toward the ground. They both held down their triggers and the bullets flew out of both sides of the transport as they pushed their backs up against each other. A thousand casings clanged as they bounced off the steel floor of the cargo hold while Ryan screamed with a falsetto pitch and Angie held onto the controls for dear life. The force of both guns evened out, and the transport straightened and touched down heading forward on the outside of the rim wall. Angie began steering to avoid ridges at the end of the rim wall, but there were too many for a smooth landing, and they bounced up and down.

"Stop shooting!" said Angie.

Alana and Jesse put down their guns and held onto the cargo hold with both hands as Angie brought the transport to a stop.

"Over there," said Ryan, pointing to the open plain, heading west.

Angie accelerated the transport west toward the opening when a motorcycle came through the open plain and rode straight at them. Then there were motorcycles coming over all sides of the rim.

"We're surrounded. Stop the transport," said Jesse.

CHAPTER TWENTY-EIGHT

DEPARTMENT OF SPACE

OCTOBER 25, 2070

"Unbelievable," said Martin.

"Sir?" said Dale, standing in front of Martin's desk.

"Wasn't talking to you."

Martin started walking around his office. Dale tried to stand at attention and turn to face him as he walked, which did not work and made him feel more awkward than usual in the undersecretary's office. He moved to an 'at ease' position, perfected in a past life in the Army. Dale had a short but remarkable military career. He attacked each challenge with the same energy; one of us was going down, and it was not Dale. This worked well until he was promoted to lead a team and proceeded to abuse every one of his team members.

No one was good enough at their job for Dale. Although many of his team excelled at their jobs, Dale felt praise would weaken them, so he criticized everyone at every opportunity, to keep them strong. His supervisors then 'transitioned him out' to the exciting world of bodyguards, even getting him a job at the hottest agency in the federal government, the Department of Space. Dale snapped up the role and pursued it with the same vigor as in the Army, even after being counseled that the private world, including government roles, did not require the same level of intensity as the Army. And by intensity, they meant harassment, bordering on assault.

Fortunately, the significant down-time of being a bodyguard lowered Dale's testosterone levels just below manic and kept him from abusing most civilians. The occasional aggressive tackles and drawn weapons did give him a chance to relive active-duty moments. He was on his final probation before being fired when Martin saw him tackle a reporter for asking a congressperson a question as a congressional staffer closed the doors of an elevator. Martin thought it was masterful.

For Martin, Dales was the perfect asset. He needed someone that would follow orders with zeal and no critical thinking. Martin saw Dale as that type of person, especially if the goal involved a little physical activity. Dale had dutifully followed Martin for the past three years, thinking his boss would eventually be the secretary of Space and have him flying across Earth and space in a dark suit and sunglasses. Dale would be seen as one of the toughest security guards, no, bodyguards, no federal agents, anywhere. He could not wait to get in the gym after this meeting to work out the adrenaline.

"What a mess," said Martin. "They get to the Gateway. Then Niko allows them passage to the moon. Just like that. Niko thinks he's smarter than any of us, but I know what he's doing."

"What's that?"

Martin looked at Dale, then kept walking and talking to himself.

"He's flexing before the summit. Unfortunately, that puts Ben's team on the moon, where I did not want them. And that Steele won't listen to anything, especially reason."

"How about the cartel members?" said Dale.

Martin stopped. Dale provided a useful comment. He noted the date and time in his head.

"In the past they never wanted to work with me on anything. But maybe, I can convince them it's in our mutual interest. Something that threatens them as much as me."

Martin did another slow loop around Dale, while Dale decided to go with quarter turns to keep up. Martin stopped walking and turned to face Dale.

"You're going to the moon."

"I am? I mean, yes, I am." Dale stood back at attention. The moon! He heard bullets flew for miles up there. One of his Army buddies said you could even shoot a bullet at the Earth, and it would get all the way to the atmosphere before burning up. So cool.

"This will officially be a reconnaissance mission. You'll be identifying what mining Sky City is performing in order to know how it will affect the contract between them and the DOS. This means taking notes, photos, and there will be paperwork upon your return."

Dale shuddered.

"Unofficially, you need to stop them from whatever they're doing, which is almost guaranteed to not be lunar mining. Understand?"

Dale almost smiled.

"Oh, yes."

"You will approach the cartel members for a teaming arrangement. I will put out feelers to find who is most receptive. But don't wait for me. Pursue your own path to stopping Ben's team, and if they do not want to work with us, find your own team, understand?"

"Absolutely."

Dale looked forward to managing a team again. He had thought once about what went wrong and immediately decided it was a lax attitude on his part. Dale could not wait to try his new, hardened management approach on a team of lunar mercenaries.

"I'll arrange for LEO Transco to take you to HOSS 2. You'll have to land at New Shanghai and take the MoonTrak shuttle to Galileonia. Get your sleep on the flights because there'll be no time once you land."

"I'll be ready to go in fifteen minutes."

Dale saluted, unnecessary and outside of protocol. Martin took it as a sign of enthusiasm for the mission and saluted back.

"Excellent. Go get what you need. I'll send you the details."

CHAPTER TWENTY-NINE

TELESCOPER TRAIL, FAR SIDE OF THE MOON

OCTOBER 27, 2071

The motorcycles were closer to beach bikes than typical motorcycles. The wheels were extra-large to get over the rough terrain. Harley-Davidson looking handlebars connected to the front wheel with a long flat seat that ended next to a trunk above the back wheel. There was a gun mounted between the handlebars of each bike, which some of the riders took off as they dismounted and approached the transport.

Ryan spotted the familiarity of the wheels, like some of the largest dump trucks in the bone yard. The appeared to be thin layers of the original wheels, sewn, or perhaps fused together to make the smaller, balloon looking wheels for these moon bikes. Ryan remembered some of the trucks were missing their tires and wondered how somebody removed them and for what. Made sense now.

Their space suits were tight, as far as space suits go. Close to their bodies. Gray, just like the lunar surface and everything else about them.

If they stopped walking, they almost disappeared. Their helmets were round and tight against their skulls. No way there were multiple layers of protection. If their suits ripped, that had to be fatal. And they must have strong heating systems built into suits, powered with the small pack on their backs. The face shield was a broad semi-circle with a mirror reflection to it. Weapons were attached to the small backpacks, their hips, and then they all had the large detachable gun. The group was made of various-sized people including some women, but with the weaponry each one appeared equally dangerous. They walked at the same pace toward the transport. One walked in front of the rest and stopped about a hundred yards away. Raising his left hand, the other riders stopped.

He spoke over a speaker in Cantonese.

"We're American," said Angie from the driver's seat.

"Ah, American," said the leader, changing to English. "Americans who are fools to be here."

"What do you want?" said Ryan.

"I ask you the same question."

"We're prospectors," said Angie.

"For what?"

"What do you mean?" said Ryan. "We looking to mine."

"I repeat myself, for what? Metals, water, helium-3? All quite different mining techniques."

"Why do you care?" said Alana.

"My name is John Han. I am the leader of the Dark Space Mining Team. We mine the far side and make claim to it."

"The entire half of the moon?" said Ryan.

"Why not? No one else is here."

"We're here," said Ryan. "How do you get to claim half a world?"

"Well, to be more specific, we are the Overseers."

"More like the Tongs," said Jesse as he walked to the front of the transport, hands still in the air.

"Whatever your fancy. You choose. I don't care. Understand we are in charge here."

"Do you allow others to mine?" said Angie. "It's too large for one organization."

John Han took a few steps toward them, slung his gun on his back, pressed the side of his face shield and the mirror screen turned to clear glass. He had a thoughtful face with hard lines in it. Appeared to be in his late thirties. He walked up to the transport.

"Can you all come down please? You in the storage area as well."

Angie and Ryan jumped out of the cab onto the ground. Alana stepped down from the cargo hold.

"You going to kill us like all those astronomers?" said Angie.

"We didn't kill them, they joined us," said John Han.

"Joined?" said Jesse.

"It's open for interpretation," said John. "Please, put your hands down. But they are part of us now."

"Why did you take down the telescopes?" said Ryan.

"We didn't. They still work. They work for us. Remarkably interesting in fact. Regardless of the rumors, we are not barbarians out here. This is not some cannibalistic cult that abhors humanity or other nonsense like that. We are pioneers, wanderers, searchers, and thinkers. This is the true frontier."

"There are some that would argue that," said Angie.

"Who? The cartel members? They are as much a part of the frontier as Wall Street," said John Han. He walked closer to look at each of their faces. "So, why are you here with your fancy space outfits and very odd mining equipment that most certainly will not work? Shouldn't you be sipping drinks on the deck of Sky City?"

"Man, do I hate interplanetary social media," said Ryan.

"We have our reasons," said Angie. "And we are open to working with you, not against you."

"That's good," said John Han. "Smart. I like how you posed it as a choice."

"So, what would working together look like?" said Angie. "The cartel approached us when we arrived but felt more like a takeover. We want control. This is an exploratory mission. If it goes well, we want to expand significantly and quickly."

"One step at a time," said John Han as he started walking around the transport, looking at each item strapped down. "Let's focus on your exploratory mission. Most likely it fails, and we never see you again. That takes care of the first ninety-nine percent probability. Then,"

He stopped at the rocket engines.

"Why do you need rocket engines?"

"Helps us dig," said Alana.

John looked at Alana, smiled and looked back at the rocket engines.

"These obviously work from your recent demonstration. I'll take two of them."

"What, no," said Angie. "We need those."

"For digging?" said John Han. "Then I think two will be just fine for an exploratory mining mission. I could ask you exactly how you'd use them for digging, but the incredulous answer might be too much to take even on the far side of the moon."

He motioned his men over to the rocket engines.

"Two engines and you can continue on. It's a fair deal."

Angie started moving toward John Han when Jesse held her forearm.

"It's fair," said Jesse. "What's included in the deal besides safe passage?"

"That's about it," said John Han. "But that's worth everything, don't you think?"

"Yes," said Jesse. "Yes, it is."

Jesse jumped on the transport and began loosening the straps on two of the engines.

"Alana, can you help me with these?"

Alana climbed onto the platform and began pushing one of the rocket engines off the transport. She did not care if it fell and broke, in fact she preferred it. Some of John Han's team ran over to catch the first engine and lower it to the ground. Then they worked with Jesse and Alana to bring another engine safely off the transport. Alana threw the straps at them. Then John Han's team called for their own transport to move the engines back to wherever they came from. They stared at Jesse and Alana with their mirrored face shields as they waited, and Jesse and Alana stared back. A flat-bed transport showed up much faster than the team expected. It came over the crater, stopped behind them and John Han's team loaded the engines on it. They strapped them down and rode away without looking back. The rest of the team walked back to their lunar motorcycles.

"Good luck with your exploratory mission," said John Han. "I expect it will be very exciting."

"Already has been," said Ryan.

John Han was the last to leave, getting on his motorcycle and climbing an impossibly steep crater wall as he launched his motorcycle and dropped out of sight. The four of them got back into the transport and headed out of the crater. Ryan drove while Jesse sat in the passenger's seat of the cockpit. Angie and Alana got into the cargo hold.

"How are we going to get to the asteroid now?" said Jesse.

"I think we're actually going to have to do some mining," said Angie.

As Ryan traversed the bumpy far side terrain, Angie and Alana were bent over their tablets in the cargo hold calculating how to get the spaceship to El Dorado on two engines.

"I found ilmenite," said Alana.

"Excellent," said Angie. "Close by?"

"It's kind of everywhere, but there's a dense patch close by."

"I was pretty proud of my hydrazine monopropellant catalytic decomposition engines," said Ryan. "Not surprised John Han wanted two of them."

"Show off," said Jesse.

"Yes," said Angie. "An elegant solution. One fuel source makes for a simpler rocket engine. But we had four of them with a specific impulse of two-hundred forty per engine. Now we have half that, so we need to double the thrust. Did that calculation work out Alana?"

"Ya, it's tricky but it can work."

"What? How are you going to solve this?" said Ryan as he hit another bump in the road.

"You're the worst driver of the bunch," said Jesse.

"It's going to be a few steps," said Angie. "Essentially, we need to change to a liquid engine with hydrogen and LOX."

"What's LOX?" said Jesse.

"Liquid oxygen," said Ryan. "How do we go from hydrazine to hydrogen and oxygen?"

"This is where it gets tricky," said Angie. "We're going to burn the hydrazine and break it down to nitrogen and hydrogen. Then we,"

"Hold on," said Jesse. "We're burning all our fuel as step one?"

"You ask a lot of technical questions for a security guy," said Alana.

"It's a good question," said Ryan.

"He's right," said Angie. "We have to do it slowly to avoid an explosion and to capture the exhaust. Then we liquify the hydrogen while we mine for ilmenite."

"What's ilmenite do for us?" said Ryan.

"We'll use the hydrogen to break it down into iron, titanium dioxide and water."

"Uh-huh," said Jesse.

"Then we can electrolyze the water into hydrogen and oxygen, cryogenically store them, and voila, we have our liquid propellants!"

"Wow," said Jesse.

"Oh, and Ryan, you'll need to rebuild the rocket engines to add the oxidizer tank. You have an extra power source in that trunk of yours?"

"I always bring an extra nuclear reactor along; just in case we need to liquify some oxygen," said Ryan.

"Always thinking ahead," said Angie. "Once we're done, then we will have doubled the specific impulse for each engine to four-hundred eighty and we're back on track to get to El Dorado in the same amount of time."

"The way I figure it," said Alana, "there are only three steps in this process where we can blow ourselves up. That's not too bad, eh?"

"Not too bad at all," said Angie as she smiled and put away her tablet.

CHAPTER THIRTY

NEW SHANGHAI LUNAR COLONY, BAY OF RAINBOWS

D ale landed in New Shanghai, passed through customs, and checked his messages. Martin told him to go see a guy at the coffee shop. He would be wearing all black. Dale grabbed his duffel bag, slung it onto his back, and left the shuttle bubble into the main dome and walked to Huaihai Road. Much busier than he expected. People were walking everywhere, and the shops were one after another, looking more like kiosks than shops. A head taller than most of the other pedestrians, Dale spotted the sign with a coffee mug after walking two blocks. He went inside.

"No bags inside," said the barista without even looking up. "Keep it outside."

Dale stepped outside, set his bag to locked and secured it to a pole. It flashed a red bomb signal near the zipper, letting any interested persons be aware that it would explode if tampered with.

All the patrons wore white, gray, or black. Dale looked around and saw one man all in black. He walked to his table and sat across from him. The man was sipping a coffee and reading. He put down his book and looked at Dale.

"Get out of here with that space suit. Now!"

Dale stood.

"Buy some regular clothes. Out!"

Dale walked out, looking around as he left. No one paid attention to the outburst, or at least seemed to, but the man was upset. He pretended to go back to his reading, glancing around the store.

Dale came back thirty minutes later in gray slacks and a gray long-sleeve T-shirt. The man was gone. Another man walked by him.

"Go to the noodle shop," he said without breaking stride.

Dale looked around, the man who walked by him was somewhere in the middle of a group waiting for their drinks, he had no idea who it was, since everyone here wore the same outfits, like a bunch of robots. He left and looked for a noodle shop, which turned out to be directly across the street. He went inside and saw the man in black eating noodles and, again, reading on his tablet. He walked over.

"Seat taken?" said Dale.

"Sit."

Dale sat. He stared at the man as he ate his noodles and read.

"Should I get some noodles?" Dale said.

"No."

He continued to eat and read.

"I need a team," Dale said.

"No kidding," the man said not looking up.

"What can you offer me?"

"Whatever I can provide you with will cost double because of the scene you caused over there."

He pointed at the coffee shop with his chopsticks, which flung drops of soup on the table and floor.

Dale leaned forward, pushing the man's noodles and tablet aside.

"I'm sorry for whatever loss of face you think you suffered through across the street, but let's get down to business or I can make a much bigger scene here."

The man looked at Dale and leaned back. Then he smiled.

"Okay, let's talk. I heard you're looking for somebody."

"A group. Four Americans on a mining mission."

The man sat up straight. Andre was killed by four Americans. Andre wasn't technically his brother, but anyone that you have stolen, kidnapped, and killed with is as close as you are going to get to brotherhood. Unless there was a large bounty on your brother. He wanted to go after the Americans, that is, once a clue to their whereabouts surfaced. And now, he thought this homie could get that clue, he could avenge Andre, and get paid for doing it.

"You know where they are?"

"I do. I've got an intercept on their communications back with Earth."

"So. Where are they?"

"The dark side of the moon."

So much wrong with that statement.

"It's the far side and it's half the size of Asia. By going there, you very well might get us all killed. Do you have anything more specific?"

"Not at the moment."

The man stood.

"Let me know when you get more details on their location. You can find me around here most days."

A few minutes after the man in black departed, Dale left the noodle shop and found a room at the Oasis hotel. His 'room' was a pullout drawer the size of a large coffin with a similar sized space underneath to store his gear. An entire wall at the Oasis had these sort of rooms along with automated ladders that ran across the wall whenever a guest opened their drawer. He thought it would freak him out until he got in. He laid down on the gray yoga type mat and the drawer closed. As the drawer closed, the full body screen above him lit up. With the three-dimensional background it made him feel like he was in a room. He had enough space to lift his hands to touch it. He connected the screen with his table and called Dr. Myers.

"You don't need to check in," said Martin. "In fact, I'd rather you didn't."

"Sorry Dr. Myers, but I need more information. I can't hire a team without knowing their exact location."

"They didn't tell Ben their location?"

"No, just that they were on the far side of the moon. By the way, you don't call it the dark side of the moon. Also, it's much larger than we thought, like the size of Asia."

"I don't care. As if I would visit that wasteland in my lifetime. Okay, I'm going to need you to visit Chussia Mining. We're going to have to make a deal with them. Go see Ms. Shi."

"Got it."

Dale didn't know who Ms. Shi was or where to find her, but the tone in Dr. Myers' voice told him to figure it out on his own. Also, he had hung up. As it turned out, Ms. Shi found him. She was in the lobby when he got down from his drawer and asked him to walk with her. They went back out onto Huaihai Road where the crowd parted as they walked. No one got within three feet of Ms. Shi. Dale became more nervous the longer they walked.

"I can find the Sky City team for you," Ms. Shi said. "Actually, I already have."

She laughed, but there was no humor in it.

"Great, what do you want in return?"

"Their mine, their equipment, everything must be turned over to me. You cannot take a thing beside the people and the suits they're wearing."

"Sounds great, that's all I wanted anyway."

"Oh, then maybe this is too easy for you?"

"No, that's not what I meant."

"Well, I'm also going to need the DOS to drop their latest lawsuit against Chussia Mining."

"Uh, that's not something I can approve."

"Of course. I understand," said Ms. Shi as she stopped and turned around. "Once you do, I'll be back in touch."

She left Dale standing in the street and people began walking by him now that Ms. Shi was gone. In fact, so many bumped up hard against him even he was afraid of getting mugged. Dale walked into the nearest store until the crowd leveled out on the street.

CHAPTER THIRTY-ONE

WEST OF THE EASTERN SEA, FAR SIDE OF THE MOON

"And we're here," said Ryan as his tablet lit up.

Angie stopped the transport. Everyone jumped out to see what their mining area looked like. The sun fell over the horizon, giving them the last view of it for two weeks. Their location was relatively flat, for the moon. They were near the south pole with ice and frost in spots where the sun never shined. The team couldn't see how any one spot looked more advantageous than another for mining. But that was always the case with mining, what sat below the surface was not indicated by what was above. Ryan's data would point them to areas to begin digging cores and home in on the best mining location.

"We need to light this place up," said Angie.

They pulled out several light sets from the cargo hold and placed them in a large circle to create as even an illumination as possible, ending up with a rough circle the size of a convenience store parking lot.

"Now, let's see what actual mining tools we have," said Ryan.

Jesse went into the cargo hold and dropped several duffel bags onto the ground. The team zipped them open, and Jesse began pulling items out and putting them on the ground.

"A small drill, that's good." Said Ryan. "A larger drill, better. Vintage sluice box, difficult to use without water. Think you could have passed on that purchase. You brought an actual pickaxe."

Jesse kept pulling items out, ignoring Ryan's comments.

"What's that, a mud filled aluminum alloy drill pipe with diamond studded bits?"

Ryan went over and picked up the drill bit.

"Now we're getting somewhere. What else? Wait, leave that bag alone, it's the solar fabric, very delicate.

Jesse emptied the other bags, and they had more drills, cutting tools, aluminum sheeting, nuts and bolts, hammers, rope, and measuring tools. They set up their tents and put the tools inside one of them. The sun went down as they finished, and everyone decided to break for the day. Once the tent pressurized, everyone went inside and removed their spacesuits. Angie emptied a full can of air freshener in the tent.

"How about some cooked food?" said Angie.

"Absolutely," said Jesse. "I'll get it started."

Jesse, who fancied himself a cook, prepared a three-course meal, and everyone realized how much they appreciated not eating energy bars. The typical meal plan on the moon was drinking some sort of shake for breakfast, eating energy bars during the day and finishing with a cooked meal at night. Although the shakes and bars provided all the nutrition a body needed, human nature craved the social time of a sit-down meal. If a person had the evening meal to look forward to, they could shrug off breakfast and lunch. The four of them fell asleep almost immediately after finishing. Twelve hours later they woke up to Jesse reheating bacon, eggs, super nutrified toast and coffee.

"I know we don't do breakfast, but I felt like we all deserved it."

No one argued, they just dug into the food and coffee. The mood was the lightest it had been since they left Galileonia.

"All right," said Ryan. "Let's get to work."

They cleaned up, suited up, and went outside. Ryan had Jesse and Alana drill sample cores out of the ground three hundred feet apart in a triangle. Whatever two samples had the highest concentration of ilmenite became the start of new triangle as they homed in on the richest location. After sixteen cores they found the spot. Ryan had them dig out a hole wide enough for two people to work in. They took turns either digging or crushing the rocks they brought up and preparing them for separation.

While Jesse and Alana dug cores, Angie burned the hydrazine, slowly. As the hydrogen and nitrogen gases exited the catalyst bed at the bottom of one of the rocket engines, she filled a tank. Then she set it upright and connected a gas sensor pump with two-stage compression that Jesse found at Mining Tools and Supplies. After the nitrogen gas settled at the bottom, it pumped the hydrogen gas into another tank connected on the other side of the pump. That's what she liked about Jesse, very practical. And kind of cute.

At the same time, Ryan, using his portable nuclear reactor, built the heater, tanks and pipes for the separation process. Ryan connected the heater to the tank of ilmenite, which would raise the temperature inside to a thousand degrees Celsius, causing the ilmenite to break down into iron, titanium dioxide (rutile), and oxygen. Attaching the hydrogen tank via a valve to the ilmenite tank, the hydrogen released after heating to combine with the oxygen creating steam that traveled through another pipe at the top of that tank into the condensation tank, which would drain into the electrolysis tank, separating the oxygen and hydrogen through an electric charge.

A pump would condense the oxygen into the next tank as a liquid, while the hydrogen was pumped back into its original tank at the start of the process. After several rounds of the separation process, they had enough fuel for a test. Ryan and Angie added the oxygen tank to the rocket engine, along with a second pump to combine it with the hydrogen and moved the igniter to the bottom of the engine where the hydrogen and oxygen combined. They placed the updated engine a hundred yards away from the mine site for testing.

"So, what we're doing is a very small test with the hydrogen and oxygen fuel combination. Making sure the ignition process is stable," said Ryan.

"Is that far enough away?" said Alana. "Doesn't seem far enough away for a rocket engine test."

"It's a very small test," said Ryan. He pushed the countdown on the tablet, and they looked at the location of the prototype, sitting in the dark. When the countdown reached zero the oxygen tank exploded, shooting the rest of the rocket into the air as well as a half-ton of rocks. They covered their heads as debris fell down a few seconds later. Alana glared at Ryan.

"We're going to need a bigger tank," said Ryan.

Ryan reinforced the tank walls, cut the fuel test size in half, and then placed the engine two hundred yards away from the mining site. He ignited it, the engine launched straight up, stopped firing, and fell back to the ground.

"So, that part's done," said Angie. "We have our new engine."

Jesse and Alana continued to mine for a week, filling up the fuel tanks with the modified propellent. Ryan and Angie put the spaceship together, connecting the cockpit, cargo hold, fuel tanks, weapons systems, and two remaining rocket engines. Then they all did a visual inspection.

"Is it ready?" said Angie, stepping back and looking at the beetle-shaped spaceship with the tiny head and large body.

"It's ready," said Ryan. "Let's test it tomorrow. Now, I need to eat."

Angie kept walking around the spaceship.

"You need all eight of those missiles?" said Angie.

"You don't need them until you need them, then you need them all," said Alana.

"Is that a laser in the nose?" said Jesse.

"Yes, and a ball turret gun underneath the cockpit just like World War II bombers. Cool right?" said Ryan. "Bringing the old and the new together in one ship."

"Not exactly, the gunner is a sitting duck."

"You know, I believe in you," said Ryan as he slapped Jesse on the shoulder and went into the tent.

As they were preparing dinner in the tent, Ryan got a message on his tablet.

"Max says there's bad chatter about Chussia Mining sending a group out here. Led by some American that just arrived."

"Gotta be one of Myers' people," said Jesse. "How long do we have?"

"Don't know, assume the worst."

"Okay, then we take off now," said Alana. "Time to go."

"I agree," said Angie. "We have to leave in the next twenty-four hours anyway."

"But I just reconstituted our last apple crisp," said Jesse lifting the lid off the pot on the induction stove.

The smell of apples and cinnamon filled the tent.

"Five minutes," said Ryan, "we leave in five minutes."

CHAPTER THIRTY-TWO

NEW SHANGHAI

NOVEMBER 5, 2071

"I know where they are."

Dale sat across from the man in black, now wearing all white, and placed his steaming bowl of noodles on the table, spilling some of the soup, out of respect for what seemed to be protocol in the noodle shop. Dale grabbed his chopsticks and started eating before the man could respond. The man stopped chewing and looked up at Dale. He set his chopsticks down beside his bowl, still looking at Dale. Then he sat back.

"That's good."

"Yeah, it wasn't easy. I won't have a job if we don't bring them back."

Martin had one of his classic meltdowns when Dale told him about Ms. Shi's demand. If Martin was not such a distinguished PhD and undersecretary for a major federal agency, i.e., if he was in the Department of Commerce, it would have been called a temper-tantrum, and he would be called a bully, maniac or possibly even psychopath.

But because he was a member of the elite technocrat society, the more civilized term, meltdown, was used. It was almost cute.

Martin first asked what exactly Dale was doing, what he was thinking, then questioned his intelligence, his ancestry, his masculinity (totally uncalled for), and finally threatened his future employment both at the DOS and anywhere else for that matter, except recycling waste on Mars, which was always hiring. After another round of the same insults, with a bit less vigor, Martin took a breath. Then he sat and asked if that was exactly what Ms. Shi said, which Dale affirmed. Martin got quiet, questioned his entire team's intelligence, started to get wound up, held back, and then told Dale to give him a day. A few hours later, Dale received a cryptic message from someone located in Chussia Mining with nothing but coordinates.

"Of course, it won't be easy," said the man. "They've shown themselves to be formidable. Normally I would double the team, but we need even more. I will bring thirty men for this job."

The man had no intention of bringing anyone back, including Dale. Dale focused on his meal and waved his chopsticks in assent. Who would have thought you needed to travel to the moon to get such good noodles?

"And many more weapons," he added. "You can get them, yes?"

Dale sat up. He had killed people before, of course, but Dr. Myers specifically told Dale he needed each of them captured and returned to Earth safe and healthy. No one, especially Ben Dawson, was going to buy any 'accidents' on the moon nonsense.

"I need them alive."

"All of them? Maybe just two?"

"No, I have specific orders to capture all four of them and bring them safely back to Earth."

"But accidents happen all the time."

"That's exactly what is not allowed to happen."

"So, how are we supposed to go about this, ask nicely? They took out ten of my brothers, some died; did you forget?"

Dale put his chopsticks down and pushed the noodles away. He sat and looked at the man.

"You know, I don't think this is going to work. You appear to have a grudge. And, I think you might be a homicidal maniac."

The man jumped up and grabbed Dale's collar. Both noodle dishes fell spilling onto the table, Dale's pants, and the floor.

"What did you call me?" said the man.

Dale stood and pushed the man's hands off his collar. He shoved the man back hard enough that he fell onto his chair, which tumbled to the ground. Dale leapt over the table and began pummeling the man's face with his fists. Everyone in the shop stopped and stared.

"I said," with a swing between each word. "You. Are. A. Homicidal. Maniac."

The man was unconscious before Dale finished. Dale kicked the man in the ribs as he got to his feet. As Dale left the noodle shop, he looked around. The other patrons avoided his gaze and focused on their meals.

CHAPTER THIRTY-THREE

SKY CITY EXPLORATORY MINING SITE, WEST OF THE EASTERN SEA

NOVEMBER 6, 2071

The spaceship was on the edge of the makeshift runway. Jesse had bent some of the steel sheeting to create a makeshift plow and secured it to the front of the transport. Then he moved the largest boulders out of the way to create a quarter mile long runway that ended at the rim of a crater. He ran over the runway multiple times to smooth it out, but as Alana looked at it from the cockpit window, it was still quite rough. Angie sat next to her reviewing the launch calculations while Ryan and Jesse were testing each connection between the cockpit, cargo hold, fuel tanks, and engines one more time. Ryan and Jesse then checked the weaponry.

Jesse looked over the controls for the guns mounted under the body, checked that they could swivel three-hundred-sixty-degrees and flicked them between armed and unarmed. Ryan scrolled through the control panel on the missiles attached to the sides of the spaceship and the laser canons placed in the nose of the cockpit. All green. Ryan and Jesse went outside for one more walkaround. Alana finished her pre-flight check. She looked at Angie

"Ready?"

Angie nodded.

"How's it look outside? Good to go?" said Alana.

Ryan nodded but he was spent. He wanted more time; he always wanted more time. But, again, they were out of time. The ship needed to launch. Alana and Angie could die. He and Jesse could die. Of course, we all die at some point, but we're not supposed to accelerate it. Maybe all this was stupid. Why push everything to the absolute limit? Couldn't they have done something else with the DOS? Something besides trying to do the impossible, again? They were so arrogant, all the time.

Ryan never questioned himself. He solved problems no one could solve. And he walked around like that. It made him unlikeable to most, but to Ben Dawson, it made him critical. Standing here on the far side of the moon in absolute darkness, except for their own lights, sending the closest thing to a daughter he'd had out into space with a trunk of mini nuclear warheads, Ryan felt ashamed. Ryan turned away from the spaceship and sighed. Then he shook his head, clapped his hands, and turned back toward them.

"Okay, time to go," said Ryan.

"Just one more thing," said Jesse.

He pulled up a ladder to the side of the spaceship and with some of the drilling oil he wrote on the side of his ship. Ryan looked at it, gave Jesse a thumbs up climbed on board. Jesse threw the ladder off the runway, jumped in the cargo hold and sealed the door. While they buckled in, Alana started the airlock process, which took several minutes. Once completed, a series of green lights lit up on the control screen.

"Jesse, what were you doing out there?" said Angie.

"Gave our ship a name," said Jesse.

"And what is that?" said Alana.

"*Committed*," said Ryan.

"Let's do this," said Alana. She hit the big red 'start' button on the control panel, which back when Ryan modified the crane cockpit programming seemed amusing. Now, thinking about it made him a little sick inside. The engines began humming.

"Everyone ready for a little trip?" said Angie.

"How far away is the asteroid?" said Jesse.

"Just under twenty-five thousand miles," said Angie.

"You have a strange definition for 'a little trip'," said Jesse.

"Remember, start with the minimum power and gently increase it as we approach the crater rim," said Angie.

"I don't know how many fancy degrees you have, but this is like taking off from a carrier. First you go fast, then you go faster," said Alana.

Alana looked at the runway, too rough. She looked at the crater rim, too steep. Then she thought about the spaceship and stopped thinking.

"Here we go," said Alana as she ignited one of the two engines.

The spaceship shook but did not move, then as if the chocks were removed from the landing gear it began racing down the runway, bumping up and down. She lit the second engine when they were halfway down the runway and the spaceship screamed toward the crater rim. Then the front wheel hit one too many rocks and snapped off. The cockpit nose hit the ground sending a wave of sparks into the cockpit windows.

"This was a bad idea!" said Ryan.

"Hold on!" said Alana.

"I'm strapped in!" said Angie.

Jesse looked at the sparks with a raised eyebrow, sat back and closed his eyes.

One of the lights on the control panel went from green to red, then another. They reached the crater rim and the ship turned up toward space. The entire spaceship shook. Alana tried to ignore it.

"Ah, it's going to be close," said Alana.

The windows were entirely blocked with sparks as the nose breached the edge of the crater rim. And then the sparks disappeared, and they were looking into black space. *Committed* was airborne.

"All right!" said Alana, pumping a fist in the air.

"We did it!" said Ryan, starting to laugh.

"We actually did it!" said Angie.

"How are we going to land?" said Jesse.

"I don't know," said Ryan between laughs. "But we've got forty-eight hours to figure it out."

Committed lifted straight up from their mining site, lights still lit and shining on their tents. The ship hit 1.2 miles per second (4,320 miles per hour) and exited the moon's gravity field with the moon blocking any view of them from Earth. And then they headed into space to look for a black dot flying through a never ending black nothingness.

PART III

What part did the Dawson family play in the creation of Sky World? Obviously, Sky City, but beyond that, it was the sibling feud that eventually created the world we know today.

SkyWorld, Jubilee Celebration (2150)

CHAPTER THIRTY-FOUR

VERDI, NORTH NEVADA

NOVEMBER 7, 2071

Ben heard his dad's ring tone on his earpiece.

"Hey, Dad. What's up?"

"Ben, thought you might want to get lunch today."

"Today? You know what we're in the middle of."

Ben heard a voice say, 'Add me in,' and then Bobby Walker's voice was in his earpiece.

"Hi, Ben, its Bobby."

"Why are you with my dad?"

"This lunch is a strong request. As a favor for me. All three of us getting together. Sounds great, right?"

"No, sounds awful. I don't have the time."

"Please, make the time, Ben, for your dad's sake."

"Are you threatening him? If you hurt him, you will regret it."

"Ben, you know I'm not a physical guy. Just look at me. I'm more of a legal and finance type."

"What do you mean?"

"He's holding a harassment filing in front of me Ben," said Neal.

"That's ridiculous and you know it," said Ben.

"Is it? It probably is. Okay, I made it up. But it will get headlines, I can make sure of that. And your dad's sterling reputation will be ruined. All because you won't have lunch with me. Seems short-sighted, don't you think?"

"Meet me in an hour," said Ben.

"You'll need to bring the book," said Neal.

An hour later Ben, Neal and Bobby sat in a booth at the Granite Street Eatery near Midtown Reno.

"This is nice," said Bobby. "I'm buying a place in town, by the way. On California Street. My home fell into the ocean after your quake. Not much to talk about with the insurance company if your entire property is gone."

"What do you want?" said Ben.

"Let me tell you a story," said Bobby.

Ben got up.

"I'll be back when you're done with your story, and then you can tell me what you want."

Bobby motioned him down.

"No, no. You will like this. I promise," said Bobby as the waitress set glasses of ice water in front of each of them, saying she would come back for their orders.

"When I first decided to take over all low Earth orbit transportation, I had my eye on a space exploration company. They were not focused on transportation but had some tech that would be a great starting point. And they were financially distressed. They had a chief scientist that believed he could make them all rich if he could just find the right rock floating in space. He ignored that you need to find it, get to it, mine it, return it, sell it, and probably a bunch of other steps. No, he was dead set on finding what he said would be the 'El Dorado' of space."

Ben sat up. Neal did not as he already knew what Bobby was going to tell them.

"He never found it, sadly. Except the last probe, the one just before I bought them, had some odd behavior. It went off its flight path, only one to do that, ever. And it continued to perform its mission functions, supposedly in empty space. But this chief scientist had to watch it land, even though it was the middle of the night and the end of his time with the company. And when it landed, it fell over and exploded, right in front of him. Lucky for him he wasn't killed. And nothing was left.

The explosion was hot enough to melt the rocket and everything in it. I'll have the burger, no fries, please. Same for you two? Okay three burgers, but fries for that guy, I know he loves them. Anyway, as far as I knew, there was nothing left to talk about. Until that chief scientist showed up working with Neal here and let it slip that he did find the rock."

"Conjecture," said Neal without conviction.

"Maybe, but then the Dawson family decides to explore moon mining, ten years after the last lunar gold rush, actually a helium-3 rush. Got a tip, some say."

Bobby paused, leaned forward over the table and lowered his voice.

"I say you're going after El Dorado. You got the coordinates from Robert Stewart, God rest his soul, and want to save Sky City with it."

"Ridiculous," said Ben with less conviction than his dad.

"I don't think so. You're clever, Ben, I always knew that. And you almost fooled me. But you're not going to risk everything on a ridiculous moon mining expedition, can we all agree on that? Now, here's what you two are going to do. Give me Stewart's notes that show the location of El Dorado and I'll be on my way. I'll even pay for lunch."

"Even if we had them, why would we do that?" said Ben. "No one would."

"But if you had a team on the moon, or somewhere else, and they needed to get back to Earth, and you wanted to make sure they could actually get back to Earth, you would give the guy that can get them back safely the coordinates."

"You can't stop my team from returning to Earth."

"It's called a monopoly Ben. Yes, I can, and I will. They can spend the rest of their days floating on a space station or in one of those loser moon colony domes. Your choice."

Ben looked at Neal, who nodded. Ben pulled out Professor Stewart's book and his own calculations of the coordinates. He slid it across the table to Bobby.

"There," said Neal. "Now, you let my granddaughter back home."

"I knew it!" said Bobby. "Fantastic."

"How is this going to do you any good?" said Ben. "It's two-hundred sixty thousand miles away. You can't get there in time."

"And that's why I had a rocket launched yesterday from the Gateway in the direction of the moon. It will be circling, waiting. Just need to signal them with the details based on these coordinates, and we have ourselves a space race. That is, if you have a working spaceship."

"But, you have a working asteroid-mining spaceship?" said Ben.

"It's a prototype. Like your guy Ryan says, 'everything interesting is a prototype.' Now this just got exciting, didn't it?"

CHAPTER THIRTY-FIVE

SPACE

Alana checked her instruments. The ship was still in one piece, check. They appeared to be on the path to the asteroid's orbit, check. The fuel was running a bit lower than expected, not check. She began going through plans to make sure they could complete the return trip. It would have to involve some coasting, which would delay them.

Oxygen shouldn't be a problem, since space travelers always brought twice what they needed, sometimes triple. Food was an afterthought since the super-nutrient bars came out decades ago. Each one a meal, even if it didn't seem like it. Water was more of a concern, being heavier and bulkier. They had enough, but not as much to spare as the food. Alana looked over at Angie. Her head tilted back and to the side.

"Angie, you asleep?"

"Huh, oh, yeah."

Angie hit her faceplate with her hands, trying to rub her eyes. She blinked instead.

"You want to lower your helmet?" said Alana.

"It's protocol to keep your helmet on when you're flying through space in a fabricated spaceship. Otherwise, you're one seal failure away from suffocating."

"Your call," said Alana, with her helmet down and gloves in her side pockets.

"If you do take any equipment off, it should be right next to you," said Angie.

They heard laughing behind them and looked at Ryan and Jesse in the cargo hold with their helmets off and their gloves sliding across the floor away from them. Angie undid her helmet but kept her gloves on.

"We're on schedule," said Alana. "Can you check our coordinates against the asteroid's orbit?"

"Sure," Angie said as she pulled up the map on her tablet.

After exiting the moon's gravity Alana had slowed their spaceship to a thousand miles per hour and expected interception of the asteroid in four hours. But she would have to continue to slow down, matching the asteroid's speed and orbit before Angie and Ryan could jump onto the rock, while also keeping in mind the rotation of the asteroid.

"Hang on, we're getting a message. Looks like from my dad," said Angie. "It says '*BW in the race*.'"

"BW in the race?" said Ryan. "Ah, what does he mean? I told Ben everything's encrypted. Why is he encoding the message too? So much paranoia."

"He has his reasons," said Angie. "It's Bobby Walker. It must mean he's looking for El Dorado too."

"How?" said Jesse. "We're the only ones with the coordinates."

"Not anymore," said Alana. "I see another ship coming in range on our radar."

Ryan and Jesse unbuckled and entered the cockpit to look over Alana's shoulders.

"How far?" said Ryan.

"About nine thousand miles. Nine hours."

"And when do we make contact with El Dorado?"

"Just under four hours."

"How is that going to work?" said Angie. "We need at least eight hours to sink the silos into the asteroid. Probably twice that."

"We'll distract them," said Alana. "Right, Jesse?"

"Right."

They sat silent while the spaceship flew toward El Dorado. If it weren't for the light pull created by the engine thrust when Alana altered course, they felt like they were going nowhere.

"It's coming up," said Angie. "let's get the mesh out. Keep your eyes open for anything heading toward us. This is a very dark rock. Remember, once we match the orbit, Ryan and I will send the trunks down, followed by using the cables in the cargo hold to work on the rock while Alana maintains the ship's distance around it as it rotates."

Ryan and Jesse swiped their tablets to release the straps securing the solar fabric wrapped around *Committed* at the center of the spaceship. Then they sent the micro-poles out to extend the fabric around the spaceship like a square net. The solar fabric was the width of a human hair, but even that was several layers of the base material, which gave it enough strength to alert them when the asteroid blew through it. Then they extended the same fabric at the front and back of the spaceship to create a three-dimensional matrix layout of panels that would detect any movement. After thirty minutes, the fabric and poles were extended a mile in each direction. Still an impossibly small area to hit the asteroid.

Alana watched the coordinates on her screen for the asteroid's orbit. There would be no visual sighting of the asteroid, she had to trust her instruments, like pilots learning to fly through fog in the 1930s. While the calculations timing the asteroid's location on its orbit were precise, they could easily end up with miles of variance.

"There it is!" said Ryan looking at the control screen. "Just went through the fabric above us, almost right where we mapped it."

"Hard left," Alana said as she pulled the spaceship to the port side with as much torque available to her.

After turning, Alana zoomed in on her map. She approached the asteroid and zoomed in more. Then she turned on the lights at the front of the spaceship and they all looked down at the map, then up at the window, waiting to see El Dorado.

"I see it!" said Angie as it reflected the light from the spaceship. It appeared to be a hundred yards in front of them, or it could have been a thousand. Depth perception was hard in open space.

"That's a trillion dollars? It looks like any other rock," said Alana.

"Believe me," said Angie. "there's more in there than you can ever imagine."

"Then let's get started," said Jesse. "Come on back to the cargo hold and I will hook you two up."

Angie unbuckled, walked into the cargo hold and Jesse grabbed one of the two tethers she and Ryan would use to keep attached to the ship. He secured it to the back of her suit, while Alana released the solar fabric from the ship.

"Let's get this support on you," said Jesse as he had Angie step into essentially a zip line support. He tightened it, and then tightened it a bit more. He clicked in the cable on her back, added a secondary backup cable clip, and moved over to Ryan. While Jesse secured Ryan's gear, Angie checked the trunks. She attached a cable to the two trunks and moved them toward the door. Then she got her helmet on and checked her suit. Ryan was hooked up and walked over to Angie.

"Here, you'll want this," said Ryan as he wrapped a grapnel launcher around her chest, same as he had on his chest.

"You've got a thing for grappling hooks," said Jesse.

"They're very handy to avoid floating away in space," said Ryan checking that Angie's hook was secure.

"Everyone ready for me to open the cargo door?" said Alana.

"Ready," said Jesse, seeing thumbs up from Angie and Ryan.

"Opening the door," said Alana as she swiped the control panel.

They all held on as the air sucked out of the cargo hold. Being a small space, it equalized in a few seconds. They looked out at the asteroid, holding onto the handles in the cargo hold. Alana traveled at the same speed as the asteroid, but the asteroid was still rotating, adding complexity once Angie and Ryan landed on it.

"Shooting trunk cable," said Jesse.

He aimed the pneumatic launcher down at the asteroid. Focusing on one spot as it rotated, he exhaled and fired. Ryan pushed Jesse from behind keep him steady after firing, but they still fell backward. The cable shot down to the asteroid and the diamond studded point of the grapnel hit the rock and went in a quarter inch to the right of where Jesse aimed. Then the tip layered with one-hundred sixty laser-cut diamond points began drilling into the rock while the side points launched out from the shaft and touched the rock's surface. As the tip drilled into the rock, the side points were pulled in and once their barbs entered a half inch into the rock, the drilling stopped. Jesse pulled on the cable.

"It's secured, jump when ready," said Jesse.

"Check," said Angie.

Angie looked down at the asteroid. It appeared much further than the fifty yards where it sat below. She took a few breaths, grabbed the cable, and jumped out of the cargo hold. Aiming herself at the asteroid with both hands on the trunk cable, Angie pulsed her thrusters to send her downward. She had to thrust herself down, but not too fast, onto the surface. That meant landing with no more than five miles per hour velocity, like the NEAR landing on the Eros asteroid back in the day. Her speed displayed on the upper right of her faceplate. It showed three miles per hour.

She pulsed the thrusters again, holding the pulse a half-second longer than before. The faceplate changed to five miles per hour, then seven, then nine, and she was just above the asteroid surface. She did not slow down. Letting go of the trunk cable, she curled into a ball and bumped the rock's surface with her back, rolling along the surface and landing on her stomach. Then she bounced up and looking down seeing the asteroid moving away from her.

"You want us to pull you back for another try?" said Jesse.

"No, I got this."

Angie aimed the grapnel on her chest and fired. It went straight at the trunk cable and hooked itself against it.

"Is that where you were aiming?" said Ryan.

Angie ignored Ryan and began pulling herself to the trunk cable She went hand over hand, as slow as she could to not overshoot the trunk cable. Once she reached it, she began the same process moving down the trunk cable toward the asteroid.

"Steady," said Jesse.

"Is she not on the rock yet?" said Alana. "What's going on?"

"Almost there," said Jesse.

Angie pulsed her shoulder thrusters as short as possible to direct her body straight back to the asteroid. Zero gravity was not as much fun as they made it seem in those videos. Her hands slid off the cable, and she aimed for landing with her feet flat on the ground but came in at an angle on her stomach. As her body hit the asteroid, she spread her arms and legs, dragging her hands and feet to stop moving. A few seconds later she stopped. She jumped up with her arms raised high. The asteroid's rotation gave it a modicum of gravity, but not enough to stay on the surface if you jumped.

"Did it!" said Angie, and then realizing she left the asteroid's surface again, hit her shoulder thrusters lightly and pushed herself back down to the surface where she walked over the trunk cable and held on.

"Fantastic," said Jesse. "Ryan, your turn."

"Is that wire still holding?" said Ryan.

Angie pulled on the trunk wire; it did not budge.

"Solid," said Angie.

"I'll use the wire and see if I can get on the surface in less than three tries. Not that I'm judging."

"Sure," said Angie.

Ryan did not jump out the transport. Instead, he crawled out using the trunk wire, pulling himself to the asteroid's surface. It was slow going.

"No thrusters?" said Angie.

"Leave me be," said Ryan. "I'm doing great."

"Ryan, I'm getting old," said Alana.

"Fine," said Ryan as he pulsed his rear thrusters, which were not aimed directly away from the asteroid and pulled his body away from the trunk cable, almost making him lose his grip. He pulled himself back, breathing hard and after a wait, resumed pulling himself down the cable hand over hand.

"No more thrusters," said Ryan.

A little over an hour later, Ryan stood on the surface of El Dorado next to Angie.

"Don't say anything," said Ryan.

"About what? It's been so long since you left the cargo hold, I don't remember what we last talked about," said Angie.

"Send the trunks down," said Ryan.

Jesse started the cable retrieval on the trunks, which would retract the cable between the trunks and the asteroid into a spool attached on the back of the second trunk. They slipped out of the cargo hold toward the asteroid. The pace of the cable winding was calculated by Ryan to not crash the trunks into the asteroid. He had to keep tension on the line, but not too much. Like when he fished for salmon in British Columbia. Always keep tension on the line. If it gets too tight, the line snaps; if it goes loose, you lose the fish. In this case, if the cable goes loose, two trunks of nuclear silos ram into you. Angie grabbed the line to help bring the trunks down. She pulled once with her right hand and was about to pull with her left hand when Ryan yelled.

"Angie, no!" said Ryan. "Don't touch the line." He could have sworn they discussed this part. But there were a lot of parts to this plan and many, many changes. Either way, this was bad.

"What? Sorry," Angie said as she released the wire and put her hands in the air.

Ryan saw the slack in the line. It continued to grow.

"Look out!" said Jesse. "They're coming right at you."

Ryan and Angie looked up at the trunks coming straight at them. They moved to the edge of the asteroid as the first, then second trunk, hit the surface. The trunks bounced away from them and they turned to chase them down. The trunks lifted off the surface and Ryan and Angie grabbed the guide wire.

"Gently now," said Ryan.

Hand over hand they pulled the trunks back toward them. They kept the wire taut the entire time they pulled the trunks back to the asteroid's surface and the trunks still slammed into them. They rolled onto their backs as the trunks pushed them down to the ground, and then bounced off them.

"Grab the handle," said Angie, holding onto the handle of her trunk and sliding across the ground. She tried to dig her feet into the ground, but there was little to dig into. The trunk hit a bump and stopped. Angie looked up as Ryan slid past her with his trunk. The cable between them was about to tighten up and drag her again. She turned the other way and began pulling her trunk. The cable tightened and dragged her back, but slowly. She kept pulling, using her free hand and feet to move forward. Then she felt no drag on her trunk. She stood and saw Ryan lying on the ground, face up with his hand on one of the trunk handles and the trunk on top of him. Two people and two trunks not moving and on the surface of the asteroid.

"Everything okay down there?" said Alana.

"Just like we planned it," said Angie.

CHAPTER THIRTY-SIX

NEW SHANGHAI

"Contact Undersecretary Myers," Dale said from inside his sleeping area. "Secure line."

Dale waited and the screen lit up with Dr. Myers face at three times normal size.

"Ah!" said Dale as he pinched the screen to shrink the unsmiling head of Dr. Myers back to normal.

"Is something wrong?" said Martin.

"No, all good." Dale took a breath. "I have an update."

"What?"

"The team is ready. Its big, almost thirty men. Several vehicles, all with weapons."

"Dale, if you don't bring everyone back alive, don't come back. What do you not understand about this? How can you possibly control nearly thirty armed cartel members?"

"I've made it very clear sir. No fatal shots. Everything is set to stun."

"And you believe they will follow you why?"

"I said there was a five-million-dollar bonus for each of them when we get all four back unharmed to New Shanghai. No bonus if even one person is killed."

"You said you'd pay out a hundred-fifty million dollars?"

"That's how they do it in the CIA. Well, maybe not that much, but the DOS has a bigger budget, right?"

Dr. Myers leaned his head down and rubbed his temple. Dale waited. He knew this was over the top, but success would mean forgiveness. But failure, well, he didn't think about failure. After a while Dr. Myers looked up.

"Just get it done."

"Oh, I have some photos as well; sending now."

Martin looked at his screen.

"These were taken by a team that tried to ambush them on the road between Galileonia and New Shanghai. They failed. Here's the front of their vehicle. And one from the side; another from the side."

"What is all that they're carrying?"

"I was told they made a transport and carted several junk items for mining."

"They're going to mine with a crane cockpit?"

"Oh, and here's the back, taken from a truck's rear camera just before it was blown up."

Martin could see the projectile heading straight at the camera. A bit shocking; but once he looked past the projectile, he saw what was on the back of the transport."

"Are those rocket engines?"

"I believe so, yes, that's what my cartel contact said."

"Who mines with rocket engines?"

"That's what my contact asked. She thought it looked more like items for a spaceship instead of mining."

"Spaceship?"

"Yes, sir."

Martin mouth went dry.

"They're actually going for an asteroid from the moon! That's a spaceship. How long have they been out there?"

"Just over two weeks."

"Two weeks? Are you kidding me? How are you not there?"

"It's complicated sir."

"You did not just tell me something was complicated. Stop them. Immediately. This is worse than I expected. Go. Go!"

"Roger that."

Dale shut off the channel before Dr. Myers could yell at him anymore. He got out of his sleeping pod, grabbing his duffel bag as he jumped on the moving ladder. He exited the coffin motel, headed to the end of town, went through an airlock to where the commuter launch pad sat, and walked into one of the two lunar rockets waiting for him. Ms. Shi's personal protection service of men and weapons filled both rockets.

As soon as Dale was on board they lifted off. An hour later they began their descent west of the Eastern Sea where the Sky City mining expedition had been located by Ms. Shi's drones. She had used five dozen drones to fan out over the far side to locate them. An expensive venture in that those drones were used to maintain order in New Shanghai, but because they were always in New Shanghai, no one noticed their disappearance for the thirty-six hours it took to locate the mining site. Since the lunar wars, Ms. Shi, like everyone else, had no formal contact with the Tongs. And every random interaction they did have ended up with at least one fatality, rarely on the Tong side. She and the other cartel members left the Tongs to their business. There was plenty to mine without venturing into their territory.

When her drones went into the far side, she expected to lose some, maybe all of them. But each drone returned without damage, along with the location of the mining expedition. But curiously, after covering over eighty percent of the far side, no small task, there had absolutely no indication of the Tongs location anywhere. Something Ms. Shi would think about more at another time.

"We're approaching the location," the pilot said over Dales' and everyone else's earpiece.

"Okay everyone, listen up," Dale said. "This is a capture only operation. Absolutely capture only. Understood? Now, here's how we're going in." Dale pulled out his tablet to create a hologram of the mining site.

"Hey, homie," said one of the team members sitting across from him. "We'll take it from here."

"I'm no homie," said Dale.

"Yeah, that's what a homie would say."

They all laughed. Like *Cheechako* during the Klondike gold rush, homie expressed the derision felt toward all newcomers. The moon was a dangerous place, and anyone's ignorance could endanger everyone's safety. If a homie did not kill himself, or others, after six months they would refer to him as such less often. After a year, because by that time all newcomers had left or died, they were accepted.

The first plane, in front of Dale's, began to land, shifting its engines for a vertical landing. As it was nearing the ground a surface-to-air missile hit it, split it in half with the front exploding in flames. Ms. Shi's plane landed, more like flew into the ground. The back door lowered, and a ten men team headed out to check on the downed plane. They came back with three survivors.

"Set your weapons to maim," said Ms. Shi. "Let's have no more casualties."

"Wait, we can't kill them," said Dale.

"That's why I said maim," said Ms. Shi. "Breathing is acceptable, yes?"

"Not really," said Dale, "but I'll take it."

The remaining team went back up the ramp of the second plane and came down with a transport carrying a large gun turret on its back and three motorcycles. Three of the men on foot removed their lunar weights from their boots with two jumping left and one right to, spreading out. The remaining four went two and two walking on either side of the transport. Ms. Shi walked with Dale as they headed down the ramp.

"If you do decide to engage," Ms. Shi said to Dale, "try not to get killed. You really don't know what you're doing."

Dale shrugged, pulled his gun off his shoulder, and walked behind the transport next to Ms. Shi. As they approached the mining site, he was impressed with the precision of Ms. Shi's team and how the transport, motorcycles and jumpers converged on the lights of the mining site in a semi-circle. He thought they might know what they were doing. When they were within a hundred feet of the site the transport stopped.

"Okay, everyone. Hold up," said the driver.

The soldiers crouched, as did the jumpers after landing.

"We're going to lead with,"

"Incoming!"

The driver never finished his sentence as the transport blew up from a bazooka shell.

"Attack!" yelled one of the soldiers.

"No, wait!" said Dale. "No fatalities."

"They just killed three more of our guys, I'm killing three of them," someone said on the channel.

"Stand down," said Ms. Shi and everyone stopped. "If you are afraid of dying, back off now. But you cannot kill them. Yes, they will try to kill you and that is not a fair fight. This was explained many times before we left. I'm disappointed to be repeating myself. If any of you kill one of them, I will personally deal with you."

After a few seconds of silence, one of the motorcyclists said, "Re-engage with targets using spread maneuvers and stun or maim settings. Circle the camp before going in."

They resumed their movement toward the camp and the mining site lights swiveled out toward them, blinding them momentarily until their faceplates transitioned. Then the lights went out.

CHAPTER THIRTY-SEVEN

DEPARTMENT OF SPACE

Martin rarely threw things in his office. Once a week, at most. Today, there were several broken items along the bookcase and near the trash can, where they would stay until housekeeping showed up that evening. He thought damaging a few useless government awards and spaceship models would improve his mood for the day, but it was fleeting. He called Don on his monitor.

"I need you to access the near-Earth objects map, or whatever it's called."

"It's up," said Don, who always the Near-Earth Asteroids (NEA) grid on one of his screens, one of his hobbies.

"What is close to the moon right now?"

"What do you mean by close?"

"Don't get smart with me, something you can fly to!"

Don did not ask for clarification on what *fly to* meant. He looked for any asteroids within fifty thousand kilometers of the moon for the past week and next week. Being a three-dimensional grid Don had to rotate around the moon in all directions to identify the NEOs that met the criteria. Once he completed his visual inspection, he looked at the calculated read-out, which matched his visual inspection.

"What is taking so long?" said Martin.

"Interesting," said Don.

"Don't play games with me Alfred Hitchcock, what do you have?"

"You don't have to be rude," said Don for the first time.

"Are you lecturing me? I could have you fired immediately for your unauthorized consulting with Sky City. Is that what you want?"

"Actually, I did get authorization,"

"Shut up and tell me what you see! I swear I'm about to come through this monitor."

Don looked at Martin and folded his arms.

"You know, actually, I don't see anything. That is interesting, don't you think? Absolutely nothing."

Martin realized he could either have an aneurysm or try being polite. Tough choice.

"I'm sorry for losing my temper Don, you didn't deserve that. I know Ben Dawson's team is on the moon and looking to mine an asteroid near it. If they somehow were able to bring it back to Earth, that amount of wealth will change the global economy."

Don did not believe Martin's apology for an instant, but it was a first. So, they were in fact mining an asteroid, fascinating. Don never believed the moon mining expedition story. But four people were not going to mine an asteroid. At least not anything large. If they were mining an asteroid, it would have to be small, very small, because of the size of the team. He began looking at his asteroids again.

"Too big, too far, ice based, carbon based, worthless rock."

Don kept crossing off the NEOs inside his parameters until he was left with nothing.

"Huh."

"What, what is it?"

"Nothing, that's what doesn't make sense. They could not be going after any of these asteroids, at least not to change the world."

"It has to be there."

"Let me do some digging and get back to you."

"Hurry."

Don hung up and went through his asteroid logs. He had compiled every known recording of an asteroid through terrestrial, space, probes, Moon, and Mars observations. He even had the missed observations, which is where he focused now. Much smaller list than the tens of thousands of known NEOs. He filtered to those misses with a location at or less than fifty thousand kilometers beyond the moon's aphelion. The list shrank more. He filtered to misses by teams otherwise successful and the list shrank to under a dozen. So many cranks filing reports, always messing up the data. Don looked only at those guys that knew what they were doing and had a miss.

He went down the list and stopped at John Stewart. One miss in his entire career. And while he was at Outside Earth Exploration. How did no one see this before? Probably because no one ever asked the question. He dug in more. The 7A probe went off its mission coordinates, performed a core test, supposedly in empty space, and flew back to Earth only to explode in front of Stewart. Odd did not describe that situation. He rang up Martin.

"Could be nothing, but there was a probe that failed to find its asteroid twenty-seven years ago. Only time ever for this scientist. One failure in his entire search history."

"Happens," said Martin. "Why wouldn't this be anything but failure by a washed-up scientist?"

"Because he never missed before. And this was his last probe."

"That explains it. Massive failure; couldn't recover. What else do you have?"

"Oh, I also noticed LEO Transco launched a rocket toward the moon yesterday."

"Why didn't you start with that? Where is it heading?"

"Behind the moon. That is, behind the moon relative to Earth."

"Can you give me precise coordinates?"

"For where the rocket is heading? Based on their deceleration pattern, that should be possible."

"Send them over. I'm very concerned this mystery asteroid could be an ELE."

"I highly doubt whatever we're talking about would be large enough or with a trajectory that,"

"You are not the Department of Space. I am and I have determined it is an Extinction Level Event."

Martin referred to the asteroid ELE prevention project. Initially funded in 2030 and put into general practice in 2050 after commercial asteroid mining was outlawed, missiles were placed in GEO orbiting satellites, ready to launch and stop any two-hundred-fifty-meter diameter or larger asteroid from impacting Earth. Depending on the size of an actual ELE asteroid, one or all the ELE rockets would need to be fired, months, if not years, in advance. More likely, the satellites would be sent to where the asteroid was going to be, and then they would launch the ELE rockets. If, instead, they were surprised with a small asteroid coming at Earth from the direction of the sun, then it was bombs away immediately.

The goal was to adjust the asteroid's orbit by a maximum of four minutes. Since Earth travels its diameter every seven minutes, even an asteroid heading toward the center of Earth only needs its orbit adjusted three and a half minutes to miss the Earth. With any asteroid that could hit Earth having at least the orbit of Earth, and likely much longer than that, it means shifting the asteroid's orbit less than 1/130,000th.

That could be done by moving the asteroid to the side, speeding it up or slowing it down. But what they didn't do was try to blow it up, and in the process create dozens of asteroids heading toward Earth, which likely increased the damage to the planet by a factor of ten. That is, unless it was a small asteroid, which could be blown up into small enough pieces that would either burn up in the Earth's atmosphere or have limited damage upon impact like the Ensisheim meteorite of 1492. An asteroid behind the moon, besides not being a threat, would test the guidance capabilities of an ELE rocket to its limit.

Regardless of the blah, blah science behind the ELE prevention project, Martin realized he would be setting precedent with his historic and courageous single rocket ELE launch. Never had the Department of Space acted independently to protect the Earth. In the past they would delay acting by seeking counsel from teams of experts, and then what? Destruction, tragedy, bad press. Martin thought it should be named The Myers Plan or The Myers Doctrine. He would have time to wordsmith later. First, get rid of the asteroid before the Dawsons reached it.

"We need to destroy that asteroid," said Martin. "For the sake of all humanity."

"Bit heavy," said Don. "Also, we don't have the coordinates of the asteroid, just where the LEO Transco spaceship is calculated to stop."

"That's a start. We'll shoot it there."

"You want to shoot an Extinction Level Event rocket to a location in space without actually identifying an asteroid?"

"Great, we understand each other."

"I wouldn't say that. Regardless, you don't have authorization. It has to come directly from the secretary."

"Fine. Don't go anywhere."

Martin hung up and left his office.

"You, you and you," he said to three of his personal security detail as he walked to the secretary's office.

"Follow me and do what I say. You just made your careers today."

Martin walked into Kerry's office with the three guards behind him.

"What is this?" said Kerry as he saw the guards.

"Kerry, I cannot tell you how much this hurts," said Martin.

"What do you mean?"

"Kerry, it has come to my attention that you have been receiving bribes from Sky City to allow them to keep their intellectual property."

"That's preposterous, and you know it."

"Unfortunately, I have documents and audio of you and Ben discussing this."

"Impossible."

Martin put his tablet on the table and played a doctored recording of Kerry and Ben agreeing to terms.

"That's not real. Guards, arrest Martin. Now!"

"Criminals never admit their crimes, do they?" said Martin as he waved the guards over to Kerry. "Based on the authority of the undersecretary to prevent corruption in this agency, I have no choice but to take over as acting secretary of the Department of Space."

The guards had Kerry stand up, handcuffed him, and forced him out of the office.

"I knew you were a weasel! You won't get away with this!" said Kerry as the guards shoved him down the hall.

Martin sat at Kerry's desk and went through approving the temporary authorizations for him to become acting secretary. Technically, the president should be approving such authorizations, but when the 51st president was losing a power struggle to the alliances, she abdicated the process for the federal agencies to manage. And, because the secretary was never going to authorize a temporary secretary, how ridiculous, it was handed down to the undersecretary, expected to never come into play. Martin lit up a conference screen with Don.

"I am now acting secretary of the DOS due to the unfortunate arrest of Kerry Reid for conspiring with Ben Dawson. And I will be issuing a warrant for Ben Dawson's arrest. Due to the emergency nature of the situation and the threat to national security, I am ordering the launch of one of our ELE asteroid rockets to a previously unidentified asteroid's location. Confirm the launch. I will stay on the line."

CHAPTER THIRTY-EIGHT

SKY CITY EXPLORATORY MINING SITE

After the lights went out, Dale knew he needed to take charge.

"Listen up people," he said over the channel. "We're doing this my way. Those people are smart. Set your timers for two minutes, and then we all rush the site simultaneously. Yes, it will be dangerous, but we're still ten to their two.

"What do you mean two?" said Ms. Shi.

"The other two probably took off in a spaceship," said Dale.

"And you did not tell me this? How could you not tell me this?" Ms. Shi's voice lost her steady pitch for the first time since Dale had met her. Her team lowered the volumes on their devices, knowing what was coming.

"They will be back, they couldn't go far with a fabricated ship like that," said Dale. "We'll get them when they come back."

"But where are they now and what are they doing?" said Ms. Shi at volume.

"Dr. Myers' thinks they're mining an asteroid."

"What? What!" Ms. Shi let off a litany of Mandarin. "Get those two now! I need to talk to them immediately! And our deal is changing, Mr. Dobbs. Changing significantly."

"Everyone, go. Go!" said Dale. "We need them alive."

The team began moving simultaneously toward the mining site, guns out. When they reached the edge of the mining site shots rang out from the west side, behind large rocks. Three of the team members went down. The rest headed for cover.

"What was that?" Dale said to anyone that could answer.

"Hello, Dale," said the voice from the man in black, then white. He had cut into their channel.

"We will take over now," he said. "After we eliminate all of you."

Thirty men charged over the rocks on the west side toward the mining site. As they charged, the mining transport started and began rumbling away from the mine site into the dark. Both groups of men went after it, shooting at each other as they approached from opposite sides. The wheels were shot out, and it slowed but did not stop.

One of Dale's men jumped to the driver's side door and another man jumped on the passenger door. They both entered the cab at the same time and realized there were no passengers and focused on each other instead. Handguns were drawn and hit out of each other's hands. Fists were thrown, knives drawn, and the two wrestled for control as the transport crept forward.

"Report, what's going on?" said Dale.

"Empty," said his team member while struggling with a knife near his face.

Dale's man was kicked out of the cab and the other began driving it toward his team where he stopped, and they surrounded it. Dale's team held back and aimed their weapons at the others. The man thrown from the cab came up to Dale.

"The transport was empty. It had been rigged to drive away."

Dale paused.

"They're in the mine," Dale shouted over the channel. "Back to the mine!"

Dale's team began running back to the mine site, followed by the other group. They were running and leaping to be the first to the mine when everyone heard a roar above them. They turned to see two modified transports with jet engines coming up behind them, fast. All the men pulled their weapons to aim at the makeshift rocket ships. The men on the ground fired, but the rocket ships had already launched multiple missiles at them, and then veered away.

Everyone yelled on the channel to take cover. The four missiles hit and scattered the men. Most were down, including Dale. The few that did not get hit dropped their lunar foot weights and leapt away into the dark. The rockets turned and came back, picking off the jumpers one by one until no one moved. As all the missiles and bullets went flying, Ms. Shi stood in the middle of the mining site observing, because she knew, as did everyone else, that you don't point your weapon at Ms. Shi.

Dale's leg was hit, his suit torn open, and his faceplate cracked. His suit resealed around the leg and sprayed medicinal super glue into his wound to stop the bleeding. The faceplate covered with goop to reseal, which eliminated his view except through the micro camera mounted on top of his head. It automatically illuminated on his faceplate. He sat up to see the rocket ships land and a dozen men come out. Two men came out of the mine, moving the steel plates. They gathered up everyone that wasn't dead, including Dale, who stumbled as they dragged him into a circle.

"Ms. Shi," John Han announced over the channel, "we have what's left of your men. Do you want them?"

"No, they failed. I have no need for failure."

Ms. Shi walked back to her rocket alone, went up the platform, and it closed behind her. The pilot started the engines, preparing to launch. John Han looked at the group. They were all on their knees in a row facing him. Injured, but recoverable.

"Looks like you all have a choice. You can come work for us."

"Or?" said one of the men.

John Han pulled out a gun and aimed it at his head.

"Or don't."

He put the gun back.

"What, are we going to be your slaves? Old Testament style?" said one of men.

"More like indentured servitude," said John Han. "You can work it off and earn your freedom back. Of course, most end up staying. It's nice."

"Why shouldn't we just escape?" said another.

"From the middle of the far side of the moon?" said John Han. "Feel free. We like to bet on how far one of you gets. Some make it a week on foot. No one gets back from where they came."

The men's heads fell. They knew what fate awaited them. Except Dale.

"I'm an American, you can't do this to me," said Dale.

John Han walked over to him and bent down to get right in front of his camera.

"And exactly who is going to stop me? Who? Be specific."

John Han stood and walked around the group.

"One of the reasons I came here was to never hear someone say something like, 'I'm an American'. Take them."

John Han's team cuffed each of the men, including Dale, and marched them onto the rockets.

"Ms. Shi," John Han said. "I hope you enjoyed your visit to the far side; it's been too long since we've seen you."

Ms. Shi's rocket had already lifted off toward New Shanghai. She did not respond.

CHAPTER THIRTY-NINE

DEPARTMENT OF SPACE

"You sit here, and you sit there," said Martin to Ben and Daniel. Ben took his directed chair in the conference room as did Daniel. Martin had a wild look in his eye, keeping Ben and Daniel quiet for now.

"If you agree to stay in this room, I will allow it. Otherwise, you will be sent to a proper jail. Do you understand?"

"I don't understand any of this," said Ben. "Why are we here?"

"Okay, then, off to jail," Martin touched his tablet to make a call.

"Wait," said Daniel. "Wait."

Martin looked up, but the call connected.

"We agree, Ben and I. Whatever you want, we'll sit. Why do you want us here though, instead of in jail?"

"If you cooperate, and I mean really cooperate; not like that game-playing you've been doing for the past year, I can still offer you a clean slate for the future."

"Of course, your honor," said Ben.

"It's secretary, and that is precisely what I do not want to hear out of you Ben Dawson," said Martin.

"Sir, can we help you?" said a voice from the tablet.

"Yes. Have two security guards sent to the secretary's, I mean, my conference room to secure the prisoners I am holding inside."

"Yes, sir."

"So, we're prisoners," said Ben, arms still folded.

"You are criminals," said Martin. "And this is your one and only opportunity to avoid prison. So, pay attention!"

Ben and Daniel looked at each other after Martin's outburst. They both thought he lost it. Martin turned to the windows, looked outside, took a breath, and adjusted his suit jacket. He turned back to the two men.

"I want to show you something."

Tapping on his tablet, he brought up a picture of El Dorado on the screen. Martin zoomed out to show the perspective of the asteroid to the moon, and then the Earth.

"Recognize this?"

Ben's eyes went wide, but he kept his voice level.

"It's a rock."

"More correctly, it's an asteroid. One near the moon right about now. Very close. So close it could be reached by a short space trip."

"And your point?"

"My point, Benjamin, is that as secretary of the Department of Space, I can authorize missile launches to obliterate asteroids on a dangerous trajectory with Earth."

"That small of an asteroid would never make it through Earth's atmosphere," said Daniel.

"Actually, that's a subjective matter," said Martin.

"No, it's not. It's science. That rock poses no threat whatsoever to Earth," said Daniel.

"But that is where you're very, very wrong. That rock, from what my astrologists tell me,"

"You did not just say that," said Ben.

"From what they tell me, is that small rock may be the densest collection of rare Earth elements, platinum, gold, silver, and who knows what else, in the history of mankind."

Ben and Daniel stared at Martin.

"Probably not gold or silver," said Ben.

"You're really going to make me walk through this? Fine. If some rogue group were to acquire this asteroid and somehow bring it back to Earth, it could upset the global economy, and I can't have that. The RAA has already irreparably damaged the country with all this 'we need transparency and accountability' nonsense.

"Sounds like oversight," said Ben.

"Sounds like meddling," said Martin. "And then we lose the moon and maybe Mars. The space stations are acting like whiny little brats and your Sky City shows up acting all independent? No, no, no, no, no. We've always been in charge, and it is not going to change while I'm here. And especially now that I'm secretary,"

"Acting," said Ben, regretting his crack the moment he made it.

"And now that I'm secretary of the Department of Space, which is tasked with defending the interests of the United States across the skies and space, I will see to it no on interferes with the government's plans."

"These plans," said Ben. "Who came up with them?"

"I did."

"And how are they the government's plans?"

"My plans are the government's plans. I'm the government. Why is this so hard for you to understand?"

"Because you're just a guy, with a new title. One guy. And you want to speak for the country?"

"That's how it works Benjamin. Did you sleep through Civics or do rules just bore you?"

"You bore me and your speeches."

"Well, who is in charge here? And who is the criminal?"

"That's relative for the moment," said Daniel.

"What matters," said Martin, "is that I have sent a rocket to blow up your precious rock. It will be gone in," he looked at his watch, "ninety minutes."

"You what!" said Ben getting to his feet. He headed toward Martin and the two security guards outside rushed in, grabbed Ben, sat him back down and handcuffed him to his chair.

"Thank you, gentlemen. Him, too," said Martin, pointing at Daniel.

They walked over to Daniel, handcuffing him. Daniel sat quietly while Ben fought with his handcuffs, cutting his wrists.

"Is there something you want to tell me?" said Martin. "You're going to be my guests for a while, all the way up to the handover, so you might want to open up."

CHAPTER FORTY

SURFACE OF EL DORADO

Angie and Ryan secured the two trunks to the surface of the asteroid using concrete bolts hammered in with a pneumatic gun, which shot Angie and Ryan into the air each time they fired it. However long Angie thought this would take, now she doubled it. Opening the first trunk, Ryan pulled out a nuclear solenoid. Sixteen of these needed to be set at specific locations, complicated even more with the asteroids uneven surface. Alana flew *Committed* around the asteroid to maintain the tension on Angie's and Ryan's tether cables, holding tight against the rock and keeping them on the surface. Ryan handed Angie the solenoid, pulled out his tablet and looked for the location of solenoid number one.

"Okay, walk straight, one step to the left," said Ryan as he looked at his tablet. "Set it down. Over a foot. The other way. Stop. Pull out the securing cable. About six inches on either side. That's it, bolt the cable into the ground. And the other side. Perfect. Now, and this is delicate, you need to initiate the drill, but not the nuclear device."

"I know this, Ryan," said Angie as she entered the drill codes on the LCD control panel.

"Better safe than crispy," said Ryan.

The silo's drill began spinning. She watched as it sped up. The bit spit dust up. Then it entered the asteroid. It went slow.

"Should I move onto the next one?" said Angie.

"We need to watch the first one," said Ryan.

"How far into the rock does it need to go?" said Jesse.

"Each solenoid goes halfway down into the rock, entering at a forty-five-degree angle. We'll drill four solenoids into the center of the asteroid on four lines equally spaced along the rock."

"It's smoking," said Angie. "Should I shut it off?"

"Wait for a spark," said Ryan.

"I am not waiting for a spark," said Angie as she shut it off.

Angie pulled the silo out and checked the bit, which had a small amount of wear.

"Bits okay."

"Let's drop some mud into the hole, needs lubrication," said Ryan.

Ryan grabbed a canister of oil-based drilling fluid consisting of diesel, brine, lime, emulsifier, wetting agent, viscosifier, and a filtration control additive. No longer legal to use on Earth, it had become the mud of choice for drilling on the moon and now, asteroids. Ryan walked over to the silo and handed it to Angie. She poured it into the hole and placed an aluminum pipe around the silo to speed the movement of mud and debris out of the hole. After entering the drill code, it moved much faster into the rock.

"That's what we needed," said Angie.

Thirty minutes later the silo was in position. Ryan entered the securing code for the silo. It drilled four foot-long stainless-steel posts out from the sides, near the tip of the silo, to secure it in place after the asteroid broke up into chunks. The silo drilled just past the center of the rock because the drill bit would be blown off during the splitting of the asteroid. The engine portion of the silo sat behind the drill bit. While the first silo secured itself, Angie went back to the trunk and pulled out another silo and more mud. Ryan pointed her to the next location and after it was in place, she did another, then another. Angie and Ryan continued for six hours placing eight out of sixteen silos around the rock. She sat for a break. Drinking water and amino acids through a straw, going to the bathroom in a spacesuit, sleeping in a spacesuit. It was getting old. Halfway done. Eight silos to go, and they could get out of here. Then the day ride back to far side of the moon, the nine-day bumpy transport ride back to Galileonia. Then a glorious thirty second shower and sleeping on a bunk. Better not to think about any of that, just the silos. Eight silos and done.

"Hey," said Alana.

"What's up?" said Angie.

"Just got a message. Not good."

"Not good how?" said Angie.

"Something about an asteroid rocket."

"Asteroid ELE Prevention rocket?" said Ryan.

"Ya, how did you know?"

"Was in one of my scenario analyses. Low probability."

"Huh, what other low probability scenarios involve us getting blown up?" said Alana.

"Few more," said Ryan.

"Who sent the message?" said Jesse.

"Just says 'Don'. Message say DOS launched it toward this asteroid almost twelve hours ago."

Angie wondered how this Don, who her dad said nearly blew them up, got a message to Alana and why. Something about that guy. Then she focused on the more critical question: how close was that missile?

"Where was it launched from?" said Angie.

"ELE Satellite."

Angie knew a dozen ELE satellites were stationed around the equator at GEO synchronous orbit, twenty-two thousand miles above the Earth. They would use the one closest to them. Likely two-hundred forty-one thousand miles away when it launched. It would be traveling at fifteen thousand miles per hour. Sixteen hours to reach them assuming minimal deceleration when curving around the moon.

"Alana, that rocket will be here in four hours," said Angie. "We need at least that to finish and I'm slowing down. We should get out of here and figure out how to make it work with half the silos."

Angie didn't believe it could work setting half the silos. The asteroid had to be broken down into sixteen chunks for the mini bots to create the right-sized reentry shield and for Jason to be able to capture them. And she and Ryan had been setting the silos all over the asteroid, not on one half.

"Keep going. I'm going to take out that missile," said Alana. "Jesse, secure Alana and Ryan to the asteroid."

"That's crazy Alana. How can you take out a satellite missile?" said Jesse.

"By blasting it into dust."

Jesse heard a tone in Alana's voice that told him not to argue. He picked up the pneumatic launcher, attached a hook to the end of Angie's tether and put it into the barrel. Jesse aimed and fired. It went into the center of El Dorado and the drill bore into the surface while the side hooks flared out and entered the rock, just like the trunk cable. He did the same with Ryan's tether.

"They're secure," said Jesse.

Alana turned the spaceship toward the coordinates sent by this Don person. Don's numbers were precise, Alana was impressed. She had the ship's computer calculate the missile's trajectory and location. Then she had it set a course to intercept, which the computer would not do until she overrode every protection Ryan had built into the software. As the ship accelerated, she went over the weapons system again. Eight AGW 583A Arrow missiles, two terawatt ultrashort pulsed laser weapons and an M197 Gatling gun placed in a rotating ball turret underneath the cargo hold.

"This is random set of weapons," said Alana. "Jesse, I'll need you to man the gatling gun."

"Got it," said Jesse as he opened the panel to sit in the turret seat.

Alana checked the firing procedures for the missiles and lasers, then breathed deeply, like she always did before battle. Thirty minutes later, Alana saw the other spaceship approaching them.

"We're coming up on the other asteroid hunter," said Alana. "Get ready."

"Ready," said Jesse.

The two ships approached. If Alana did not have them on radar, she would not have seen them. No one fired. They passed by each other, several hundred yards apart, looking through the windows, waiting for the other to engage. Then the other spaceship left their view and Jesse relaxed off the triggers.

"What's with the space standoff?" said Jesse. "I mean, it's better than a firefight, but odd."

"They probably think we're going in the wrong direction and wanted to avoid the potential of us hitting them."

"How long until they reach El Dorado?" said Jesse.

"Less than an hour," said Alana.

"How long until you intercept the missile?"

"Too long. Angie and Ryan are going to be exposed."

"Then let's speed it up," said Jesse.

*

Ryan pointed to the edge of the asteroid.

"The next one goes near the other side, over there," said Ryan.

Angie looked where Ryan pointed. She placed the solenoid, mud, and aluminum sleeve into her backpack, zipped it up, and jumped. Angie flew off the asteroid and floated away until the cable tightened around the asteroid and began pulling Angie back toward it. She landed on El Dorado with both feet and started running, following the directional arrows superimposed on her faceplate. She pulled out the pneumatic gun and put a stake into its barrel. She held a security cable in her other hand.

With each step she came down lighter on the asteroid, leaving its surface. Once her screen showed her above the silo's drilling location, she stopped, dropped to her knees, and put the security cable on the ground. She fired the stake into it and held onto the cable as the recoil of the pneumatic gun pushed her off the asteroid. She holstered the pneumatic gun, pulled the silo out of her backpack, and placed it in position on the ground.

Then she pulled the cable over the end of the silo, pulled out the pneumatic gun, let go of the cable for half a second to load a stake and pumped it into the ground, securing the silo and herself. She pulled out the drilling mud and sleeve, wrapping the sleeve around the silo, pouring mud into it, down the side. Angie entered the drill code and watched the silo dig into the rock, spitting out mud and dust. Because this silo was further out on the asteroid it had less distance to drill down to get into position. After thirty minutes, it was in place.

"Secure," said Angie.

She let go of the silo security cable and jumped up away from the asteroid, back toward the trunk. Four more to go.

*

Alana saw the light of the ELE missile's fuel as a tiny bright dot in the distance, like a star. She looked on the control panel, which displayed a frontal and aerial view of her and the missile's locations. She had the screen add the range of her AGW Arrow missiles as a dotted line around her ship on the aerial view. She looked at the ELE missile's flame, then back at the screen. Almost there.

"How many missiles do you need to blow it up?" said Jesse.

"Four," said Alana.

"Cool."

"So I'm dropping all eight."

"Even cooler."

Alana stopped talking and ignored Jesse. The closer they got to the missile, the more intense her anger. She was furious at the person shooting a missile toward her and her friends. She knew Martin Myers did it. How dare he? Alana did not make a lot of friends, and she was okay with that. Most people bothered her, and she had no patience. It took a lot to break into her small circle, dominated by her family. Not that her family did not annoy her, but they were family.

This team, while annoying most of the time, had her back. And they put their faith in her. Some people said they believed in Alana, but she knew they needed something from her and would dump her as soon as she slipped up, not that she did. These people had put their lives into Alana's hands. And now she had a chance to do something about it. Nobody comes after her friends.

The missile came into range. It showed up on her screen as an Aegis Missile Defense System, SM-3 Block V, three stage solid fuel model, speed of Mach 20 (15,000 mph), with smart guidance and avoidance systems. Alana initiated the full release sequence for two of the Arrows. They acquired their target, completed the power transfer and umbilical disconnect. After the missiles separated from the spaceship, their four popout fins clicked into position and the oxidizer fuel mixture ignited. The two missiles shot ahead of *Committed*, sending their thousand-pound warheads toward the ELE missile. A half second later she did the same for two more Arrows and a second after that released the final four.

The ELE missile adjusted its trajectory to avoid the first two Arrow missiles, and then adjusted again for the third, which sent it into the path of the fourth. That Arrow missile made impact at the nose, destroying the ELE missile's guidance system and turning it into a dumb torpedo. Then the final four Arrow missiles converged upon the ELE missile, detonating their warheads, and igniting the ELE missile explosives, creating a spherical shockwave that rattled *Committed*. Alana flew into the debris firing the ultra-short pulse lasers. To an observer, the rapid shots would have appeared random, but she was dissolving large chunks of the missile remnants until nothing larger than a coffee cup remained, making good on her space dust claim. Before turning back to El Dorado, Alana turned on her comms to an international public channel, typically used for distress calls, which would be picked up by basically anyone in humanity with a radio.

CHAPTER FORTY-ONE

DEPARTMENT OF SPACE

Ben had been struggling with his handcuffs for fifteen minutes when Martin threatened to personally administer him a sedative and let him wake up with restraining belts. Ben stopped trying to get out of the handcuffs, but his face remained beet red. It gave everyone, including Martin pause when they looked at him. Martin stopped looking at him and spoke to the window instead.

"I don't know why you are so upset with me," said Martin as his coffee was brought in. He methodically stirred in two small spoons of brown sugar for a full thirty seconds, then took a sip, and continued to stare out the window while Ben and Daniel glared at him.

"You brought this on yourself. Always the entrepreneur, creating the future. That's how you like to think of yourself, isn't it? Didn't you know most small businesses fail? But guess what does not fail? Government. And more specifically, a federal government agency. How many government programs, let alone agencies, get closed? Let me help you, none. Even after the alliances, all they could do was shrink budgets."

"Martin if you don't stop lecturing, I'm going to kill you twice," Ben said. "Your garbage philosophy of the World According to a Bureaucratic Idiot named Martin is just that, garbage."

"A threat?" Martin looked at Ben. "I believe we now have a physical threat against me."

"It's not a threat," said Ben. "And I'm upset about not winding my chronometer. First day I've ever missed."

"Ben," said Daniel. "This isn't the time."

Martin's earpiece notified him that Bobby Walker was calling. He answered, hoping to drop in the fact that he had Ben and Daniel in handcuffs.

"Martin, what are you doing?" said Bobby.

"I've got Ben and Daniel here, according to protocol."

"That's not what I'm talking about, you fired a missile into space?"

"Oh, that, yes."

"I've got a team out there. They're in the flight path."

"Then I guess you better tell them to move."

"Martin, you can't do this! You have no idea the damage you are causing."

"Yes, I do. And you need to know your place. Goodbye Bobby."

After Martin hung up and turned to gleefully explain the situation to Ben and Daniel again, the conference room door opened. A soldier walked over to Martin, leaning over to whisper in his ear.

"What? What!" said Martin waving him away from his personal space, which no one invaded, ever.

"A message, sir," said the officer at attention.

"Yes?"

"It appears to be personal."

"From whom?"

"That is the issue, sir. It was over a public broadcast station. Across space. It came from outer space."

"And you are saying it is personally for me?"

"That's the consensus, sir."

"Consensus from whom?"

"The consensus from the combined communications analysis teams of all the intelligence agencies. With some agreement from NATO countries. And China. Also, Russia."

Martin sat up.

"What's the message?"

The officer stood as straight as possible to avoid any possibility of personal inflection in delivering the message.

"*Take that, Marty.*"

Ben raised an eyebrow to Daniel.

"Out, out!" said Martin to the soldier, who was outside the room in two steps.

"Daniel, what could a message like that mean?" said Ben.

"I have no idea," said Daniel. "You think it's our first alien contact? So odd."

"Just an opinion," said Ben. "But my guess, Marty, is that you lost something."

"I agree," said Daniel. "Something big. What is it you think you lost?"

"Quiet, both of you," said Martin as the red increased in his face while it left Ben's. He tapped his fingers on the windowsill and fumbled his coffee cup as he took a drink.

"Marty, you win some, you lose some," said Ben. "It happens."

"You still need to bring it down here," said Martin.

Ben said nothing.

"That's right, I know you need it down here, not just up on the moon or in a Gateway storage box."

Martin began pacing.

"Where will you bring it down? Over the ocean, of course."

Martin stopped and turned to Ben.

"I'll be ready. Probably your son, right? Well, that's not going to happen. It will be a sad day when your son's floating boat falls into the ocean. A sad day that is very soon in the future. Call Don. Don!"

Martin looked straight at Ben as he talked to Don LaRue.

"Set up a search over the Pacific for Skyboats. Ones that aren't moving. Like they're waiting for something to fall out of the sky. Have your drones ready."

Ben sat back.

"You don't want to do that," said Ben.

"It's done."

"You know," said Ben. "Jason' mother has been watching this entire time. And she's also Angie's mother. Do you forget you tried to shoot down our rocket leaving Earth? Yes, it was our rocket. How many times do you think you can threaten our children before Paige Dawson unleashes on you? Here's a hint, once; and you've done it twice with a third on the way. You think I'm mad? I'm a Boy Scout compared to what's coming for your team."

"Hey Marty," said Daniel. "You're going to keep that screen up the entire time, right? This is going to be fun once the show starts."

CHAPTER FORTY-TWO

SKY CITY

Paige sat at the desk inside the cabin of *Firefly*. Streaks of tears had dried on her face from watching the launch of the ELE rocket. She had banged the table, shouted, and finally sat back staring at the screen as the blip moved closer to El Dorado. Helpless, again. Then the blip disappeared, and she sobbed uncontrollably. Angie was gone. Her little girl, gone. She felt empty. Paige's radio crackled but she ignored it. Nothing mattered. She blamed Ben, she blamed herself, Ryan, Daniel, even Angie. Why did they agree to do this? Why? How could it ever be worth losing someone?

"Take that, Marty!" came over the speaker.

The sound wasn't clear, the pitch uneven, but Paige knew Alana's voice. She grabbed her microphone.

"Alana, Alana is that you?"

No answer.

"Alana! Answer me!"

She looked over on her message board and saw a one-word text.

"Yes."

Then another.

"Hi, Mrs. D, it's J. All safe."

A wave of relief swept over her followed by exhaustion. She fell back in her chair from the stress of the situation when Jason flew *Sky Dancer* up next to her and jumped onto *Firefly*'s deck. He dropped into the cabin.

"Mom, they've got Dad."

She sat up.

"Who has him?"

"Who else? That guy Myers. Daniel, too. Under arrest, can you believe that?"

Paige felt a spark ignite inside her. It began in the center of her body, a red-hot pinpoint. Then it grew. The heat flowed across her body into her arms and legs and finally throughout her head. Her breathing went shallow and fast, and she tried to slow it down. But she could not slow it down, so she stood. Did not help, she sat back down. The anger was white hot inside her. Paige could not see, could not hear, could not feel.

No, she could feel, feel the anger of everything in her past racing forward to this moment. Every wrong she thought she forgot, every slight made to Angie or crack about her looks or their odd family. Paige felt all of it and nothing else. Then the heat receded. Draining from her head, her arms, her legs, back into the pinpoint. Sounds echoed around her, the cabin walls appearing again. Paige closed her eyes. When she opened them again, the anger was gone, but only because it was replaced with resolve. Jason touched her on her shoulder.

"Mom, are you okay?"

"Yes I am."

"I can't retrieve the meteorites without Dad."

"We'll do it. You and me."

Paige stood.

"We've got ten days, right?"

"About that, assuming everything goes as planned up there today."

"It will. Time to get ready because I've had enough of this."

"Me too."

"Where does Ryan keep all his protypes?"

"On *Nautilus*. Everything's in coolers. He's not so good at documentation."

"We'll figure it out."

CHAPTER FORTY-THREE

SURFACE OF EL DORADO

Angie was at the northern pole of El Dorado, about to set the thirteenth solenoid when the spaceship came into her field of vision. It surprised her, and she let go of the solenoid. The solenoid floated up in front of her face, bringing her back to the job. She grabbed it, shoved it on the ground and pumped the two stakes for the securing cable around it and started the solenoid's drill. Then she leapt back in the air and wrapped her tether around the asteroid, sending her toward the trunk.

"It's here," said Angie, out of breath.

"I see it," said Ryan, putting away his tablet.

Angie landed at the first trunk.

"What do we do now?"

"Keep going," said Ryan. "Set number fourteen. Also, we need to hide."

He handed Angie another solenoid and put the last two in his backpack. Then Ryan turned off all the lights on his suit, released the trunks from the cable and kicked them. Angie watched the two trunks float away.

"Hide?"

"We need to stay on the other side of the asteroid from the spaceship until Alana shows back up."

"Ryan, that's a least an hour, probably two or more. If they even come back."

"If they don't come back, we're goners. Might as well assume they're coming back. Now, here's the coordinates for that silo," said Ryan.

She leapt off the asteroid and had her tether whip her around the opposite side from the oncoming spaceship's path. Ryan followed, less refined in his jumping since he had been standing next to the trunks all the while they were on the asteroid.

"If you can't see them, they can't see you," said Ryan. "Look for lights, they'll probably shine down to observe."

"Won't they see our tethers? And our solenoids?"

"Maybe, yes. Probably. But they might think we're gone."

"Until they see the cables move," said Angie.

She went to the location for the fourteenth solenoid and began the drilling process.

"The tethers moving might be a giveaway," said Ryan. "But it could also be a robot. Keep them guessing as long as possible."

The spaceship passed the asteroid. Angie and Ryan watched as she finished inserting the solenoid into the rock.

"Should we get to the edge and see if we can hide?" said Angie.

"I'll do that, you take this," said Ryan, handing her number fifteen.

The ship passed the asteroid and made a lazy loop to head back toward its center. It kept moving past the asteroid and its lights illuminated most of the rock facing the spaceship. It was making sure it could see pole to pole as El Dorado rotated.

"We're going to have to cross that light beam to finish," said Angie.

"Maybe if we crawl down the underside, we can find an overhang and,"

"Time to go," said Ryan, and he jumped, crossing the light beam for half a second then he was out.

"I guess I'm crossing the beam," said Angie, and she jumped into the light.

*

"They're at the asteroid," said Jesse from the co-pilot's seat, looking at the control screen showing the other ship next to Angie and Ryan on the asteroid.

"I see that," said Alana. "We'll be there soon."

"How soon?"

"Soon."

Jesse sat back, frustrated at being able to do nothing. If there was any way to make the ship go faster, he, wait a second.

"What if I shoot the gun below to speed us up?"

"Won't do much."

"But it's something, right?"

"Ya, but don't waste our ammo."

"Yes, Captain," said Jesse as he jumped out of the co-pilot's chair and into the gun turret. He turned it to the rear of the plane and let out a few hundred rounds.

"How's that?" he shouted from the turret.

"Fine, you feel better?"

"Much, here's some more."

Jesse shot another hundred bullets and hopped back into the copilot's seat.

"How much faster are we going?"

"You wanted me to measure it?"

"Well, yeah, that was the point."

"The point is to get back and save our friends."

"Right; so how long until we get to our friends?"

"Soon."

*

"Do you think they saw us?" said Angie as she landed next to Ryan, and then laid down on the ground of the asteroid.

"Probably, but let's act like they didn't. Here's the last one. C'mon, let's keep moving."

"Wait, look at the back of the spaceship," said Angie.

Ryan looked up and saw a large Kevlar bag extending out of the back of the ship. It appeared like a chute used to slow down drag racers. The bag continued to move further from the spaceship until it almost became too far to see.

"They're going to bag it!" said Ryan. "How lame."

"Now what?" said Angie.

"Get ready for a ride."

The LEO Transco Spaceship drifted over them and adjusted its trajectory to place the asteroid inside the four cables coming out of the back of the ship. Angie drilled the final solenoid with Ryan next to her when the bag touched the asteroid. They felt a slight pull as the spaceship had aligned with the asteroid's orbit. Angie and Ryan did not feel much change in velocity or acceleration, but they were trapped.

*

Alana approached the LEO Transco spaceship from above. Passing at a rapid speed, they were well past the ship when Jesse saw the bag.

"What's that?" said Jesse. "Are they pulling the asteroid?"

"Looks like it," said Alana. "Ryan, Angie, can you hear us?"

"We're stuck," said Angie.

"I guess we'll meet you at the Gateway," said Ryan before their signal cut off.

Alana began turning *Committed* around.

"What do you think?" said Jesse.

"Not sure, might have to blow up the spaceship."

"Angie and Ryan could get hit."

"It's either that or cut those cables. And those aren't normal cables."

Jesse sat for a second and looked toward where the spaceship was as the bag came into view.

"I can cut those cables."

He got up and went back to the cargo hold. Alana heard him throwing things around. Sounded like he threw everything in the cargo hold. Jesse was angry.

"Careful," said Alana.

"Don't worry, your spaceship is safe."

"Not what I'm talking about."

Then she heard the hook and loops straps. No way they had that many on board, but then, Jesse loaded them, not Alana. They approached the space bag. Jesse shut the door between the cockpit and cargo hold. Then Alana heard the cargo door open.

"I'm jumping, cover me," said Jesse as he aimed at the cables and hit his thrusters.

Alana slowed *Committed* to keep pace with the LEO Transco spaceship. She looked out her side window to see Jesse heading toward the cables and loaded with so much gear he looked like a walking armory. He reached one of the cables, put his arm around it, and latched himself to it. Alana saw a side door of the spaceship open. She aimed her lasers at it and fired for five seconds. The door closed.

"They're going to come out," said Alana. "You better hurry."

"I am," said Jesse as he pulled out a plasma torch, turned on the power source, opened the liquid oxygen/nitrogen tube which ionized into a plasma jet and began heating up the cable.

The door opened again, and Alana fired the laser at it. This time a shield hung outside the door, so she put *Committed* on autopilot, secured her helmet and gloves, went into the cargo hold and dropped in the gatling gun seat. She fired at the shield and whoever was holding it lost their grip, the shield flew away from the door, hitting the spaceship before bouncing into space.

"Running out of tricks," said Alana.

The wires holding the Kevlar bag were a carbon nanotube and graphene composite fiber, which Jesse heated to forty thousand degrees Fahrenheit with his plasma torch. Then he pulled out his assault rifle and put it right on the blue heated section, firing a series of bullets through the wire. The bullets created a tear pattern but left over half the cable intact. And the recoil sent Jesse back away from the cable. He aimed the gun at the holes in the cable and emptied the magazine. After that, the cable hung by a few hairline threads, each of which still had a good portion of the wire's original fifty-thousand MPa tensile strength, versus nine-hundred MPa for a stainless steel cable. Jesse replaced the clip, aimed it behind him, shot it once to thrust himself back into the cable. Wrapping his legs around the cable, he pulled out his knife and the plasma torch. As he heated the remaining threads of the cable, he sawed at them with his knife. One, two, three, and the cable was cut. He hit his thrusters, moving over to the other cable connected to the top of the LEO Transco spaceship.

*

"We can't let them take us all the way to the Gateway," said Angie as she and Ryan sat on the asteroid while being pulled in the space bag. "Was this in your probability scenarios?"

"Everything was in my probability scenarios," said Ryan. "But I have thousands, so I had to apply probabilities. This one was pretty far down the list."

Angie looked up, her default reaction to being on Earth and looking to the sky for answers. Then she saw the cable on the right begin to slack.

"Look!" said Angie pointing at the cable.

"It's cut," said Ryan.

"Let's try to pull the bag down."

Angie crawled to the back of the asteroid, next to the space bag and tried to grab it. Her gloves could not get a fold in the bag. She tried pushing on it, but the bag was too big, it went out and settled back against the asteroid.

"Grappling hooks to the rescue, again," said Ryan.

He pulled out his hook and shot it up above their heads at the bag. It hit the bag but did not pierce it. The hook bounced away from the bag.

"That material's too tough," said Ryan.

"Let's shoot over the top and pull the bag down," said Angie.

"May be too high."

"I'll see."

Angie hit her thrusters, aiming the grappling hook at the edge of the slack cable and the bag. When her tether tightened, she shot the hook. It went past the corner of the bag but as she came back down to the asteroid it hooked around the cable. Ryan grabbed her ankle and pulled her onto the asteroid.

"Quick," said Angie. "it's at the corner, we can pull it down."

Ryan and Angie pulled her hook down and grabbed the corner of the space bag. It folded over them and starting to cover them and the asteroid.

"Push it down," said Ryan. "Behind the asteroid."

They kept folding the bag, pushing it behind the asteroid. It was huge, and they did not feel like they were making any progress, but they were doing something, so they kept doing it.

*

Jesse was heating the second cable when the spaceship doors opened again. He ignored them and Alana pulsed the lasers at them. This time multiple shields came out with spacesuits behind them. Jesse finished heating the cable, aimed his gun at it and shot holes through it like the last cable, propelling him back. The four spacesuits spread out from the ship and Alana could not hit them all. Jesse emptied his gun's clip into the cable, leaving five threads, and put his last clip into the gun.

The spacesuits oriented themselves toward Jesse and aimed their weapons at him. They pulsed their thrusters while he fired a shot behind him and moved back toward the cable. He threw three grenades at them, ignoring their shots as he heated the threads and cut them with his knife. They were approaching him when the cable broke, and he let the plasma torch go, grabbed his gun, and fired at them. They scattered away from the cables.

"It's cut," Jesse said. "Let's go get Angie and Ryan," Jesse said as the recoil pushed him further away from the cable and the spacesuits. He emptied the clip at them, sending him closer to *Committed's* open cargo bay.

"Roger that," said Alana as she began the wide turn to send *Committed* toward the asteroid bag a quarter mile away.

*

"The second cable's cut!" said Angie.

"Keep folding the bag!" said Ryan. "We can get out of here!"

The started pulling against the other side of the space bag where the other cable had just been cut. The adrenaline pumped, and they doubled their speed. The bag was large, but now they were pushing tens of yards down each second.

"We're above you," said Alana.

Ryan and Angie looked up to see Jesse hanging from below *Committed.* He thrust his jets to get back into the cargo hold.

"We're coming," said Ryan. "Just a little bit more needlepoint work down here."

"Hurry up," said Alana. "Hostiles coming your way."

"Goes without saying," said Ryan.

Angie and Ryan pushed the bag down behind the asteroid faster and faster. They were working too fast for their spacesuits climate controls to keep up and their sweat dripped on their faceplates.

"Almost there," said Angie.

And then the asteroid was clear of the space bag. It did not move any differently, at first. But the LEO Transco spaceship was turning around, so in a few seconds the bag was underneath the asteroid, and then over to the side.

"Time to go," said Jesse. "Those spacesuits are coming up on you."

"Okay, we're going to have to thrust into the cargo hold," said Angie. "Without the tethers. Ryan, aim like you're diving off a cliff, hands out front, head forward."

"I got it, let's go."

Angie unclipped Ryan's harness, and he unclipped hers. Ryan aimed at the cargo hold above them and fired his thrusters. Angie did the same right after Ryan was above her. Ryan looked through the sweat droplets on his faceplate at the cargo hold, hands in front. He began drifting left and was about to hit his thrusters to correct.

"Don't do it," said Angie. "You're too close. Jesse, can you grab him?"

"I got him."

Jesse stepped out of the cargo hold, held onto the edge with his right hand and grabbed Ryan's right wrist with his left hand. He pulled him back into the cargo hold, throwing him inside, and Ryan hit the bottom corner of the back wall and bounced up to hit the ceiling.

"Really, Jesse?" said Ryan.

Jesse ignored Ryan and placed himself in the center of the cargo hold opening as Angie approached. He grabbed her by the waist as her arms and upper body passed through the doorway. He stopped her movement and set her down on her feet facing him.

"You okay back there?" said Alana.

"I guess," said Ryan.

"I'm perfect," said Angie as she smiled at Jesse through the condensation on her faceplate.

"Then can someone blow up that rock?"

"Happy to," said Ryan, pulling out his tablet.

Ryan swiped the tablet into hologram mode and the screen illuminated a panel above the tablet. Everyone watched as he went through the checklist.

"Solenoids online," said Ryan. "Angie, you want to do the honors?"

"What about those guys down there?" said Angie. "Can't we warn them?"

The spacesuits were crawling over the asteroid, trying to come up with a way to put it back in the space bag.

"I'll warn them," said Jesse.

He jumped into the gunner's seat and fired at the asteroid, intentionally missing the spacesuits. They looked up and began firing back, but Jesse's continuous stream of bullets forced them off the asteroid. They floated a few feet away and reoriented themselves to head back to the asteroid.

"They've been warned," said Jesse.

Ryan pressed the red button hovering over his tablet. A confirmation box came on the screen 'So, you want to blow up El Dorado?'

"Now?" said Ryan.

"Yes!" Angie and Alana yelled back at him.

Ryan pressed the confirmation box. They looked out at the asteroid. A smoke ring came out of the center, and then it split into two. Ten seconds later, after the two rocks had moved several yards apart, they saw two identical smoke rings in the center of each of the two smaller asteroids. There were four pieces, like an asteroid sushi roll. Then each of the four slices split into four boulders. Sixteen almost equally sized rocks floated below them.

"Not so hard," said Angie.

Ryan issued the configuration protocol and each boulder's solenoid began firing to spread them out and line them up, making sure each boulder's solenoid engine pointing in the same direction. The spacesuits were scrambling to grab the boulders.

"How do we stop them going after the rocks?" said Angie.

"I gave them something else to worry about," said Alana. "See their spaceship?"

Angie, Ryan, and Jesse looked at the rear of the LEO Transco spaceship and its engines were smoking.

"You burned up their engines?" said Jesse.

"Only two of them," said Alana.

"Time to send these babies home," said Ryan.

Ryan started the thruster protocol that fired the first of the sixteen solenoids, beginning its descent toward Earth. A minute later the next one fired. This continued for a quarter of an hour until each were heading toward Earth. The spacesuits could not hold onto or keep up with a boulder once the solenoid fired. Not for lack of trying. At one point, all four spacesuits were thrusting against one boulder when it fired, and they slid off like a muddy rock rolling downhill. The spacesuits headed back to their spaceship, empty-handed and staring at their smoldering engines.

As the boulders raced toward Earth, the mini robots inside the solenoid rolled out onto each boulder to create a heat shield on the opposite side for reentry protection. Earth's gravitational pull would accelerate the boulders as they approached, and the solenoids would do correction burns throughout their journey to reenter at the location Ryan programmed. Ten days later they would enter Earth's atmosphere where Jason and Ben were waiting for them. At least that's what Ryan told everyone during the briefings.

"So, that's it?" said Jesse.

"Believe so," said Ryan.

"Okay to head back?" said Angie.

"Absolutely," said Ryan.

"Well, that's good since I've been heading back for half an hour," said Alana.

Angie looked for a final twinkle of the El Dorado boulders solenoid engines, but they had already faded from view.

"Jason, it's up to you now," she said.

CHAPTER FORTY-FOUR

SKY CITY EXPLORATORY MINING SITE

NOVEMBER 8, 2071

John Han was at the mining site when Alana landed *Committed* next to him. The newly indentured servants, including Dale Dobbs, were on board one of the Far Side Mining modified rocket ships with the rest of John's crew, next to the mining site, ready to head to their underground facilities. FSM had mined out an underground living area years ago and continued to carve out space underneath the surface.

The mined regolith was scattered across the surface, looking virtually identical to the rest of the regolith because on the moon, with no organic material, atmosphere, or water, everything looked the same. They learned to spread the mined regolith during the two-week lunar night, after removing any valuable minerals, so when the sun came up, it all looked like it was before the sun went down. There would be a point where FSM's location was discovered, but it could be years or even decades. The team exited the spaceship and John Han walked up to them.

"Sight-seeing?" said John Han.

"Yeah. Did you know the far side of the moon looks the same everywhere?" said Ryan.

"Perhaps to you. Find what you were looking for?"

"Maybe," said Angie. "Not that I'm saying we were looking for anything."

"Look around you, who am I going to tell? Do you not trust that my interests are here and here alone? And did I not protect you as promised?"

"That you did," said Angie.

Alana and Jesse were walking around the mining site and came back to John Han.

"What happened while we were, uh, sightseeing?" said Jesse.

"Like I said, I protected you, and your equipment."

"You're a rare man, Mr. Han," said Ryan. "You did as you said, don't see that much. I respect that."

"You four have my respect. This is a harsh place. As bad as it gets."

"Great, mutual respect," said Ryan. "Tell you what, you want a spaceship? Maybe help with the astronomy?"

"That's very kind of you," said John Han. "I'm in your debt."

"A first," said Ryan. "Alana, you mind giving him the keys?"

"Ya, there's no keys. You know that."

"Thank you," said John Han. "Might change the name though."

"Wouldn't do that," said Jesse getting into the driver's seat of the transport. "Bad luck."

The rest of the team followed Jesse into the transport.

"Safe travels," said John Han.

They waved knowing if John Han wished them safe travels on the far side of the moon, then that was what they were going to get.

CHAPTER FORTY-FIVE

SKY CITY

NOVEMBER 17, 2071

"Everyone, listen up!" said Jason on the Command deck of *Horizon*, standing next to Roger. "Handover is in thirty-six hours, and I want a bigger celebration than 1997 Hong Kong."

"Is that really an appropriate comparison?" said Roger.

"It is and I do!" said Jason.

"Do what?"

"Want a perfect handover!"

"You don't need to yell."

"Stop questioning me!"

"It's not a, forget it."

Jason pulled the microphone off Roger's console and turned it onto broadcast. With less than a hundred Skyboats left in Sky City, he did not need more than a Bluetooth speaker out on the deck of Command for everyone to hear him. Sky City was down to one level, primarily the service Skyboats. Less than a dozen individual owners, the diehards, remained for the Sky City transfer of control.

"Hello Sky City, it's Jason Dawson. I'm excited to announce our handover to the glorious and merciful Department of Space will be tomorrow night, precisely at midnight. We will have the largest celebration in the history of Sky City for this memorable occasion. No expense has been spared, which is why I sent our cargo Skyboats out at top speeds across the globe for the finest cuisine. And there will be fireworks. Thank you."

Jason dropped the microphone on the floor.

"That's how you announce a handover."

"Jason, I appreciate your engagement in the process," said Roger. "In fact, I wish the rest of your family realized, like you, how important it is to embrace the process of rehabilitation. But enthusiasm is not a substitute for process. I have a detailed checklist, hundreds of pages long, and we need to get through it all before tomorrow night for this to be official. Can you help me with that?"

"I would," said Jason. "Sounds fantastic; but I have one more special package to pick up personally, for the handoff. You're going to love it."

"What is it?"

"It's a secret, a present for the new owners of Sky City. Don't worry, I'll be back well before the handover. Besides, who could do a better job than you of all this government paperwork?"

"Thank you Jason I appreciate that. It's been a way to keep me focused. And it will be exciting to have your dad and Dr. Myers here together tomorrow. Very reassuring to hear they are able to spend this last week of transition working together."

"So great. I cannot wait to see Dr. Myers again."

"Any word from your mother?"

"No. I guess she doesn't want to deal with the new reality."

"She'll come around."

"Yes, that she will. Anyway, gotta go. See you tomorrow!"

Jason walked outside Command and jumped onto the deck of *Sky Dancer*, which was floating next to the deck of *Horizon*. He grabbed the wheel and headed south, away from Sky City.

CHAPTER FORTY-SIX

GALILEONIA

NOVEMBER 18, 2071

The transport hobbled up to the north side of the dome. Everything creaked and the only item still on the platform was the crane used to take everything off the transport. Jesse drove in the front seat with Alana beside him. Angie and Ryan sat on back of the platform, legs dangling off the side. Sherriff Steele waited for them outside the dome. He had one of his Vigilance Committee men stationed at the door, preventing others from coming out while the transport approached. Jesse parked the transport in front of Steele, and they all jumped down to the ground, stretching after a long ride.

"Any trouble?" Steele said.

"Not on the way back," said Jesse.

"Nice job keeping everyone safe out there," Steele said to Jesse.

"Wasn't just me," said Jesse, "but thanks."

Steele walked around the transport, looking over what was left of it and the gear on top of it.

"Missing a few items."

"Donated," said Ryan.

"For what?"

"Science."

"No littering, right? You bring out what you brought in. That's the rule on the moon."

They all looked at each other, and Steele laughed.

"And how did your mining expedition turn out?"

"There's potential," said Angie. "We will have to file our claim."

"So, you're going back to work that mine?" said Steele.

"Well, not right away," said Angie.

"Then I wouldn't file that claim. If you don't work it, you'll lose it. And I guarantee someone else will go work it if you file and don't work it," said Steele.

"I don't know if anyone would go work that claim," said Ryan. "But we'll wait on filing it. Right now, we need to get back home."

"I figured that. You have seats on the next shuttle to the Gateway. How much you taking with you?"

"Just this one trunk," said Jesse. "Souvenirs."

"Do I have time to drive this back to the boneyard?" said Ryan.

"Well, hold on," said Steele. "I can take this off your hands if you won't be needing it. Nice craftsmanship. Can always use another transport."

"How about I loan it to you?"

"Is it even yours to loan?"

"Fine, take it. I'm ready to leave."

"Follow me, then."

Steele took them into the shuttle dome. Jesse loaded the trunk in the bay underneath, which the porter promptly unloaded, and they waited for the other passengers to board.

"This ship will get you back to the Gateway," said Steele, "but I don't know how you're getting back to Earth. There's a lot of chatter about the problems you and your team down there is causing."

"Couldn't be helped," said Alana. "And we didn't start it."

"Well good luck," said Steele. "Seems you keep needing it."

Steele shook each of their hands and the four got into the shuttle and strapped in. Steele stood outside the shuttle watching them as Max entered the shuttle dome and walked up to ask Steele something. Max smiled at the response, looked at the windows to find Ryan and gave him a thumbs up.

"What was that?" said Angie.

"Oh brother," said Ryan. "It's nothing."

"You think we'll be able to get back to Sky City from the Gateway?" said Jesse.

"Oh, we're getting back," said Alana. "Even if I have to blow more stuff out of the sky."

"That makes me feel better," said Jesse, sitting back in his chair and closing his eyes.

CHAPTER FORTY-SEVEN

ISLA PINTA, GALAPAGOS ISLANDS, SOUTH PACIFIC OCEAN

Jason had his lights out on *Sky Dancer* as it landed at the southeastern coastline of Pinta Island, just after midnight. He parked in between the sixteen cargo Skyboats sitting along the beach and walked up to the forest line where *Firefly* sat.

"Permission to come aboard?" Jason said, seeing a light on in the cabin.

"Oh, good, you're here," said Paige from inside the cabin. "Come on in."

Jason went to the stern and climbed up the ladder onto the deck. He walked down the ladder into the cabin and saw his mom bent over a computer screen at the dining table.

"How's it looking?" said Jason as he walked down the cabin stairs.

"I was going to ask you."

"Well, there's no one left at Sky City that doesn't get a paycheck. Roger's still a robot. Haven't heard from Dad or Daniel for a week, and sixteen two-hundred-ton meteors are about to drop into the atmosphere six hundred miles west of here, which we need to catch. Seems everything's going according to plan."

"Great," said Paige as she stood. "I need you to check the re-entry coordinates and timing. I'm going to get our cargo Skyboats ready."

Jason sat and looked at the laptop. His mom had loaded the same program he had on *Sky Dancer*, written by Ryan and Angie, for the meteorite re-entry. They dubbed the program 'Melvin', some sort of acronym for Meteorite Entry Level Vectoring... but then it fell apart and they resorted to a name everyone could pronounce. Jason had turned off the audio feature long ago since it used Angie and Ryan's voices. Melvin continuously received the pinged data from the meteorites' solenoids and provided them with real-time re-entry data. It calculated re-entry beginning in six hours. After that, a two-hundred-ton rock would fall out of the sky every fifteen minutes for four hours. Tricky was an understatement. And he wasn't going to get any sleep tonight.

Paige walked down to the cargo Skyboats on the beach. Vali had retrieved, then sent out, the entire fleet of cargo Skyboats for supplies needed for the handover. The reconfigured cargo Skyboats traveled with cargo Skyboats picking up actual cargo but broke off under drone canopies at various locations to travel to Isla Pinta. The plan had its flaws, but Jason created enough distractions of his own at Sky City to avoid extra scrutiny of the cargo Skyboats.

"This is a nice place. We should visit after it's all done," said Jason walking down to the shore next to his mom.

"We'll have to," said Paige. "I agreed to pay them about half a boulder to be able to land on this island. Could have used Daniel's negotiation skills to lower the price."

"You did great Mom. I'm sure all those public relations skills helped out."

"Former life."

Jason looked around at the arid landscape, barely visible.

"Not like we're damaging anything."

"Tell that to the environmentalists that spent the last seventy years bringing those grasses back."

"Grasses, huh? The tortoises walking around are cool."

"We're going to head out soon. Did you confirm the location of re-entry is programmed into all the cargo Skyboats?"

"It is. Should take about two hours to get there."

"I want to be there two hours before the first one drops."

"Then we might as well get airborne."

Jason and Paige walked back to forest line, got in their Skyboats, and lifted off. Jason positioned *Sky Dancer* next to *Firefly* and launched the canopy drones. He remotely started each of the cargo Skyboats one by one, putting them underneath *Sky Dancer* and *Firefly*, increasing altitude as each one lifted off. Once Jason had the eighteen boats airborne, they headed west, flying over the water without using any lights and only the glow of their hull engines providing illumination. With little moonlight, the night was almost completely black. After two hours, Melvin piped up.

"Stop your boat here," said Angie's voice.

"I thought I turned that off," said Jason.

He scrolled through the program settings and saw an override feature re-engaged voices for the re-entry period of the program. He looked for the documentation, found a '*readmedummy*' file, refused to open it, and shut the voices off again.

"Mom, we're stopping," said Jason, setting the cargo Skyboats to hover.

Paige stopped *Firefly* and looked up at the clear night sky. In this remote part of the South Pacific, the stars filled the entire sky. Hopefully one of those bright spots was Angie, Ryan, Alana, and Jesse, coming home. She continued to look up and realized how immense everything was above her.

"I trust all of you," said Paige, still looking at the stars, "but this is kind of ridiculous. I mean we're supposed to catch a falling boulder from the sky?"

"Sixteen of them," said Jason.

"Exactly," said Paige as she sat on a bench looking out at the dark ocean, barely visible.

The adrenaline dropped in her body. She soaked in the fact that it all came down to catching a bunch of falling meteorites before they landed in the ocean. Then her optimism sank. It was her and Jason. Against the elements, against the government, against gravity. She had always been the realist in the family. Someone had to pump the brakes on Ben's crazy plans. Yes, he created the impossible, but only after Paige got him to focus. 'Walk before you run' she repeated over and over.

Eventually it would sink in, but not after a heated argument where Ben claimed no one believed in him, not even his wife, and he stormed out to fish on the Truckee. A few hours later he would appear with his rod and reel and a mopey look apologizing for losing his temper, and that as usual, she was right, he needed to focus. And he loved Paige more than anyone, but it was a toss-up between her and *Blue Darter*. Happened time and time again. Paige leaned her head back and fell asleep. The sunrise woke her an hour and a half later, shining in her eyes. She blinked at looked at her watch, five-fifty am.

Sixty miles above Paige the first of the meteors began entry into the Earth's atmosphere. The solenoid fired to position the meteor's carbon fiber shield, wrapped around a third of the boulder, to face Earth as it accelerated toward the ocean. The solenoid's radar began looking for an active instance of Melvin. As the speed and heat increased, it connected with Jason's laptop. The solenoid fired, pushing the meteor's trajectory in line with the laptop. And then it broke through the lower atmosphere.

"I see it!" said Paige as she pointed up at sky and ran onto the deck.

Jason ran out from the cockpit and looked up.

"Where?"

Paige pointed at it.

"There."

Jason turned his head and saw the tiny fireball.

"Okay, we need to connect."

"Which side, starboard or port?" said Paige.

"My starboard, your port," said Jason.

Jason brought *Sky Dancer* around lining up its starboard side next to *Firefly*'s port side, and they connected their wings. The solenoid sensed the reduction in heat after entering the Earth's atmosphere and extended its base fins, which rotated the boulder one-hundred eighty degrees to point the solenoid engine down at the Earth's surface. Then it began firing all its remaining fuel to slow down.

"Here it comes," said Jason, looking through the binoculars. "Coming right at us!"

Meanwhile Paige looked at the connected wings between their two Skyboats. They looked weak. No way they could hold this incoming rock.

"It's not going to hold Jason," said Paige.

"Mom, the solenoid is slowing the rock down. It will hold. And we have the grapnels."

Jason pointed at the pneumatic launcher on the deck of *Firefly* and held his up to the sky. The meteor flew down toward them. It was difficult to tell if it was slowing down at all. But the fact that they saw it coming toward them sent a small wave of relief through Paige because at least they had a chance.

"Now!" Jason said as he shot the grapnel toward the meteor way too soon.

Paige struggled to position her launcher on her shoulder and before she could aim it the meteor flew past the port side of *Sky Dancer* and splashed into the ocean.

Paige looked at Jason.

"My port side! Your starboard side!" said Jason as he detached his wing from *Firefly*. Jason moved *Sky Dancer* over to the other side of *Firefly* and connected the wings again. Jason avoided Paige's glare as he reset his launcher while waiting fifteen long minutes.

"I see the next one. It's coming!" said Jason looking through the binoculars.

They aimed the launchers as the meteor approached.

"Now!" said Jason, and they fired the grapnels at the rock as it came between the boats. The grapnels shot under the meteor and could not re-direct themselves fast enough to connect. The meteor fell into the wing net and broke through it, hit the deck of the cargo Skyboat below them and bounced off like a basketball, splashing in the ocean.

"Well, there's another sixty-three billion dollars gone," said Paige.

"Oh, come on!" said Jason to himself as he recoiled his grapnel. "What gives?"

Jason looked at his laptop and saw the Melvin program flashing. He pressed it.

"Would you like to engage pneumatic launcher timing notification?" said Angie's voice in a loud volume across the water.

Jason went red as Paige looked at him.

"You know, instructions aren't a bad thing, even from your younger sister," said Paige.

Jason scrolled through the rest of Melvin's settings. 'Meteoroid re-entry notification', turned on; 'Collection Count', turned on; 'harpoon shooting accuracy', not turned on. He looked up at the sky. Fourteen more rocks were coming. He was zero for two on his part of the mission. Everyone else did their part and now they needed him to finish the job. Then he saw the cargo Skyboat beneath them floating empty with a dent in the decking.

"I know what to do," Jason said. "I'm going to move the cargo boat down as the meteor lands on it. Like catching a ball in your mitt."

"Can you do that while you're harpooning the rock?"

"Give me a little credit Mom."

Jason had no idea if it would work, or if he could do what he said. He opened his tablet, put the altitude bar for the cargo Skyboat at the center of the screen and set it on the ground. Then he took off his right shoe and sock and practiced lowering the bar with his big toe.

"That's your plan?" said Paige with the launcher on her hip.

"Meteoroid three approaching," said Ryan's voice out of Jason's tablet.

"Here it comes!" said Jason as he picked up his launcher and aimed it at the sky. "Let's do this!"

Paige looked through her sight, watching the rock approach.

"Fire harpoons now," said Angie's voice.

They fired, hit the rock, and dropped their launchers on the deck. The grapnels hit the rock and the point of each grapnel drilled into the meteorite's surface at fifteen hundred cycles per second while the mini-spider drones flew around the rock looking for each other on the other side. Once they collided, they connected using tiny metal hooks with their trailing micro cables tightening onto the meteor. As the grapnels were securing themselves to the rock, the zing of the two retracting spools rang out and Jason grabbed his pole.

"Mom, your pole!"

Paige took the carbon fiber pole out of its stand. She set her right foot in front, bent her knees, and held on. The motorized reel managed the tension between the cable, the meteor and the winch bolted on the deck of *Firefly*. Jason ran around the deck of *Sky Dancer* like he snagged a sixty-foot marlin. When the meteor hit the connected wings, the motorized reels went tight. They whined as the meteor pulled out ten, twenty, thirty feet of cable. The meteor fell through the wings toward the cargo Skyboat. Jason had his big toe on the screen, but it was too slick to be recognized. He threw his pole down and picked up the tablet as the rock hit the deck.

Jason pulled the cargo Skyboat down as the rock began to recoil up, but the downward movement of the Cargo Skyboat took most of the force out of the rock's bounce, and it fell straight back down instead of rolling. The cargo Skyboat hit the one below it as the rock hit the deck for a second time. It bounced and rolled but not high enough to get over the railings. The rock continued to roll around the deck pushing on the railings until Paige had the reel on her pole pull it back to the center. Then the meteorite came to a standstill.

"Yes!" Jason said as he pumped his fist and slapped the railing. "We caught one. We actually caught one!"

"Nice work, honey," said Paige. "How many more do you think these cargo Skyboats can take?"

"All of them! Let's send this one home."

Jason called Vali.

"First package coming your way. ETA of seven hours. You got a good storage spot for it?"

"Oh, ya, it will be in your room on *Horizon*."

"Meteor four approaching," said Ryan's voice.

"Sounds great, gotta go," said Jason.

After Jason sent the first cargo Skyboat to Sky City, he and Paige hit the fourth meteor with the grapnels, and it went through the wings at the same speed as meteor three, cracking more boards on the next cargo Skyboat deck but did not bounce off.

"First problem," said Paige. "Drone approaching."

"Right as I'm getting the hang of this, too."

"I got it."

Paige opened one of the benches and took out Ryan's boulder drone along with the control tablet. The drone flew past them, then circled back as it rotated its turboprop to maintain a vertical position over the Skyboats. The drone reduced altitude until it was fifty feet over Paige and Jason, hovering, with its cameras scanning them. It appeared to be an improved DarkStar drone that the DOS had rebooted from the grave because of the cool name, unlike their Predator variant. Paige fired up the drone ball and sent it toward the DarkStar drone as fast as she could. The DarkStar drone flew left, and the drone ball missed it.

"You are ordered by the Department of Space of the United States Government to cease your maritime activities and return to Sky City immediately," said a mechanical voice out of the drone's speaker.

"I don't think so," said Paige as she sent the drone rock down to hit the drone.

The rock drone flew on top of the DarkStar drone and bounced off.

"What?" said Paige as she looked at her tablet.

"I repeat," said the DarkStar drone, and then Paige heard a gunshot, looked up and the drone was smoking. It lost altitude, got shot again and burst into flames, falling onto the deck of *Sky Dancer*.

Paige saw Jason hit the remains of the drone with the butt of his twelve-gauge Remington until the fire went out, and it was in several pieces. Paige looked at the tablet and kicked the drone ball.

"Mom, what are you doing?" said Jason.

"Apparently nothing," said Paige as she threw the tablet on the deck.

"Fire harpoons now," said Angie's voice.

They grabbed their launchers and shot the grapnels straight up, hitting the next meteor. The zing of the retracting cables rang out while the meteor hit the wings. It fell through and hit the deck of the cargo Skyboat as Jason grabbed his tablet and yanked the altitude lever down, again crashing the cargo Skyboat into the one below it. Paige fought the meteorite with her pole, managing to keep it from falling off the deck.

"Cool, that's three," said Jason.

"Eleven more," said Paige.

"We're going to see more drones."

"Let's do this one at a time. I've got a better plan for the next wave."

They had recovered six more meteorites when another drone showed up on *Firefly*'s rangefinder. Paige saw it coming at them much faster than the previous drone. And it was four times larger. She hit the emergency release to disconnect the wings from *Sky Dancer*.

"Jason, hold tight," said Paige. "I'll handle this."

Paige jammed *Firefly* to maximum speed toward the drone. As the Skyboat accelerated, items not strapped down flew off the deck. Paige walked over the multiple white coolers littering the cabin and dragged out the only blue one, sitting under the dining table. Ben always supported Ryan's projects, after all, that was how the skyboard was invented. And of all Ryan's Skunk Works projects, like the original Lockheed 1943 F-80 fighter jet, the one in the blue cooler had a ridiculous price tag.

She undid the rubber lid latches and flipped open the lid. Inside was a helmet, gloves, heavy backpack, and Ryan's handwritten instructions. Paige had practiced with the helmet and gloves while waiting on Isla Pinta. She wasn't proud of blowing a few dozen seagulls into feathers, but she needed to get used to the device. Then she walked over to the side wall, unhooked her skyboard, and set it next to the cooler. She opened the closet and pulled out a body armor jacket. She put it on over her T-shirt, zipped it up, and flipped off her tennis shoes as she grabbed the body armor pants and put those on over her shorts.

Looking at the control panel, she saw the drone was bearing down on *Firefly*, and then it flew right past. Paige slowed *Firefly* down and went up on deck to look at the drone as it headed away from her. A Predator variant, Department of Space code name, 'Custodian'. Paige walked back down into the cabin and looked at the control screen. The Custodian drone continued its path away from her but now she saw twenty-four smaller drones approaching from the Custodian's flight path. They were in what appeared to be a 'W' formation in front with a 'V' formation trailing, actually six sets of an echelon formation, half-right and half-left.

Paige did not care about formations. Everything was going down. She aimed *Firefly* at the eight drones approaching on her left and set the autopilot. Paige then went to the aft stateroom, her master bedroom, and pulled the emergency exit lever behind the bed. The back wall of *Firefly* flew off. She went to the front of the bed and kicked it off the Skyboat.

*

"Uh, Johnson, what are we looking at?"

"It's an approaching Skyboat. Prepare to apprehend."

"I mean what fell out of it. Is that a bed? And nightstands? Coolers, chairs, a mini-frig?"

"Dropping ballast, likely a pre-attack move. Heads up everyone."

The twenty-four rotary drone pilots sat together in a small room across the hall from the Predator pilots. Unlike the Predator pilots, treated like royalty in the drone community of DOS, with their plush seats and mission control like settings, the low-range rotary drone pilots sat at six sets of four desks packed together in a room. Various levels of apathy across the team.

Drone pilots were notorious for burnout in the early years, forcing an overhaul, particularly around getting drone pilots the prestige they craved. After an extensive public relations campaign, both internal and external, drone pilots became cool. That is, if they flew extended range drones with eight active hardpoints. Short-range rotary drone pilots did not make that cut.

Training for the rotary drone teams was not a priority, filling seats was, and many of the team were military dropouts. And it didn't help when Predator pilots called them their *spider spawn* because they released them from the belly of their planes. Demeaning and gross.

All of which meant most of the team members considered this job a paycheck, not a calling. And when the morning briefing explained they were going after high priority targets that turned out to be the Dawsons, no one, outside of the team lead, felt like they were really protecting America's interests. The orders suggested fatalities would be acceptable, but then there would be much more paperwork, so consider that. They did consider it as they sipped their Lattes and Espressos, stolen from the Predator pilots' break room, and decided to give a pretty solid effort with this pretty meaningless mission.

*

Paige took the helmet from the cooler, put it on and pressed the power button on the side. It formed to her skull, strapped under her chin, and dropped lenses over her eyes. Then she put on the backpack, which nearly toppled her over. She stood back up and put on the gloves, connecting the pneumatic tubes from the backpack. Paige clicked the dial on the back of each of her hands to the maximum setting, which was eleven, because Ryan thought he was funny. The gloves hummed.

Paige picked up her skyboard and walked up to the deck. She set the skyboard down and stepped onto it in her bare feet, right foot in front, pressing both heels into the board, signaling to strap in. The board had her feet sink into the board and straps pushed out over her feet. She could see the drones in front of her.

"Okay, let's go."

She pressed her front foot down and the skyboard shot out of the starboard side of the bow of *Firefly*. She flew straight at the drones on her right while *Firefly* flew into the left group of drones. *Firefly* continued straight past the drones as they swerved to avoid it. The eight drones near *Firefly* turned to pursue.

At the same time Paige aimed her arms at the front drone on her right. She looked directly at the drone, which like the other twenty-three, was armed with a B&T APC sub-machine gun mounted underneath the drone's body, along with stabilizing legs on either side of the gun. Her glasses identified it as the target. She made a fist with her right hand and the tube from the backpack filled with micro radar guided missiles approximately the size of a 9mm bullet.

The micro missiles pulled into the bolt on the top of her hand and began shooting out of the barrel resting between her first and second knuckle. Once airborne, the residual propellant cap at the rear of the micro missile allowed the guidance system to alter course as the seeker dome headed for the target. Just before impact six micro carbon steel blades extended below the tip, spinning at the speed of sound. Each micro missile lacked a warhead component, but the force of the blades shredded the interior of the drone as they blew through its frame.

Instead of looking to see what happened to the drone, she pressed her back heel on the skyboard and headed up above the drones. Looking down she saw seven drones turning toward her. As she moved further up in the sky, she pointed her arms out at her sides toward the two closest drones and fired. Her glasses picked up the empty space around the drones and modified the micro missiles paths to hit something solid, which gave Paige one hundred percent shooting accuracy. After the micro missiles flew out of each barrel, trashing two more drones, she focused on the next five drones coming after her.

The remaining five drone pilots put down their coffee cups and decided to get serious, regardless of the paperwork.

"Go after her," said the commander, whose drone was one of the first shot down. He stood, looking at the other two groups of eight drone pilots. "You all, keep back. And you, chasing that Skyboat; blow it apart."

Paige weaved in the air to avoid the drones' machine gun fire while the eight drones chasing *Firefly* shot it into oblivion. *Firefly*'s automated system notified Paige.

"Imminent failure of all systems," said the automated system. "Beginning shut down procedures."

"No, proceed with modified end of life protocol," said Paige.

"Modified end of life protocol does not include safety shut down, please confirm with passphrase."

"This is goodbye *Firefly*," said Paige.

"This is goodbye confirmed. Stay clear."

The eight drones surrounded *Firefly* and continued to empty their guns into the Skyboat as it listed port side. After the confirmation from Paige, *Firefly*'s coolant pump shut down, which stopped the pressurized liquid sodium flow inside the mini nuclear reactor. The liquid sodium coolant was then purged onto the hull floor while the ceramic encapsulated uranium, carbon, and oxygen fuel pellets were released from the control rods inside the core, instantly increasing the internal temperature of the reactor from fifteen hundred to twenty-seven hundred degrees Fahrenheit.

The fission process continued to heat the reactor, and seconds later reached thirty-three hundred degrees Fahrenheit, which melted the dual layer metal containment vessel, including the steam generator tubes. Steam blasted out of the melted tubes, touching the liquid metal of the containment vessels, and exploded. The pressure of the steam explosion rippled through *Firefly*, blowing it apart in a spherical shape and sending Skyboat shrapnel into each of the eight drones surrounding it. The drones either smoked or exploded, but all eight fell into the ocean.

Paige heard the explosion and a tear rolled down her cheek. Then a bullet hit her in the ribs. Another hit in the same spot, cracking it. The pain snapped Paige back to the moment. She aimed her right arm back and let loose a hundred missiles. The drones chasing her were too far away and the micro missiles fell into the ocean. She pressed on the board with her front foot and the rotary blades adjust their positions, accelerating to top speed. The drones also accelerated and closed in. Paige felt another bullet, this one on her helmet. It rang like falling on concrete.

She pressed the heel of her back foot and braked hard enough to snap the strap on her front foot. The drones came up behind her but needed a moment to recalibrate their aim through the cameras on their screens. She turned the skyboard vertical and flew above them. They spread out to angle their submachine guns up at her.

She pressed her back foot again and turned upside down. Paige fell toward the drones. She aimed her arms down and fired, angling toward each drone. She stopped firing as she fell between them. Once below the drones, she pressed her back foot again, turning the skyboard upright and heading away from the drones behind her as they broke into pieces and fell into the ocean.

The final eight drones advanced and began shooting at her. There were too many bullets. Paige got hit again and again, the pain searing through her body. She bent down into a ball on the skyboard and the drones surrounded her, halting their fire as the commander spoke over his loudspeaker.

"Final warning. Give yourself up."

Then one of the rotary drone pilots dropped his cup on the keyboard and emptied a clip of bullets into Paige's bent leg. The body armor failed, and Paige slumped onto the board.

"Stop!" said the Commander's voice.

Paige was on all fours with only one way out. She turned her heard, extended her arms, and fell almost face first onto the board. Then she pressed her back foot to begin spinning the skyboard with her fists clenched, emptying the backpack of its micro missiles. The drones began firing at her, but after two seconds, they were all incapacitated. One by one they fell into the ocean. The last one sparked and smoked as Paige glided over to it, still lying on the skyboard, punching its camera, once, twice, a third time, until it cracked.

"Stop coming after my family!"

She turned and flew back to *Sky Dancer* as the last drone spun out of control and into the ocean. Paige landed the skyboard down on the deck of *Sky Dancer* and rolled off the board.

"Mom, that was amazing."

"Yes, I know," said Paige as she took off her helmet and gloves. She tried to stand and fell onto the deck. Jason helped her to a seat.

"I got this, you rest."

Jason had captured meteor twelve solo while Paige shot down the drones. He used one of the cargo Skyboats as the other part of the wing net. Then he caught thirteen, fourteen and fifteen with one final meteor incoming.

"How are we going to capture the last one?" said Jason aloud, looking at *Sky Dancer* barely floating in the air with only one more cargo Skyboat that was being used as the second part of the wing net.

"We have another problem," said Paige, looking at the control screen in the cockpit. "More incoming drones. A bunch of big ones."

Jason looked up at the sky.

"Maybe we just let the last one land on the cargo Skyboat?"

"We have to go now."

"Then we've got to move to Melvin 2.0."

"What's that?"

"Dad wants any meteor not in our possession blown up immediately."

"Okay, blow them up and let's go."

"I have to know which ones we have first."

"Doesn't Melvin already know that?"

"Yes, but it wants a confirmation before it detonates the nuclear reactor in each solenoid. Safety feature."

"Fine, do it on the way back."

"Aye-aye, Captain."

Jason started *Sun Dancer* toward Sky City then began scrolling through the meteorites on the cargo Skyboats. Melvin registered the solenoid numbers as he clicked on each of them.

"Here goes."

Jason hit the detonate tab on Melvin.

"Are you sure?" said Angie's voice.

Jason hit the confirmation button.

"Not to be a pest," continued Angie's voice, "but you are absolutely certain you want to blow up the unaccounted for meteors, right?"

Jason hit a second confirmation button. Then a third, fourth and fifth button.

"Angie, I'm gonna kill you when I see you again!" Jason yelled.

After the sixth confirmation button Melvin's screen burst into flying multi-colored confetti, which Jason thought was in bad taste. The meteor above the remaining cargo Skyboat exploded. At the same time, beneath them, on the ocean floor, the first and second meteors' solenoids clicked but did not explode. The damaged solenoids attempted to complete the self-destruct command three times, but when they continued to be unsuccessful, they sent out a failure notice and shut down.

"Jason, get under something!" Paige said.

Jason jumped under the cockpit covering next to his mom as pieces of the sixteenth meteor rained down on *Sky Dancer*. After a few seconds, it stopped, and the deck was littered with millions in rocks. Jason started the autopilot on the last cargo Skyboat, wondering how much of blown-up asteroid rock it had on its deck as it started on a path back to Sky City. Paige texted Ben while looking at the wrecked deck of *Sky Dancer*.

"What a mess. I'm glad that's over."

CHAPTER FORTY-EIGHT

DEPARTMENT OF SPACE

The screen in the conference room was split between the twenty-four drone cameras. High-definition quality gave fantastic views of Paige demolishing each drone. Martin was in a slow burn as each camera went dark. The final screen went blank after Paige's repeated beating.

"Well, that was clear" said Ben,

"Crystal," said Daniel.

"Enough," said Martin. "I'm sending in all the drones. You did this Ben, you brought this onto your family, not me."

He motioned for a soldier to come in when one ran in front of the other soldier.

"Sir, it's the Rural American Alliance."

"Who cares?"

"The commissioner of the RAA wants to speak with you."

"I'm busy."

"He's patching into your earpiece."

Martin turned away toward the wall.

"Yes? I did. He broke the law. I did. Yes. There was an asteroid.

Hidden. Yes. Is he? I see. Of course."

Martin turned back toward the room and punched the soldier in the face. The soldier did not move. Martin held his hand, shook it, and put it by his side.

"Get out!"

The soldier turned and left, shaking his head in question, not pain. Martin sat. He had to make sure the drones stopped the asteroid retrieval. He called the drone team lead.

"Launch all the Custodians!"

"Sir, we have been told to stand down by the RAA."

"You don't work for them."

"Actually,"

"Let me clarify, launch the drones or you're reassigned to the LEO Transco customer complaints center."

"Yes, sir. We will launch all the drones."

"Keep me informed every fifteen minutes."

Martin was going to make them pay. Things had gone too far. He had to end this.

"You can still call this off," said Martin.

Then Ben's watch vibrated. 'El D secured' illuminated on the tiny screen.

"Okay, that wraps this up," said Ben as he showed his watch to Daniel before the screen went dark.

"Nothing is wrapped up," said Martin.

"I beg to differ," said Daniel. "Can you release me so I may hand you a document?"

"Like a piece of paper?" said Martin.

"Yes, paper."

"Always with the games," said Martin. "It doesn't matter. The handoff is imminent. You two will be flying with me on the DOS jet to participate, willingly, I might add. And then, your trial."

He waved a soldier over to take off Daniel's handcuffs. Daniel pulled out a folded sheet of paper and slid it over to Martin.

"What is this?"

"A Declaration of Independence," said Ben.

"Really? Just because it's on paper doesn't make it official."

"The signatures do," said Daniel.

"Today is Independence Day for Sky City," said Ben. "Going forward to be known as Sky Nation."

"Stupid name," said Martin. "And it's meaningless. You can't create a nation out of nothing."

Martin tore up the paper.

"Like the United States?" said Ben.

Martin slammed his hands on the table.

"Don't you dare even pretend to compare your little boat marina to the greatest government in the world!"

"Government?" said Daniel. "You're leaving out the citizens."

"No, the citizens have the pleasure of living under the greatest governing body to ever exist."

"And that's why we're leaving," said Ben. "Please, remove my handcuffs."

"I will have them taken off," said Martin, "but you're not going anywhere."

After the soldier removed Ben's handcuffs, he rubbed his hands and his neck. Daniel pulled out his tablet and pressed it.

"The document you tore up has now been sent to all other existing governing bodies for Sky Nation to receive formal recognition as a sovereign entity, including the State Department," said Daniel. "You can choose not to recognize Sky Nation, but you cannot hold us as hostages. Sky Nation has not established an extradition agreement with the United States. Besides, we would be the ones to establish that agreement."

"You're traitors," said Martin. "I don't have to release you."

"Yes, you do have to release us. You are violating the Vienna Convention on Diplomatic Relations by restraining us," said Daniel. "Also, we notified the Alliance commissioners of your actions, which they found quite unorthodox."

Martin saw a team coming through the elevators and asking reception a question. She pointed to the conference room. They looked over at Martin and started walking toward him.

"Get out!" said Martin. "Everyone, get out of this room!"

"Gladly," said Ben as he stood.

Ben and Daniel walked out of the conference room. Ben held the door for the four men in suits entering the room as he and Daniel left.

"Mr. Dawson," one of them said and nodded. "We'll be talking with you soon."

"I'm sure of it."

Daniel looked back to see one of the men motioning for Martin to take a seat, which he refused. Ben and Daniel avoided the elevators, taking the stairs to the rooftop without stopping.

"Nice work back there," said Ben. "How did you get the State Department to recognize us a country so quickly?"

"I didn't," said Daniel. "But I figured Martin wouldn't calm down long enough to check."

"Clever."

They reached the rooftop where *Blue Darter* and *Serenity* sat with several armed guards around them.

"Soldiers," said Ben as he walked toward them, "I think you'll find we're free to go."

One of the soldiers called it in, listened and nodded.

"Yes, sir, you may leave."

"Thank you," said Ben.

"Ben, why don't we take my Skyboat? It's faster."

"I'm feeling nostalgic Daniel, big day for us and, besides, everyone's safe now."

"Still, I'd like to get back to Sky City as soon as possible."

Ben smiled and nodded at Daniel.

"Let's take *Blue Darter*," said Ben. "*Serenity* can follow."

Ben lifted them off the rooftop of the Department of Space in the middle of downtown Denver. Fifty floors above the ground, he flew around the sky taxis and headed west to Sky City, now the first city of Sky Nation.

CHAPTER FORTY-NINE

SKY CITY

Jason and Paige arrived at Sky City pursued by a dozen Custodian drones. Once they entered the Sky City dome the drones disengaged. At some point they would return, perhaps with people and documents allowing them to search Sky City, but for now, the drones headed back. Paige limped off *Sky Dancer* at Command while Jason went to find Vali. He wanted to be sure the rocks were spread out and hidden across the Skyboats. Hidden as much as you can hide a four hundred-thousand-pound boulder. Paige walked into Command, sore, but relieved to find everyone at their stations, including Captain Sinclair. It gave her a sense of normalcy.

"Okay, Roger," said Paige, breathing a sigh of relief. "Take us out."

"I'm afraid I cannot do that," said Roger.

"Why, is there an equipment issue?" said Paige.

"No, I cannot continue to betray my country," said Roger standing stiffly, looking forward and avoiding eye contact with Paige.

"What are you talking about? This is now a country. Like we agreed upon last week. You signed the papers," said Paige.

"I was forced to sign those papers," said Roger, "and my notes to the Department of Space reflect that. They've requested I steer Sky City over North California and land immediately outside Sacramento. And that is what I will be doing. Followed by arresting you and your family."

Roger tapped into the boat's command channel.

"Plot a course for Sacramento."

"Roger, why are you doing this?" said Paige.

"You and Ben left me no choice," said Roger. "After what you did to my family, I couldn't allow any more lives to be ruined by your negligence."

"Roger," said Paige, her voice softening, "I understand what you've been through losing your family."

"Understand?" Roger's voice lost its military flatness. "You don't understand anything. My entire family died because of Sky City. I lost everything."

"Of course, I cannot understand your loss. I only meant I know what happened, and I'm sorry. Not sorry that we caused it, because we didn't, and you know that. It might seem easy to point fingers, but Sky City's launch was not the cause. And deep down, I know you know that. Now, what do you want to do? Start a new chapter with us or send us all away and go back to being a part of the government machine."

"I spent my life in the government, which is not a machine as you suggest. I didn't see it as a waste. And I don't see it as a waste now. But you, your arrogant family and all the others; Ryan, Daniel, even Alana, who was a good soldier before you wrapped her up with your insanity. And you are responsible for the deaths of millions. Millions! How do you even sleep at night? I don't. I'm as responsible as anyone for firing up this Sky City. Don't you see? You made me kill my family! So, now I'm going to kill yours."

Paige stiffened.

"You crossed a line," said Paige as she walked up to Roger and got in his face. He was six inches taller than her, but it did not feel that way with her right next to him.

"I have had enough threats against my family for a lifetime, let alone today," said Paige. "You need to take back what you said and now."

"I take nothing back. You deserve everything you coming to you," said Roger, putting his hand on the butt of the handgun in his belt holster.

"That's it," said Paige.

She coldcocked him with a right hook on the cheek. Roger turned from the blow, but then pulled out his weapon and hit her bruised knee with the butt of his gun. Paige crumpled. Half of the crew in Command grabbed Roger and pulled him away from Paige. The other half stood back and drew weapons, aiming them at Paige and the other crew members. Roger got up, aimed his gun at Paige's head, and walked backward to the crew with their weapons out.

"We're going to Sacramento," said Roger, "like I told you."

*

Ben and Daniel were flying over Utah, still two hours away from their arrival at Sky City.

"We'll join them when they're over the water, it'll be a celebration," said Ben.

"Maybe not," said Daniel, looking at the control panel map. "They've changed direction. They're headed toward North California."

"Something's wrong," said Ben.

He clicked onto the command center speakers.

"Roger, it's Ben. Why aren't you heading to sea?"

"I can't be a part of this any longer," said Roger. "You need to be stopped."

"Ben," Daniel said, "look at this."

Ben leaned over to view the screen where Daniel had a camera of the command center.

"Roger, tell me you do not have a gun pointed at my wife."

"She started it."

"Started what?"

"Roger's lost his mind," said Paige. "He's blaming all of us for losing his family."

"It is your fault," said Roger, keeping his gun aimed directly at Paige. "You and your constant pushing. This didn't have to happen. I didn't have to lose my family. Maybe you should lose yours."

"Roger, wait," said Ben. "Put the gun down. You're not making any sense. Why are you going to shoot someone? How does that help anything? You think it's going to make you feel better? Then shoot me. I'll be there in two hours, and you can put that nuzzle right up against my forehead and blow my brains out in front of the world. We'll broadcast it and you can make a speech, and then kill me. That will fix everything won't it? You will be a hero to your family's legacy, everyone will love you for killing me and you will not be charged for murder because it's all justified due to your suffering. Do I have this right?"

"How dare you?" said Roger. "Don't mock me."

"I'm not mocking you," Ben said as he waved to Daniel and Daniel broadcast Ben's face on the main screen in the control center. "Here. Here's my face. Start with this. Shoot me now and shoot me later."

Ben clicked over to Jason, who was flying around Sky City with Vali placing meteorites like parents hiding treats for an Easter egg hunt.

"Jason, where are you?"

"Sky City, where else? Almost all the rocks are sorted. Pretty great, huh?"

"Roger has a gun on your mother in Command. He's gone nuts."

"What? I'll take care of it."

Jason stopped his cargo Skyboat and waved at Vali, who stopped next to him.

"You got a vest?"

"Plenty. You a medium or a small?"

"Come on man, large."

Vali threw Jason a soft body armor vest. After putting it on, Jason grabbed his skyboard. He dropped it, stepped on the board, and pressed in to secure his feet.

"That traitor," said Jason as he kicked into the air, heading straight toward *Horizon*. "Dad, I'm headed to Command."

"Be careful. You need to protect your mom, nothing else," said Ben. "Just keep the situation under control until I get there."

"Oh, it will be under control."

It was not going to be under control. Jason swerved around the Skyboats, skyboards, and an array of trusses to fly to the center of Sky City. He approached Command from the front, lowered himself on his skyboard and rammed the center window of Command. The bulletproof glass cracked, but held, and Jason slammed into the window then fell onto the deck. Roger motioned two of his crew outside where they grabbed Jason and pulled him into Command.

"Jason, stop it," said Roger, keeping his gun pointed at Paige. "You're being an idiot and you might get you and your mother killed."

"Oh, about that," said Jason as he pulled his arms away from the crew members and stepped between Roger's gun and his mom.

"Stop, I mean it," said Roger, pointing the gun at Jason's head.

"Wow, you really lost it," said Jason.

"This is why I'm doing this. Each of you Dawson's think you run the world. You don't run anything. Not anymore."

Ben and Daniel watched from their Skyboat as Jason got Paige out of immediate danger. But still, Roger could shoot Jason at any moment. The situation was unstable.

"I've had enough of Roger," said Ben as he clicked into the Sky City control system.

"Initiate Emergency Break-up Protocol."

"Confirm identity," said the control panel.

"Ben Dawson."

Ben put his hand on the screen and leaned forward.

"Scanning palm and retina. Identify confirmed. Do you wish to proceed?"

Ben paused.

"Confirmed."

*

Sirens sounded across Sky City, including in Command, followed by a broadcast of Ryan's voice with extra bass.

"This is not a drill. Sky City separation beginning immediately. Report back to your Skyboats. Sky City will disassemble in five minutes."

The dome began retracting as did all the trusses. The sirens continued to screech across the city. Everyone in Command tried to hold their positions and ignore the sirens, but they were ear-piercing, and most could not help flinching. Except Roger, who stared at Jason with his gun aimed at Jason's head. Then another skyboard crashed through the center window of Command, with Vali's huge frame on top of it.

Roger turned his head, Jason leapt at Roger to grab his gun, pulling it down. Roger fired into Jason's chest. Jason held onto Roger's hand and pushed him backward as Roger fired again. The two of them fell into two of the other crew members while Vali took out the rest of Roger's crew. Roger got one more shot off into Jason's chest before a pile of people jumped on Roger, grabbed the gun out of his hands, and turned him over with his face on the ground. Paige was on top of Jason, looking at his chest.

"I'm okay, Mom, I'm okay. I knew what I was doing."

"No. No you didn't," said Paige as tears fell out of her eyes.

She stood. Vali and the rest of Sky City's staff had Roger's team surrounded.

"Enough!" said Paige. "This is over. Look around you, Sky City is breaking up. What are you going to do, try to take *Horizon* to Sacramento?"

Paige walked between the two groups. She stared at the mutineers.

"Leave. Leave now. You can even take your Skyboats. If you leave now, we're done. If you don't, then whatever happens to you is your fault. You don't want to be here, and we don't want you here, so leave!" Paige screamed so loud her voice cracked.

Roger's crew looked at each other, looked at Roger, and avoided looking at the crazy lady. They nodded to each other and walked out the side door. It was over.

"I cannot say the same for you Roger," said Paige. "You will be the first prisoner of Sky Nation."

CHAPTER FIFTY

Ben and Daniel arrived at Sky City in the dark as it floated over international waters. They approached *Horizon* where hundreds of Skyboats flew around, waiting. *Blue Darter* and *Serenity* docked at the top deck of *Horizon* and Ben and Daniel headed down to Command. Jason sat on a chair, complaining a little too much, while Paige managed the crew with Vali. When Ben came in, he and Paige hugged for a full minute, crying. Daniel gave Jason a squeeze on his shoulder and ruffled his hair. The crew stared in silence. After Ben wiped his eyes, he gave Jason a hug and Jason winced.

"Shouldn't you be in the hospital boat?" said Ben.

"Yes, but I'm pretty sure you're about to make a speech," said Jason.

"Always harassing your dad."

"Always."

Ben left Jason and went around the room, starting with Vali, giving each of the crew members a hug, which was awkward for everyone, but remembered forever.

"Did you get the update from Angie? They'll be here tomorrow morning," Ben said to Paige.

"Yes, but why did you offer Bobby Walker Sky Nation citizenship for bringing them home? He didn't even ask for it."

"Maybe, but I won't gamble our families' lives again. I don't care what it costs to keep us safe, nothing else matters. This has never been about the money."

Then Ben stood in front of the shattered center window of Command and clicked onto the Sky City Public Broadcasting System.

"Sky City, welcome back! We are not, I repeat, not, having a handover tonight, but we will be having that party Jason promised. A party for our independence!"

Ben looked over at Jason who gave him a thumbs up.

"Ben, shouldn't we wait for everyone to come back?" said Paige.

"No reason we can't have two parties, even three, said Ben.

"Also, I did spend about a billion dollars on food," said Jason.

"You what?" said Ben. "How is that possible?"

"It's called a distraction, Dad. Do you know how much space that amount of food and drink takes up? Roger lost his mind figuring out how to store everything. Especially with Vali telling him all the cargo Skyboats were full."

"That was fun," said Vali. "Never liked him."

"Fine, fine," said Ben. "We all deserve it. Vali, I'd like to ask you to oversee Command. Will you do that for me?"

"You'd be surprised what I'd do for you."

Ben slapped him on the shoulder, more like the lower portion of Vali's shoulder blade, and he went with Paige to the main deck to celebrate with the rest of the crew. Exciting but hollow for Paige while she waited for Angie's return. Shortly after midnight, she turned in with Ben following her, sleeping in their room on *Horizon*. They did not expect to rest but both were exhausted, and they fell asleep in their clothes. A knock on their door woke them up seven hours later. It was Daniel.

"You've got to come see this."

Ben and Paige left the room without changing and went up to Command. They stood on the deck, looking out where hundreds of Skyboats were flying back to re-connect with *Horizon*. Each level was forming with ships locating their spots and joining their wings. Jason limped into Command as Ben grabbed the microphone.

"Just in time," said Jason as he fell into a chair.

"Hello, everyone, this is Ben Dawson. First, thank you. Thank you for believing in a dream. We've gotten here through a path none of us expected. But now we are a nation and that means much more than whatever I can say to you today. Second, all of you are free to choose. Free to choose to be a part of this nation or be here as guests. Or not at all. The choice is up to each of us."

The levels of Sky City resembled their original structure as more Skyboats arrived.

"I believe this will be the start of something greater than any of us can imagine. I also believe it will be different than our imaginations. And that is how everything I've experienced has turned out. And we will have struggles."

Paige looked at one of the cameras on the *Horizon* landing platform and saw a LEO Transco passenger rocket coming down for a landing near *Blue Darter*, *Serenity*, and the torn-up *Sky Dancer*.

"They're here!" she said. "They're here!"

Paige ran out of Command.

"But we'll finish this later," Ben said. "Congratulations Sky Nation citizens and friends!"

Ben set down the microphone, and he and Daniel followed Paige running out of Command, heading to the landing platform. Vali was behind them, almost out of the room when Jason called after him.

"Hey!" said Jason. "A little help!"

Vali turned around and went back over to Jason. He pulled him up, and with Jason's right arm around Vali's shoulders, they made their way toward the landing platform. The R9 LEO Transco passenger carrier landed vertically on the platform. Piloted by Bobby Walker, nothing but perfection was expected, along with maybe a little too much self-congratulation in the cockpit. As the passenger carrier's wheels touched down, a large female cooper's hawk perched on the platform's railing took off.

The hawk flew toward the upper levels of Sky City, where Skyboats were re-connecting. The hawk navigated through the connecting wings and trusses, then it looked down toward the platform as an older woman ran toward the group exiting the rocket and a younger woman broke away from the group, running toward her.

They met and began hugging, then an older man came out of the doorway and ran to the two women. The rest of the group came up to the three of them, and they all grabbed each other with handshakes and hugs. One man stood back, observing, until he was pulled into the group. The hawk was above Level Four when it saw two other men struggle out of the doorway, moving more slowly than the others, and the two younger women ran to them and hugged them. Then they switched and hugged each of the other men, and they all started laughing.

The hawk was at Level Five, passing by *Freedom*, the only Skyboat on that level, when the group appeared as one on the platform, smiling and laughing with each other. There was no rush for any of them to go anywhere, because at that moment, being together was the most important thing they could do.

The hawk continued up to the Sky City dome as it formed back into a hemisphere above Sky City. The hawk headed toward the shrinking hole at the top of the dome, flying through before it closed. Looking down once more, where the details of the people on the rooftop deck of *Horizon* were blurred, but their feelings for each other were not, she made a loud *whaa* call and headed out over the water.

EPILOGUE

DECEMBER 5, 2071, 08:00 — EARTH UTC

The screens each lit up with the seven pictures of the committee members.

"They actually did it, didn't they?" said Niko Genji, waiting for quorum, which for this committee was one hundred percent attendance.

"Yes, they did," said Bowler McKay, Governor of Mars. "Now it's open season on asteroid mining."

"Won't be long before there's an asteroid shuttle to the Kuiper Belt," said Sylvester Hall, newly selected Space Colony Director.

"Interesting that we have a new player on the board," said Bowler.

"Will they pick the right side?" said Wei Shi.

"Will you?" said Steele.

"Should we tell them what's coming?" said Albert Jackson.

"How about if Steele does it?" said Aiden Wolfe. "He can make it appear friendly."

"I'll think about it."

Don LaRue joined, making it eight, and completing the committee.

"I am calling this meeting to order," said Steele in the upper left picture on everyone's screen. "First order of business, please welcome our newest member to the committee, Don LaRue."

"Thank you, Mr. Steele, I'd like to—"

"Please, stop talking," said Ms. Shi. "Protocol states new members do not speak on their first call."

Don nodded.

"Even nodding is considered bad form," said Ms. Shi. "Freeze your screen to avoid further embarrassment."

Don's screen froze with his mouth open. He unfroze it and froze it again with his mouth shut tight.

"Now that we've welcomed the new member in this committee's unique fashion, onto the only other open item," said Steele. "Does anyone have changes to the declaration before we vote?"

"Did you send it to our newest member?" said Niko.

"Thank you for the reminder. Aiden, as secretary, can you send the declaration to Mr. LaRue?"

"Still don't know why we have to do our own paperwork," said Aiden.

"We've been over this," said Steele. "It was the only way to ensure confidentiality. Besides, it's a rotational position. Please, send it."

"It's sent. How about we rotate positions next meeting?"

"I'll put it on the agenda," said Steele. "Back to the declaration. Any revisions before we vote?"

Silence.

"Then all in favor, say aye."

Everyone on the call said 'Aye'.

"The declaration is now official. Aiden, please provide the members final copies before further distribution. Thank you everyone."

Each of the eight screens went black as the members logged off the call. Don's screen was the last one to log off, and it unfroze for a half second showing his shocked face, only to himself, before turning to black.

ABOUT THE AUTHOR

Alan Priest is a fan of classic adventure novels and thought provoking science fiction.

After a career in high-tech, he now spends his time writing nondystopian stories because, while humanity might make some big mistakes in the future, they will always find a path to recovery.

With degrees from Georgia Tech and Harvard Business School, Alan enjoys pretending to know something about technology, business, and interpersonal dynamics.

Alan lives in Reno, Nevada, with his wife, two daughters, and sheepadoodle. This is his first novel.

Stay up-to-date with Alan via his website:
alanpriest.com

You can also connect with him on social media:
twitter.com/alanjpriest

Lightning Source UK Ltd.
Milton Keynes UK
UKHW011925100522
402797UK00009B/483/J